The Shadow War Saga:

SOURCE

By Lee Wilson

The Shadow War Saga: Source by Lee Wilson

Cover design by Jessica Richardson.

www.TheShadowWarSaga.com

ISBN: 9781980675402

Dedicated to my wife, my friend and my colleague.

Thank you for supporting my weirdness, inspiring my imagination and believing in my dreams.

This is for you.

To

Gemma

FIRST EDITION

Prologue (Shadow War)

As I stand looking out over the battlements, I can't help but wonder how we had got to this.

I stand shoulder to shoulder with the archers, all of us fully armoured and ready for the inevitable battle before us. I turn to look down the line, the sun gleaming as it hits the enamelled white armour of my brothers at arms, the white panels blazoned across their chests and thighs signalling that they belong to the Royal Knights, the defenders of our great city and its people.

A few of the archers nearby turn to face me, giving me a small nod in acknowledgement. I am in almost identical armour to theirs, save for mine also has gilded gold feathers running along the sides of my helm and pauldrons. They are somewhat more fanciful than those belonging to the brave elves beside me, but they were designed that way by my father as a fitting way to display my rank, the General of the Royal Knights.

Turning my focus back to beyond the wall, we are all stood here looking out on the overwhelmingly large orc army that has now gathered at our gates, clad in their black armour to match their darkened skin.

We do not know much about the orcs, they are an infant race in comparison to the elves, and the details surrounding their existence all vague but horrific in nature.

The elves have been watching over this world for millennia, using the Light within each of us to protect and shepherd all life within it. When we had first set out to explore this world, we had discovered many different species sharing it with us. We had met other sentient races, who we had discovered shared elemental powers much like our own, and new alliances had been formed, and we had lived in peace. Later came the realms of men, and their unwavering thirst for knowledge coupled with their undying curiosity propelled their race into greatness and they too prospered in this world. Our alliances were strengthened, and again we had lived in peace. But for all the peace and harmony in the east, lays the dark and stormy Outlands in the west. The elves had been content to leave that gloomy place untouched, but our ever-curious allies had wanted to chart every part of this world.

We had sent scouts and scholars with the men who had ventured out past the Flaming Deserts and into that dark place. Although they always suffered grievous losses to both the terrain and the ominous creatures within, still they had ventured out, determined to make new discoveries. Over time, we had reduced our support to our allies in the north, only agreeing to send any elves that had wanted to be part of the excursions.

All of the reports from the Outlands were that the land was inhospitable and it was thought that the land itself was unable to sustain life. The dark and twisted creatures that roamed the Outlands, feasted on each other to survive; every creature both predator and prey. But no reports of sentient life had ever been given.

Over the decades, our scholars began to suspect that those that returned did not come back entirely unscathed. It was more obvious in the men and women who survived, their mortality showing the strain that the trips to the Outlands put them through. But eventually, the elves that had been on multiple excursions began to change too, imperceivably at first, but it was like their Light had begun to dim, almost as if it had been drained from them.

Even now, our scholars do not definitively know how the orcs came to be, nor exactly where they came from. But it doesn't matter, they are here now, waiting outside the walls to our great city. While our scouts had given us warning of their arrival, it had not been enough. We had not been given chance to call for aid, nor had we time to await their arrival. They have offered no parley, no chance to surrender nor negotiate. They are here for one purpose. To kill us all.

I turn away from the darkness outside the walls and look back at the castle, although it is over a mile away, I can see every detail on the bricks, the frosting on the windows and even make out the eyes of the Royal Knights posted outside. Among other things, we elves are blessed with extraordinary eyesight, and I find myself searching out the windows for signs of life. It isn't until I reach the very top that I see any, when I find King Cen'ahan stood at the top looking over the parapets, watching over his city, and his army, with deep concern clearly etched on his face.

He hasn't aged in thousands of years, another elven trait, but today he looks as old as I have ever seen him. Beside him stands my mother, Queen Elaina, unlike my father she doesn't look out over the city as she only has eyes for him today, but does share that same concerned look on her face. Stood just behind them is my wife Cara, holding our infant daughter Serah in her arms. Even at this distance, I know that she can see me looking at them; I raise my hand to my heart and then hold two fingers to my mouth, a customary sign of affection, and see her return the gesture.

On either side of my family stand two Royal Knights, both young and strong and ready, fully clad in their pure white enamelled armour much like my own, although they are carrying their greatshields with the Royal Arms of Lor'ahan blazoned across them - twin wolves chasing each other, surrounded by white trees on a field of green. Looking at the two of them stood there, I can't help but feel a sense of pride for my two sons; the firstborn Cen, named after his grandfather, and his younger brother Raf. They argued fiercely when I assigned them to guard their Grandfather, saying that I was only asking it of them to ensure they were not in the middle of battle but in reality I only wanted them to be with our family, which is exactly where I wished I could be.

Forcing myself to look away from my family, I put my hand on the shoulder of the archer closest to me and, looking into his eyes through the slits in his helm, I can see that he is afraid. I nod to him and squeeze his shoulder in reassurance although I am not sure who it helped more, him or me. I start to move along the wall, making small talk with those that turn my way and only hope that my own feeling of anxiety doesn't show in my voice. I climb down the steps to the Wolf Gate, where below me stand nearly ten thousand soldiers.

A large number to be sure, and all of them Royal Knights, trained personally by me and my Captains, but they are all that remains of the elven armies now. There used to be many more, almost triple in number, under the command of my twin brother and Crown Prince Mal'ahan, known as the Crown Army. While the Royal Knights specialise in the defence of the Kingdom, it was the responsibility of the Crowns Army to launch expeditions outside of our realm, either in the defence of our allies or as preemptive attacks on our enemies. The last time we had seen the Crowns Army, or indeed my brother, was over four years ago.

We had received word from our allies that a large unknown force had been raiding some of the outlying human settlements, so Mal had ridden out to meet them to honour our allegiance to Chancellor Eldren, the head of the council who governed the realms of men.

At first, father would send small search parties out, to try and get word of his eldest son's whereabouts, but as the months went on, he began to lose faith. We all did. Having now seen the sheer number of orcs

stood before me, I can't see how there is any hope that he survived. Even in the face of overwhelming adversity, he didn't turn away from his mission. Typical Mal, stubborn to the end.

As I reach the gate, I see my squire walking towards me and he bows to say, "Here is your horse my lord" which makes me smile. I've known the boy his whole life and have told him countless times to call me by my name, but he never has. Putting my foot into the stirrup I pull myself up onto her back.

I had let my daughter, Serah, name her. After long deliberation, she had chosen "Moonwalker" as her bright white coat and mane reminded her of the monthly walks we would often take as a family under the full moon. The filly had been born four summers ago, so I had used her to teach Serah how to ride while she was still small. Serah would go out to tend to her every morning without fail, feeding her hay and brushing her down, always with a smile on her face and love in her eyes. Once she reached her full size last winter, I took over her care along with my squire, but I would still take Serah out for rides into the forests that surround the city. I find myself smiling at the memory and reach down to touch her mane and, looking back up to the castle one last time, I find myself thinking about Serah and how I wish I could see her just one more time before I leave.

After excusing my squire, I check the shield is still secured to my back, both golden curved sabres are sitting comfortably in their sheaths on each side of my hips, and my greatsword is sitting correctly in its brace between my shoulder blades. The greatsword was crafted by my father when I came of age 872 years ago; it measures nearly six foot long from the hilt to the tip of the blade, but weighs much less than a typical sword of its size given its intricate design, it looks like several thinner curved blades have been linked together instead of being a wide solid blade like most swords that size. My father had made one for both Mal and I, twin blades for his twin sons, mine pure white with gold flourishes to match the armour I would wear in the Royal Knights and Mal's was red and gold to match the armour of the Crown Army.

I give my squire the signal to open the Wolf Gate, turning my horse back to the mounted soldiers gathered behind me, and looking into the eyes of those closest to me, I shout "Today, my brothers, we find ourselves tested by this new threat, this new darkness. Fight for your families, fight for their futures, fight for your King!" and with that I turn and charge. Straight into hell.

Chapter One

I wake up to the sound of banging. Confused and disorientated, I open my eyes to see Olive peering through the now open bedroom door with the same look on her face she has every morning, a strange mixture of mild disappointment and amusement that I haven't gotten up yet.

Looking over at the alarm clock I can see it is 6:22am. I slept in. Again. I really should set an alarm and stop relying on Olive. Throwing off the duvet, I sit up and stretch my arms. My shoulder is still sore, and the physiotherapy isn't helping as much as it used to. I should do my exercises, but they can wait until later. So I decide to have a shower instead, before heading downstairs for breakfast.

I find her sitting at the dining table with her usual helping of bagel and marmite along with a steaming cup of coffee. She points at the kettle where I see a cup of tea waiting for me and I smile as I think about how she always looks after me, ever since I took her in twelve years ago.

She has grown up a lot in that time, it's hard to think of her as the same scrawny teenager I found all those years ago now that she is a woman grown, on the outside at least as she is still one of the only people that can be as immature as I am. Now she embraces her fuzzy red hair, and her green eyes are filled with fun and curiosity about everything. I still tease her about the fact she is barely five foot nothing, but she likes being small, always telling me that it helps her to be invisible. It is the one part of her personality that hasn't changed in all those years, she still likes to hide from the world when she can. Most of it at least. But for some reason she let me in and now I see her as family and, as some of her lesser behaved boyfriends have found out, I can be fiercely protective of her.

I still remember the day I first met her, I had just moved into the area, and was walking around town trying to adjust to the new surroundings. I'd always had an affinity with the countryside so London didn't appeal to me despite working there, but I had liked the idea of being close to a town so this leafy suburb was as good as any. I was walking down the high street when I realised it was getting late, the sun was setting and there was a distinct chill in the air. That was when I saw this girl curled up in the doorway of a charity shop. She couldn't have been older than fourteen, scrawny as they come with matted red hair and green eyes that had too much pain and sadness in them for someone so young. She looked up at me to ask for money, and I stopped to look at her and instantly thought about how could she have ended up there? The longer I stood there, the more I found that I couldn't just keep walking. I remember looking into her eyes and getting the distinct feeling of deja-vu.

I had tried to smile at her and said, "I'm sorry, I haven't got any change, but the McDonalds is still open, want me to buy you a coffee and something warm to eat?"

I remember how she looked at me, as if she was trying to work out if I meant her any harm. In the end, she must have come to the conclusion that while I was a total stranger, the risk was outweighed by her need to eat.

"Umm, okay," she replied in a very quiet voice.

The girl gathered up her meagre belongings, then we went in and made our orders. I just ordered a tea as I wasn't particularly hungry, but it felt like she'd ordered one of everything, not that I could blame her, when was the last time she even ate? We got our orders and I carried the tray over to a table in the corner and she tucked straight in.

"My names Jake, by the way."

"I'm Olive," she said with a mouthful of chips, with more bunched in her hand ready to replace them.

"Well it is nice to meet you, Olive. Enjoying your food?" I said with a smirk on my face.

"Mmhmmm" she said with just as big a smile on hers.

I was about to start to asking her for her story when I noticed that some of the other people were looking, giving her strange looks. I know she had seen it too, as she had started to slow down on the chips and shrink down into her seat.

"What's the matter with you? Never seen a hungry teenager before?" I snapped at the nosey woman at the table next to us, who quickly decided to move further away. Some people are unbelievable.

I got a muffled "Thanks" from Olive's now burger filled mouth as she looked up at me with a curious look in her eye.

No one bothered to look over in our direction after that, so I started to ask her about her life, and how she had ended up on the streets. Turned out that both her parents and her older brother had all died in a car accident, and with no other family around she had nowhere else to go and ended up in the child care system. The first foster family hadn't treated her very well, so when they moved her to another home, she just ran away and had been on the streets ever since. That was over a year ago.

I wasn't sure what to say to her, what was there to say to someone who had such a hard start to life. So I said the only thing that I could think of that might help the poor girl.

"I know you don't know me, and I don't expect you to trust me yet, but I've got a spare room if you want somewhere warm to sleep tonight, somewhere to clean up. No pressure, at all, but everyone needs a friend and I'm new in town so I know I could do with one."

She stopped eating mid mouthful and looked up at me, I remember seeing the same sadness in her eyes as before, only this time it was mixed with an intense curiosity. Although she couldn't trust me yet, she obviously still didn't think I was all that dangerous.

"I'll stay tonight, if that's ok. But I'll be gone in the morning. It's nothing personal."

She has been living with me ever since.

Chapter Two

We jump in the car at 7:00am, right on time. I'm driving Olive to the train station as she has a course today in the City, before heading over to the commuter park to get my coach into Canary Wharf. I can see Olive messaging, presumably to our friend Cassie as they are practically inseparable. I've known Cassie for longer than Olive, we had friends in common during school but only really grew close as we were leaving school. Now I consider her one of my best friends.

Cassie is a little taller than Olive, with dark brown shoulder length hair and bright blue eyes, although they have specks of grey in them too. She never leaves the house without looking immaculate, always ensuring that her 'face is done' as she puts it and the outfit will have been carefully picked. I've seen her a few times without make up, and in her pyjamas and an oversized jumper when we have all been too lazy to go out, and she still looks just as lovely, not that she ever listens. The main thing that drew me to her wasn't her looks though, it was her heart, as Cassie is someone that you would describe as being beautiful both inside and out. The thing is that she doesn't let people in, as she is very guarded, but if she does open up to you then you'll have the best friend humanly possible; which I guess would make me one of the lucky ones. If you are in her circle of trust then there is nothing she wouldn't do for you. I remember when I told her about how I had found Olive and taken her in, not once did she question it, but merely embraced her as one of our group and for that I will be eternally grateful. I think even Cassie sees her as a little sister now too.

I pull up to the front of the station and turn to Olive, who is giving me another of her curious looks.

"What is it today then?" I ask.

"Just wondering, how it is that you manage to be late and early for everything," she says with a hint of sarcasm.

"It is a skill, little one" I reply trying not to laugh.

"Of course it is, just don't be late to pick me up later as I am meeting Cassie once I get back," she says climbing out the car. I can practically hear her rolling her eyes.

"Have a good day. Try not to get into any trouble this time?" I shout after her. Although she isn't the same little girl from the streets, sometimes she gets herself into trouble during certain social situations, with training courses and networking events the prime candidates.

She has a point though. Somehow I have dropped her off early for the train but I am still running late for the coach. As I park up, I can see the coach pulling in.

"Damn it," I mutter to myself, grabbing my bag before making a run for it.

A great start to a Monday morning. I pick a double seat to myself and put my headphones in, listening to the same playlist today as it has been every day for the last four years. I am a creature of habit. I close my eyes, hoping to get a little nap before work.

I wake up as the coach pulls out of the Blackwall Tunnel. I've always assumed it is the change from the darkness of the tunnel to the bright light that wakes me up every day, but today it's still dark given that it is before 8:00am on a typically cold Winter morning in England.

A few minutes later the coach pulls into Canary Wharf, so I get up and climb down off the coach, to find the harsh reality that is -1C outside and realise my coat is sitting safely in my car. Luckily I don't feel the cold all that much, something that Cassie always jokes about - me being a human hot water bottle and that it makes for great cuddles, but I only have her word to take for that. Olive isn't particularly tactile and I'm hardly going to cuddle random strangers to test the theory. I find myself smiling away to myself at the thought, like I often do when thinking of the two young women in my life.

I make the short walk to the office in just my suit while everyone around me is in overcoats, scarves and gloves. I pretend not to notice the strange looks for my choice of clothing. You tend to get used to strange looks after a while, especially when I have a scar running down the side of my face from a fight when I was much younger; it runs from above my left ear down my cheek and along the line of my jaw in a shape that aptly resembles the letter J. It isn't quite as prominent now, but it used to be much worse and people would stare at it all the time. I've learnt not to let it bother me, it's not like they gave me the scar or even know where it came from.

Chapter Three

As I walk into the ground floor reception of the office tower, I spot Nat standing against the wall by the first set of lifts. Although I can't see the person he is talking to as she is stood behind him, I know it'll be Cassie. I see him bend down to give her a kiss as she heads off in the other direction before I can catch up to them, although I am pleased for them both as I know they make each other happy, I still haven't quite gotten used to seeing them together.

I walk up slowly behind Nat. He is over six feet tall with short blonde hair and striking blue eyes, with designer stubble to complete the look. We are almost equal in height, but he is broader than my leaner frame thanks to all the time spent in the gym. Although he is quite an imposing figure, once you get to know him you laugh at the people who are scared of him as he is basically a giant teddy bear.

"Mr Smith. Tell me, do you make a habit of kissing random women in reception?" I ask him with a somewhat fake authoritative voice.

"I…" He stumbles over his words as he turns to me with an anxious look on his face "You asshat, you scared the shit out of me."

"You know me, I saw an opening and took it," laughing as I say it.

"Typical Jake, always looking for a way to wind everyone up. How are you mate?" he says with a smile on his face. It's hard for Nat to stay annoyed for long.

"Good thanks, nothing new. You?" I reply.

"Yeah, now my heart rate is back down to normal, I can't complain too much. Although Cassie is having trouble at work. I think she is seeing Olive later so I'm sure she'll fill you in." I can hear the concern in his reply. They have been dating for about four months now, and I can tell he really likes her. Of course, I already know Cassie's news as we talk every day.

"Apparently so, I have been warned not to be late picking her up…" I roll my eyes and Nat laughs as he knows Olive's favourite look of exasperation as well as I do.

I met Nat seven years ago through work. I had already been working at the bank for a number of years by that point, so I was asked to mentor one of the new recruits that was starting that summer. My first impression of Nat was that he was cocky, almost on the verge of arrogance, but I soon realised that it was just a front. We worked closely for six months as I helped to train him up in the exciting ways of corporate banking, and by the end of it we became really good friends; and now I can't get rid of him. We are no longer on the same team, but we have both been promoted fairly equally since then and still only sit about fifty feet from each other.

We jump in the lift for the canteen on level three, at this point we don't even need to ask as our morning ritual is to go and grab a tea before we go up to our desks, although Nat also gets poached eggs to help his recovery from whatever rigorous gym routine he had been doing earlier that morning.

"You got plans for tonight?" I ask as we step out of the lifts.

"Just going to make the most of having some time to myself, might watch the Spurs game as a bit of self-inflicted punishment" he says. While I follow them as well, Nat is a die-hard fan. He keeps telling me we should go up to White Hart Lane to watch a game but so far I have managed to avoid it.

"Well I'll leave you to it, wouldn't want to interrupt something so tragic" I joke back. "I'll grab the teas while you go eat every egg in London, see you by the lifts."

He waves his arm up behind his head as he walks off in what could be seen as a blasé response, but really we have just adjusted to communicating with as little words as possible just because we can. I've lost track of the amount of times we have just looked at each other and giggled like children because of some obscure unspoken joke, usually an innuendo based on something that Cassie or Olive said entirely innocently.

I grab the teas from the counter, then head to the lifts and watch as Nat scoops what looks like eight eggs into a container with his bagel. I push the lift button as he is walking over and one arrives immediately which is a nice surprise. The lifts are usually a nightmare at peak times. I

17

smirk at Nat, who is still a good twenty feet away, and dive into the lift and let the doors almost close before I hit the open button and just get to see a glimpse of Nat's incredulous face before it changes back to the same grin I get every time I wind him up. After all these years, he is still easy to prank but he has never managed to return the favour, although not for the lack of trying.

As we step out of the lifts on level 27, I turn to him to say "Have a good day buddy, fancy grabbing lunch or you seeing Cassie?"

"I'm seeing Cassie today mate, she made us both lunch. Maybe tomorrow?" he says.

"Sure, give me a shout if you want to grab a coffee later" and with that we both turn away from each other and head for our desks.

I'm lucky to have a window seat right in the north east corner of the building, so I get a good view of the O2 Arena and out over Greenwich, which is made more beautiful by the sunrise currently playing out across the horizon. I take my phone out to get a picture of it and send it to Cassie as I know she loves landscapes, nature, sunrises, even random weather effects which happen far more frequently when you are this high. The other week we had thunder and lightning with heavy snow and we were up in the middle of the clouds.

Work goes fairly uneventfully this morning, as it is the second week of January so a lot of businesses are still getting back into the swing of things after the Christmas and New Year breaks. It isn't until Nat appears at my desk at 2pm that I realise that I had been working on the same report for five hours straight and had completely missed lunch. Olive is going to kill me, followed closely by Cassie.

"Coffee time, let's go" he says, already walking towards the lifts.

I offer the girls next to me a drink, who politely say no as they always do, and then walk after Nat who I already know is going to attempt the exact same lift trick from earlier. It fails miserably as we have to wait five minutes for the lifts anyway. He struggles to hide the disappointment on his face.

We get into the next lift, and while Nat checks himself out in the large mirror at the back, I look at the same old 24-hour news that plays on the small TV panel next to the door. But instead of the usual boring updates on the worlds events, I am looking at something truly unbelievable.

"Nat" to which I get no response "Nat, Nat, NAT, seriously, look at this."

"What mate?" he says and I see him turn in the reflection of the screen, only to have the same reaction I do. Open mouthed shock.

The TV broadcasts BBC News, but instead of the usual news reporters there is a large bipedal humanoid creature with dark skin on the screen. And it is talking.

"Jake, what the hell is that thing. It doesn't look human, and is it wearing some kind of medieval armour? What the hell…" He asks a very valid question and I agree, it isn't human, and it is wearing armour as dark as its skin and covered in the bones of something else entirely, and a shiver goes down my spine as I look over the bones and notice they are distinctly human in appearance. Neither of us notice as the lift doors close and it starts to work its way back up the building.

"Just shhh a minute, it's saying something." Is all I can think to say as we both stare at the screen and listen:

"My name is Gro'alk, an orc Warchief in the service of the Shadow God" it says with a deep gravelly voice, and I try to process exactly what I am seeing on the little screen. How can this be?

"And I am here to deliver a message to the leaders of your world. For millennia, the orcs have suffered an agonising existence in the Underworld following our banishment at the hands of your long dead ancient protectors."

"But now they are gone, and with no one to protect you, war is coming to your world, and the Shadow God will bring the darkness to your lands. You are outnumbered, and outmatched. The allegiances of old are broken and now you stand alone."

"There will be no-one to die for you this time." And as it fell silent, some sort of portal opened behind him, and it turned to step through without hesitation.

I looked at Nat, who looked back at me and for the first time since I've known him, he was speechless, and scared.

Chapter Four

For what seems like forever, we just stand and stare at the now blank screen where the monstrous creature with the harrowing message had been moments before, when Nat finally breaks the silence.

"Jake. Tell me this was one of your really, really, unfunny jokes?" Nat asks, clearly shaken from what he had seen.

"To be honest, while the look on your face makes me wish I had thought of it, no, it wasn't one of mine" I reply.

"Seriously, this isn't you?" he demands sternly, although his voice gives away his fear.

"No Nat. Honestly. It's the first time I have seen it too," I say, although I'm not sure he actually believes me. "We need to get out this lift mate. I have to call Olive." Although I desperately want to call Cassie too, but I know that Nat will ring her while I am on the phone to Olive.

The lift stops back at level 27. We might have been gone for 15 minutes, but we haven't actually gotten anywhere. I pull my phone out and dial Olive. It rings but goes eventually to voicemail. I can hear Nat on the phone to Cassie as I redial. Voicemail again.

"Olive. It's Jake. Call me as soon as you get this, little one. Don't wait, for anything, just call me. Please." I can hear the anxiety creeping into my own voice. I hang up and turn to Nat, who is just finishing up the call with Cassie.

"Cassie ok?" I ask him, finding that I desperately need to know she is ok.

"Yeah, shaken and confused, much like the rest of us. But still at work, no one has been allowed to leave her office. Not sure why?" he tells me.

"Ok, thanks mate. Glad she is safe." But even as I say it, I know that I am going to text her and make sure for myself. I do trust Nat, but this is Cassie. I need to hear it from her.

"Did you get through to Olive?" he asks with serious concern in his voice this time, not just the fear.

"No. Went to voicemail. But she is on that course today. Although it is unlike her to follow the rules, especially about turning off your phones" I say, smiling slightly, Olive has never been one to conform.

"Shit. I'm sure she is ok mate. She is tough, and stubborn like you. You know that." But I think he is also trying to convince himself.

"I know, but I have to know. I can't sit around here just waiting."

"Jake, I know that tone." His response is inquisitive, but he knows what I am thinking.

"I have to go. I'll drop in and see Cassie on the way. Then carry on to find Olive. You can stay here, I wouldn't ask this of you. Or you can come with me to Cassie and then stay with her. I'll feel better knowing she has you there." I tell him, and I mean it. I know he would protect her if things go that way. When they go that way.

"You know damn well I am not letting you go alone. Olive is one of us. Cassie wouldn't let you go without her either. She loves Olive like a sister, and you too" he says, but now the fear is back in his voice. Although I can't quite tell which part of that he is most scared of.

"Thank you, Nat. Come on, let's grab our bags and stock up on water and snacks. I know how you can't go five minutes without eating." I say back to him with a sigh, trying to lighten the mood. I am already walking back to my desk so I can't tell if it worked or not.

I grab my bag and walk over to the kitchen, grabbing a couple of bottles of water, some energy drinks and a random selection of chocolates, sweets and nuts just so we have something to eat. I know it isn't exactly ideal supplies but beggars can't be choosers. I'm not prepared for this. But then who exactly would expect an orc invasion when they woke up this morning? I find myself smiling at the fact there is probably some conspiracy nut somewhere shouting I told you so at their TV. I look up to see Nat looking at me completely perplexed by the stupid grin on my face.

"Random thought, just amusing myself," I tell him. "You got everything you need?"

"Yes, and no. What the hell do we need for the apocalypse again?" he says in a sort of joking way, demonstrating our ever-similar sense of humour.

"Common sense and a can-do attitude," I reply. "So basically you're screwed. Just try not to fall behind." I definitely deserve the punch on the arm. Luckily I don't bruise easily. He normally pulls his punches but that one felt like it wasn't.

We walk back to the lifts in silence, I push the button and we wait for the lift which comes almost immediately. I guess we are the only two people crazy enough to try and leave. When we get down to reception, the entire security team is out in force and I can see the Canary Wharf armed guards outside in their crisp blue uniforms and fetching high-vis vests. I guess that is the clearest confirmation so far that the message we saw wasn't a fake. As we walk over to the side exit, I finally have signal again and take the chance to text Cassie and let her know we are coming for her, and to ask if she is ok. No one even notices us, let alone tries to stop us, as we walk outside and onto the street. Other than the security teams, there are no people on the pavements, or in the ground floor of the buildings, or in fact anywhere at all. I don't think I have ever seen this place so quiet.

"This is getting really creepy now." Nat says to no-one in particular, but he has a point.

"Let's just get down to the other end and find Cassie." I tell him and he just nods. I know that I need to see her, but in reality I know that we both do.

We pick up the pace, the unnatural silence makes me not want to be outside longer than we have to be. I kept trying to tell myself that what the orc said was that war was coming, not that it was here already. I guess most people are probably thinking, why take the risk? I know why I am doing it, Cassie and Olive. I'm certain Nat is doing it for much the same reasons.

As we come round the last corner on the west side of Canary Wharf, I can see Cassie's building and notice that there are a number of police officers outside. I look at Nat, who looks straight back at me as we both just nod and start running. As we approach, the police turn to us and I can see they are all armed with sub machine guns.

"Hold up you two. What are you doing here? You shouldn't really be outside." one of the officers says to us.

"Is there a problem here? What has happened?" I ask him while trying to catch my breath "We are only here to pick up family. We won't be staying. Can we just get inside quickly?" As far as I am concerned, Cassie is family, same as Olive and Nat. They are all I have.

"Everything is fine inside, we are just working our way down the Wharf to make sure everyone is safe and secure in the buildings. But I'm curious guys, you say you want to leave again afterwards?" he asks me with a puzzled look on his face.

"We are only stopping on our way through to the City. We need to go find someone else as we can't get hold of her" I tell him, and I can hear the pleading tone in my voice.

"Go on through, find who you're looking for. Tell you what, while you're in there, I'll try to get hold of someone I know who got posted to the City and get a sit rep for you." he tells me, while trying to give me a reassuring smile. It doesn't work, but I nod my thanks anyway.

We both run into the building and head straight to the lifts. When the doors open, we find ourselves face to face with Cassie. She obviously got my text. She jumps forward and puts one arm round each of us and pulls us into a cuddle, as I find myself relax a little. Cassie is OK, only Olive to worry about now.

"I was so worried about you two. Thank you for coming to get me," she says to us both, and I can hear her relax slightly too.

"Of course. Always. You know I'll always come for you," I tell her with a smile, like I have a hundred times before, "Have you heard from Olive? I just keep getting her voicemail."

"No, I haven't. Oh god. I'm sure she is fine sweetheart. Even if something happens, she is a survivor, you know that, plus she is great at hiding remember." Cassie says with a smile. I know she is only trying to calm me, but I can't help but worry. Ever since I took her in, Olive has been my responsibility.

"I need to go find her Cassie, I have to go. You can stay here, you both should. No need to risk yourselves. I'll contact you once I find her, and then head back here to find you so we are together." I say to them both.

"Really?" Cassie says rolling her eyes, "You know we are both coming with you. You need me to look after you, plus Nat has to come otherwise he won't have anyone to look after him." At which Nat firstly looks amused, and then slightly annoyed as he realises what Cassie actually said. But he knows she is joking when he sees her smiling away to herself. While I am worried about putting her in danger, selfishly I am glad they are both coming along.

I stand in silence by the lifts with Nat, as Cassie heads back up to grab her bag and some more supplies, so I use the time to try to call Olive again. And again. And again. Voicemail every single time. I'm sure it is just bad reception or her phone is off, but I can't help worrying. I see Cassie coming out of the lift, and I know she can see in my eyes how worried I am.

"Olive will be fine. You'll see," Cassie says to me. She is trying to smile but I know she is as worried as I am.

"I wish I had your positivity sometimes. You ready?" I ask her, and she nods, "Let's go."

We all head back out of the main doors, where we find the officer from earlier waiting for us.

"I'm glad you found your family" he says to me, and I see Cassie smile at the fact I had called her my family to get in here.

"Thanks, me too." I tell him. "Did you manage to get hold of your guy in the City?"

"That's why I came to find you. I'm sorry to tell you this, but there has been a number of attacks across London, and the rest the of the country for that matter. One of those attacks was in the City. A small number of those things came out of what is assumed to be some form of portal and went into a nearby building. Apparently, they killed everyone inside. It was brutal. Unrelenting. They've left the area now and moved into the Underground so that's been shut down too as a counter-measure," he tells me, but all I can think about is: please not Bank, please don't be Bank.

"Where in the City?" I ask, the desperation now clearly showing in my voice.

"They attacked a conference centre, just outside Bank tube station." He knows from the suddenly sullen look on my face, along with the audible gasp from Cassie, that it wasn't the answer we wanted. "Oh. Damn. I'm sorry. Listen, the tube lines are all shut down and it's too dangerous to go there on foot, so give me two minutes to call it in and I can drive you over there, ok? They are still searching for survivors, so maybe you can join in the search. It's not over yet, you might find her."

I can't even think, all I can feel is intense anger, fear and desperation all rising up inside me. I am vaguely aware of Nat taking my arm and guiding me over to the police car, and helping me into the back seat. Cassie slides in next to me, I feel her take my hand in hers and she leans in close to me.

"No Jake, we will find her," Cassie whispers to me.

Chapter Five (Shadow War)

I can hear the thunder of hooves behind me as I charge at the enemy lines, the deafening sound of the one thousand mounted Royal Knights riding behind me roaring in my ears. Three hundred yards out from the first orcs, I draw my left sabre from its sheath and lift it above my head before bringing it down to point towards the orcs ahead of me.

Right on cue, I hear the distinctive twang from several hundred recurve bows firing from atop the city walls, and seconds later I see a shadow pass across the ground as the cloud of arrows fall into the enemy ranks. The initial flurry of arrows decimates the front-most orcs, their hastily erected shield walls now easily breachable by our cavalry and within seconds I hear the familiar twang again as another volley of arrows fall into the second line of orcs that were holding the lances behind the shields.

Moments later a third volley of arrows pass overhead, this time they fall much further back, demonstrating the extraordinary range that our bows are capable of, all thanks to the mastery over nature that our carpenters have built up over the centuries. This tactical advantage allows our archers to remain effective for much longer than traditional bows, amplified by our natural eye sight. Our archers can continue to fire deeper into the enemy ranks, even after our infantry or cavalry have engaged directly.

Thousands of orcs have already fallen to our archers deadly precision, but in reality it has not made a dent in the endless sea of darkness still before me. A foreboding sense of dread fills me as I realise the sheer scale of the impossible task being asked of me and my knights; we may have the superior weaponry, but we are only twelve thousand against an army that is impossibly large.

When we first got word that a large force had been seen heading from the Outlands in the east, we sent scouts to try and understand what was coming. Most did not return. Those that did gave vague reports that it was an enemy of pure darkness, that consumed all it touched, leaving only death and darkness in its wake. As they got closer to the Lor'ahan, we had finally gotten a sense for the enormity of their armies. We counted our soldiers by the thousand, but theirs must number in the hundreds of thousands, if not more. I had sent one of my Captains out to scout their camps, hoping that by going alone, he would be able to move unnoticed, and his report stated that while they had brought horses with them, they did not appear to have any cavalry as none of the horses would let an orc near it, let alone ride it.

However, their lack of cavalry was more than made up by their infantry. For every orc that fell to our archers, there were hundreds behind them waiting to take their place.

I am only one hundred yards out when a volley of bolts fly from somewhere in the orc army, their crude crossbows being rushed forwards to counter our inevitable attack. I hear the saddening yelp from a horse just behind me as one of the orc's bolts hits its target, and I instinctively reach down to place my left hand on Moonwalker's neck, attempting to calm her. I don't turn back, unable to see who fell but sensing the loss nonetheless. All life is sacred to the elves, and all losses affect us deeply. It is why murder does not exist in our culture, and while we have been forced to take arms over the years, we do not take it lightly. Each death stays with us for eternity, both in this life and into the Eternal Lands beyond.

In response to the orcs crossbows, another volley of arrows hits with each archer picking their target carefully, and many of the crossbows topple down with the orcs who held them.

We are moments away from the first orcs, so I reach back with my left hand to unlatch my shield from my back and lock it into place on the brackets built into my left bracer. There are a few orcs that had wandered forwards in the carnage by the arrows, and I cut them down as I ride through to the army waiting beyond and I can hear the other knights doing the same behind me. More orcs fall to arrows just as I reach their front lines, dropping any orcs that had tried to reorganise the shields and lances after the initial volley, allowing us unrestricted access to those stood behind. I keep my shield up and swing my sabre at any orc that dares to come too close, all while encouraging Moonwalker to keep up her momentum. We cannot afford to slow down.

After charging through several waves of orcs, I steer Moonwalker right, trying to breach back out the front of the orcish lines; it was a tactic that my father and I had devised when we had learnt of the enemies' numbers. To charge straight in to their lines would result in an initial unstoppable wave of destruction that would decimate their ranks, but eventually the horses would tire or be cut down, leaving their riders surrounded and what would only be certain death. Instead, we would ride into the enemies' front lines, before turning to break back out the front and going back round the tail of our own cavalry still charging in our wake. We would then charge back at the front lines from a different angle, resulting in what would look like a large figure of eight if viewed from above. The added benefit was that our archers would be able to track our movements from their elevated position, and fire upon the orcs as we circle around for the next attack.

I can hear the cavalry circling round with me, and find that our quick change of direction has caught them unawares as we are attacking the orcs from behind, due to their sheer size and tightly packed numbers, it appears that they cannot turn nor react quickly enough to the unexpected movements of our cavalry. This tactic is working for now, but I know this will not go undetected forever, they will learn the pattern and we will need to adjust.

As we breach back out onto the open ground, I can see our infantry filing out of the Wolf Gate to set up our own shield wall just outside the gate, ready to engage the enemy and stop them from attacking the two gates on this side of the city. Our walls might be tall and thick, but the gates could not hope to hold off such a large army for any long period of time.

Circling round to join the tail end of our cavalry, I see more arrows flying up from behind the battlements that are followed by their telltale shadow seconds later. It is this small distraction that makes me realise that the intense noise of the battle has drowned out all the little background noises I could hear from the battlements only minutes before. All I can hear now is the ringing of steel on steel, the thunder of the horses and the screams of those that lay dying on the ground. All the beautiful sounds of nature have gone, leaving only the ugly sounds of war.

As the cavalry ahead of me enters the fray, I break off to the left as they turn to the right, breaking through into a new part of the army that had been unaffected by our initial attack. The sudden movement by the horses both beside me and following me remind me of a flock of birds dancing in the evening sky. More arrows fall in front of me, as do the orcs we hit, as we push through their lines, time and time again.

After another sweep, I can see there are many orcs lying dead and trampled by our horses, but as time wears on I can see that it is not just the orcs that are lying there, there are also the broken bodies of our horses and the dented armour of the elves that were once at my side. My heart hangs heavy as I find myself wondering how many have we lost? I can't tell, but even one life lost is a life too many.

As I begin to turn to signal the movement back out to the open, I notice an orc ahead of me, standing directly in the path we are due to take. It stands slightly taller than the others, the plate armour seemingly blacker somehow, and it covers its entire body, more like my own plate armour than the light armour of the orcs around it. As we draw closer, I can see that the armour is also covered in bones. The bones of those that had challenged him in battle, the bones of those that had fallen to his wrath. Much like my own golden feathers that adorned my armour, these bones showed his heightened rank.

The report my Captain had given about the cavalry, had also made a guess at their military structure. It appeared that the majority of their infantry were in lighter armour, with a mix of weaponry that appeared to be crudely made or stolen. Large numbers of the infantry all followed a single orc that would be in heavier armour covered in bones and other trophies. Our best guess was that these orcs would achieve the higher rank through displays of strength and cruelty, either by leading successful raids on the innocent or by killing their predecessor. The only other information we had gleaned from our scouts, was that all of the orcs answer directly to the self-proclaimed "Shadow God" although we do not know who or what this being truly is. War may be ugly, but this war is only made uglier by our enemy.

I ride towards this new threat, leaning into my shield and tightening my grip on the sabre in my right hand. As we close in, I notice that he is carrying an incredibly large two-handed mace that is easily ten feet long and I know that my shield will not withstand a direct blow.

The towering orc looks straight at me, clearly singling me out as his target as he launches himself forward, raising the mace high to his left to attack my unshielded side but I have no time to adjust my course so I raise my sabre in an attempt to get in a preemptive strike. But as I raise my blade, I realise what was going to happen and he swings the mace far too early, driving the weapon straight into the right flank of Moonwalker and I hear a heart wrenching squeal come from her as I am thrown from her saddle, landing on my back nearly ten feet ahead of the giant orc.

I am winded from the impact, but after a quick check of my senses, I am otherwise unharmed. I quickly roll over and get onto my knees in time to see the other cavalry swerving to the sides to avoid the reach of that mace, but I also know they are trying to avoid trampling me. They are simultaneously cutting down any orc that dares to run at me while I was down.

Looking back at the orc, I can see Moonwalker laying broken on the ground, the beautiful horse that I had shared with my daughter, her flank and mane covered in her own matted blood and I can see her chest heaving in a desperate attempt to suck in air, despite the obviously mortal wound sustained moments before. The giant orc glances back at me as he raises his mace high above his head and slams it back down into her side, and then again into her head. I don't need to look at the horse to know, I could feel her remaining Light leaving her body. It feels like a connection that I had with Serah has just been taken from me, and I desperately hope that Cara had spared her from witnessing this moment.

As I get slowly back up to my feet, my head and heart reeling from the loss, I watch the last of the cavalry filter past me until I am alone with this larger orc and surrounded by the innumerable orcs who have now formed a ring around us both. We stand at opposite ends of this make-shift arena, so I start to circle around the outskirts and he reciprocates the movement in the opposite direction to keep the distance between us even as he weighs up his quarry. I use this respite to sheathe the sabre and slot the shield onto its brace on my back, I won't be needing it in this fight, both it and my sabres will be ineffective against that mace. I stop as I get close to Moonwalkers now still body, and reach down to lay my hand on her side. I don't have time to mourn her here, so instead I must take this pain and anger and direct it at the orc stood before me instead.

It stands there holding the mace in both hands, looking eager to get started, seeing me as some sort of prize, a trophy to take back to his 'Shadow God'. I morbidly find myself wondering where he would put my bones on his armour before chasing away that thought.

I raise my hand to the hilt of the great sword and pull it from its brace before bringing it round in front of me, holding the hilt inches from my face, I drive the tip down into the ground. I look over the top of the blade, straight into the dark slits in his helmet where its dark eyes should be and wonder how any living thing can be filled with such darkness.

I have trained with this sword every day of my adult life, I know its weight and I know its balance, but more importantly I can wield it with extraordinary precision and power, despite its large size.

The orc lifts the mace to his shoulder and starts to move towards me at a gentle pace, so I lift the sword and hold it out in a defensive stance in front of me. Making sure to move slowly and deliberately, I stand side on to the approaching orc with my left foot forward, the hilt up by my right shoulder and the blade pointing down at an angle towards the floor.

The orc lunges forward and heaves the mace down from his shoulder in powerful downward strike, forcing me to parry the strike to my left and I reposition myself to where he had stood moments before, while he picks up the mace and turns back around to face me again. I know he is baiting me, testing my skill, watching how I handle the blade before committing himself fully. I should know, I am doing the exact same thing.

I watch him start to move towards me again, this time swinging the mace from the side in a wide arc so I parry it from below while jumping back to avoid any potential follow through, when he suddenly changes the direction of the swing with absolutely no effort and slams it down again, missing me by seconds as I move sluggishly out of the way. He is gaining confidence now, and swings the mace from its position on the floor in another wide arc, although I make no attempt to parry it and just move back out of its range. It is nearly time to fight back, but I need to time it right.

Looking up at me, the orc screams as he charges at me, swinging the mace wildly. I can see why this orc was given command. His ferocity and strength are truly a sight to behold. I continue to dodge while being careful to move the sword just enough to successfully parry his attacks without giving the orc reason to be wary of me. It is not quite time yet. He lifts the mace up to his shoulder again and a deep and harsh noise erupts from him that I can only assume is a laugh.

He moves forward with a surprising burst of speed, dropping the mace down along his side and bringing the mace back up for an upward strike. I have no option but to flip my sword horizontally to block the strike and as the mace connects with the blade, it stops dead in its track and the orc just stares at me. This is it, now or never, so I push the mace down with my blade and turn away while spinning the sword above my head in a full circle to force the orc to retreat back without attempting a counter attack. As I turn back to face the orc, I place the flat of the sword onto my right shoulder and drop my left hand from the hilt, readjusting my stance so that I am now standing in a more offensive position, still left foot forward but with my left arm out front and gripping the great sword with just my right hand.

I smile as I hear the sound I had been waiting for, although it may be a moment or two later than I had hoped, but the sound of hooves is almost music to my ears. Without hesitation, I launch myself at the orc, swinging the sword in a downward arc forcing him to block with the handle of the mace. As soon as it connects, I immediately turn back away, pulling the sword back into a horizontal swing that follows me as I spin round, putting all my strength behind it. The orc clumsily lifts his mace to block the attack with the handle yet again, but this time it throws him off balance and I push the advantage. Pulling the sword back away from him again, I feint an attack in the opposite direction and the orc hastily attempts to block my sword, but as I turn my back to him, I adjust my swing to bring the sword upwards then I heave the blade down onto the top of its helm, cleaving the orc almost in two.

After a moment of stillness, the orcs all burst forward to attack in revenge for their fallen leader, but are stopped short as they are met with the swords of the returning cavalry who charge either side of me, cutting them down as they pass.

After a moment, a number of the Royal Knights jump down from their horses to fight at my side, their horses moving on with the rest of the cavalry, who will continue the rotating assaults for as long as they can.

Knowing that I cannot yet rejoin them, I must trust my knights to weaken the frontal assault on their own and judge when best to retreat and join the infantry protecting the city gates.

While I was able to best the orc, I have now witnessed their strength.

Chapter Six

Sat in the back of the police car racing across London, I can barely register what is happening around me. Despite that numbness, I find that I am aware of the warmth from Cassie's hand still holding mine, and through that, I can vaguely hear Nat talking but I can't make out what he is saying. All I can think about is finding Olive.

I stare out the car window and try to focus. If we are going to stand any chance of finding her, I need to focus, I need to regain some control, I need to know what is happening. Not just in Bank, but across London. As far as I can tell, it was barely half an hour between the warning on TV and reports of the first attack. I take a deep breath and lean forward to talk to the officer currently driving us across town.

"Excuse me mate, quick one, you said there had been attacks across London?" I ask him, trying to keep my voice level but failing, "So not just in Bank?"

"Yes, sir, that's right. We have had seven confirmed attacks now and some other sightings but we are still trying to get more information on those. From the initial eye witness reports, it would seem that the attack on Bank was in far greater numbers than the others, but those reports aren't always reliable," he replies, and I nod along. When I worked in the branches during my first years with the bank, we were told to write down any eye witness reports as soon as possible after a raid or robbery, as the average person tends to forget the little details very quickly after a traumatic incident, reverting back to generic assumptions sometimes within minutes. And frankly, these attacks would be far more traumatic than any bank robbery.

"Thanks. Do you know how long it was between the attacks and the warning that was shown on TV?" I ask him. I have lots of questions but I am trying to prioritise anything that may be important and focus on those for now.

"The 999 calls all came in within minutes of each other, maybe five, ten minutes after the TV broadcast. But the reality is that those reports were probably delayed by everyone phoning about the thing on TV. Everyone is on edge, as you can imagine." His reply is curt, but it isn't intentional, he is just as on edge as the rest of us.

"Thanks. Look, I really appreciate you driving us over," I say to him, and I mean it.

"We all do. Thank you so much." Cassie echoes my sentiments, and I see Nat nodding while looking out the other window. I know he is worried about Olive too.

I sit back in my seat and look out of the car window, trying to process what I've been told. In the distance, I can see smoke rising over the west end and off again to the south west towards Clapham or Wimbledon, presumably a result of the other attacks. Something is troubling me about the attacks. Why attack so many targets at once, but then nothing since? Why lose the element of surprise? What would that achieve? My mind is whirling.

"How far out are we now?" I ask the driver. I know London fairly well but only on foot or via the underground. Driving across it like this is a new experience for me, even if you ignore the rest of the circumstances.

"Not far now actually, just round this corner," he replies as he slows to a stop. "Ah, looks like I might need to drop you here actually, the road is closed ahead."

"Here's fine," I say, a sense of dread starting to build inside me. "Thanks again mate, and good luck."

He climbs out the car and lets Nat out first, I feel Cassie squeeze my hand before she lets go to follow him out the other door. The officer then walks round the car and opens my door. I look up at him as I climb out the car.

"Good luck, I mean that. You guys stay safe, and I hope you are able to find who you are looking for." He says to me with a sympathetic smile, and I just about manage to nod back. I feel totally drained, but at least the numbness is starting to fade.

"Come on guys, let's get to the conference centre and see what we are dealing with here," I say to Cassie and Nat. I am trying to take control, a part of me needs to take control. For their sake as much as mine.

We all walk down the road without saying a word, there just isn't anything to say. Not yet. We just need to get there and see it for ourselves. As we round the corner, I take in the scale of the attack. There are at least fifteen ambulances, half as many police cars and a huge amount of paramedics and police officers running urgently around the area.

I look over at the steps leading up to the building that I recognise as the conference centre. Olive had asked me for help with the directions last night, so I found it on Google Maps for her and sent her the picture from street view. I notice that the steps leading up to the building have several black sheets dotted about and I suddenly realise that they are covering up the dead. I can feel the fear building up inside me again, and try to fight the resulting nausea. Now is not the time, we don't know anything yet.

I involuntarily start to run towards the building, and can hear Cassie shouting behind me but I have no intention of stopping, I need to get inside right now. As I get to the first the step, a couple of armed police officers spot me from the pavement and hold their hands out, gesturing for me to stop. As I do, Nat pulls up next to me panting.

"I'm sorry gents, can't let you in. This whole area is closed off, as there was an attack by those things here earlier. The search and rescue teams are inside now." the one on the left tells us, just as Cassie catches up to us.

"We know, one of your guys drove us over from Canary Wharf, we have someone in there and he said we might be able to join the search?" I ask him, nodding in the direction of the doors.

"To be honest, while we could use the help, I would strongly warn you against it. It's ugly in there, you aren't prepared for it. I wasn't even prepared for it," he says, and for him to even say that means that it must be even worse than I expected.

"Jake, I'm sorry, I can't go in. I'll stay out here and talk to the paramedics and the people out here, try and find out if they have seen her?" Cassie says apologetically, "If you don't mind?"

"No Cassie, of course not. I wouldn't ask you to. Look, I appreciate you being here and helping. Honestly," I say to her and when I look at her, I can see the fear in her eyes of what she may find in there. Although I know how much she wants to help, to be there for me, I can't ask her to go in and be part of this, I wouldn't be able to protect her from that. "Nat, that goes for you too, you're staying out here with her. No arguments."

Nat just nods, he knows not to argue with me right now, not that I think he wants to and I don't blame him. I turn back to the police officers and take a deep breath and start to nod my head dejectedly, before following the talkative one up the steps and into the large reception area.

"Just go straight through reception, then round that corner and follow the signs for the conference suites. That is where most of the, err, well, that is where you'll find the search team," he tells me with a grimace, and I just nod again. I can't talk, I am not entirely sure how I am even breathing right now.

I watch the officer walk back down the steps, and then turn to finally focus on the scene around me. I realise that the bodies on the steps outside must have been covered up where they fell, either as they ran for their lives or attempted to run in to be a hero.

In the large reception area, there are rows and rows of body bags on both sides of the room. Almost all of them have an initial and surname written on the bag in large white letters, and I find myself scanning each of them eagerly, searching for the one name that I am hoping beyond all hope not to find: O Shepherd.

Olive had taken my surname when she turned sixteen. She did it as a thank you to me, to show her commitment to our new little family. I suddenly remember how overwhelmed I was by the gesture, and blink back the tears forming in my eyes. I can't lose her.

I get to the end of the rows of bodies and let out the breath I didn't realise I was holding; I hadn't see her name. So either she is alive somewhere, or they haven't found her yet. Either way I feel lost, still no way to find my way to her.

I look over at the signs on the back wall and follow the arrows for the conference suites. As I walk down the corridors, I check the names by each set of doors, and desperately try to remember which conference room she said she was in. Drake? Draper? It was something like that. I round the last corner and see an open set of double doors ahead for the suite called 'Darcy'. Close enough.

As I approach the doors, several paramedics come through with stretchers with more body bags on top. I try to see the names written on them as they pass, none had the initial O. It is little more than a drop of hope, but it is still hope nonetheless. Once they pass, I move tentatively into the large auditorium style room and almost immediately regret it. There are still so many bodies strewn across the chairs and laying in the aisles, and stench of blood and death is overpowering.

I walk down each of the aisles, forcing myself to look at the faces of all the men and women who are just lying there, looking almost peaceful amongst the chaos. No one here deserved this, and it feels like the least I can do to try and honour their memory. I know it is pointless, ultimately, but it is all I can offer them. I walk down each aisle and check every face, then I walk them a second time and then a third. She is not here. She is definitely not here. Although a part of me is relieved, I can't help but think about where she might be, now that I know she isn't here.

I can't take the smell of blood and death anymore, so I head back out the way I came and into the reception area, where those paramedics are adding more body bags to the rows I had checked when I first came in. I can't imagine what these guys are going through, having a job where you are meant to use all your power to save people, but then find yourself spending the day dealing with nothing but overwhelming and senseless death instead.

As I get outside, I stop to take a breath of fresh air to try and clear the crushing stuffiness of that building. I'm glad Cassie and Nat didn't come in with me, they didn't need to see that. I look around and notice Cassie speaking to a couple of police officers on the other side of the road, but I can't see Nat anywhere. I know he'll be around here somewhere, and as I walk over to Cassie, she sees me coming and starts to wave frantically at me.

"Jake, Jake, quick come here," she shouts over to me as I approach, before turning back to the two officers "Officers, can you tell my friend what you just told me, please?"

"Sure miss, we have had some eye witness reports, they are a bit light on detail and while we haven't been able to verify them as such, several people have independently collaborated the information…" the policeman says to me, and I can see Cassie trying to motion for him to get on with it. "The monsters that left the building after the attack? Well, apparently, they didn't leave alone. It appeared that they may have had a hostage with them. We don't know who it was, but the general description appears to be that she was small and had long red hair. Now look, I don't want to give you false hope, it may not be her and we don't know what happened to her after they went into the tube station," and with that, the two of them turn and leave me alone with Cassie.

"O… k… listen, Cassie. I couldn't find her inside. I checked all the body bags, I checked the room with the, err, and nothing. She is definitely not in there. So it has to be her, right. It has to be?" I say, fully aware of the intense mixture of fear and hope in my voice.

"Until we know, one way or the other, we have to focus on the positives, ok?" Cassie says to me, and she tries to offer me a smile. I feel calmer for it, but I know the feeling won't last long. "Come on Jake, let's go find Nat."

"Ok. You're right, as usual. Any idea where he went? I couldn't see him from up there," I tell her, nodding back towards the steps leading up to the building entrance.

"He went to look for the officer in charge, I think he wanted to get an idea of what they were doing about all this." she tells me as we start to walk over to the tube station. It was as good a place as any to start to look, given the sheer amount of police currently gathering outside.

As we get closer, I can see that Nat is right in the middle of the pack of police that have formed, talking rather animatedly to one of them, as he always does when he is passionate about the topic of conversation. I push my way through the group, looking back to make sure Cassie is still behind me and I grab her hand to make sure we don't get split up, before turning back and trying to get Nat's attention. It isn't until I am right next to him that he sees me, and he just stops talking mid-sentence and gives me an expectant look that I know means: 'Did you find her?'

"Olive is not in there mate, I checked and double checked. Then I found Cassie and was told that those things took a hostage with them; a little red head," I tell Nat.

"The fact you didn't find… Anything… Is good, right? But Cassie, these things took Olive with them?" he says, turning his attention to Cassie now.

"We don't know if it was her, obviously, but it seems safe to assume that it is a strong possibility." Cassie tells him. I can see the concern in her eyes, she wants it to be true as well but is trying not to get any of our hopes up too much.

"Then we have a problem guys," Nat tells us both,. "Those monsters, creatures, what are we calling them? Anyway, they went down in to the station after the attack. The police have shut down the entire Underground, and evacuated every train, every station, and are securing all the public entrances and exits, supply tunnels, emergency entrances. The whole lot. If she is down there with them, it looks like she is staying there for now."

"Who is in charge here?" I shout at the group, putting on as authoritative voice as I can muster, "I need to talk to you, right now."

"That would be me, son. Chief Superintendent Peter Jackman. Not meaning to be rude, but, why exactly are you demanding my attention? In case you haven't noticed, we have quite a lot on our plate here." he snaps at me, rightfully so, given the situation.

"Yeah, err, sorry, I know, but my little sister was in there, and now she isn't. From what I have seen in there, and what my friends have been told by your officers out here, I am pretty damn sure that the girl they took was her." I snap back, although I know it won't help the situation. I get my phone out to show him a picture of Olive,. "Look, this is her. She matches the description."

"Yes, she does. And you are sure she wasn't in there?" he asks me, gesturing at the conference centre with a pained look in his eyes that tells me he had already been in there too.

"Positive. I checked all the tags and all the faces." I reply, the horrors of what I saw flashing in my mind.

"Listen son, I'm sorry that you had to go through that in there and I'm sorry that your sister is missing too." he says with a sad tone to his voice, his face dropping the stern look it had at the start of our conversation. "So what is it that you think I can do?"

"I want to know exactly what you are doing about the hostage," I tell him, my voice now firm and confident. "And whatever it is, I want to be part of it."

Chapter Seven

"I'm sorry son, we can't just let you go down there."
Peter tells me flatly. "With us, or without us."

"Let me? You think I was asking permission?" I snap
back at him. "My little sister is down there. so I'm going,
whether you send anyone with me or not."

"While I admire your ferocity, it actually isn't my
decision. I'm sorry, I can't help you even if I wanted to.
The gates are locked down until further orders," he replies
solemnly.

"Ok, fine," I say, taking a deep breath. "Then if it
isn't your decision, whose is it?"

"Well, the Met might be handling the initial
aftermath of the attacks as first responders, as well as
locking down the various Underground access points as
we find them. And the army is still being mobilised. Until
they are ready, it is the Met armed response unit that are
currently overseeing any planned operations to go down
into the Underground," he explains. "Let me make a call,
I can't promise anything, but at least you can explain about
your sister. Ok?"

"Yeah, ok, thanks," I say dejectedly as he walks
away to make the call. I feel like every minute that goes
by is another minute wasted. The tunnels used for the
London Underground are extremely expansive and cover

the majority of London and the surrounding boroughs. Olive could be miles away by now, or she could be at the bottom of the steps just feet away from me and I'd never know.

I look over at Nat, who looks just as frustrated about this as I am, and then down to Cassie, who just looks concerned.

"Are you Ok Cassie?" I ask her.

"No Jake, I'm not. You just demanded to go running down into the Underground. where there could literally be thousands of those… those things waiting," she tells me, with tears in her eyes, "What do you think you'll be able to do down there? You're no good to Olive dead. You're no good to any of us dead."

"I'm sorry Cassie," I say to her, and step over to pull her into a cuddle. "I just feel helpless, standing around like this, doing nothing. I don't know what else to do."

As I am holding on to Cassie, I can feel her trembling and she starts to cry into my chest. I might feel helpless in trying to get to Olive, but I can sense that she is starting to feel helpless in just trying to stay here with me. I look up at Nat and he still looks frustrated, but I was wrong, it isn't at the situation, it is at me.

"What are you thinking Nat?" I ask him over the top of Cassie's head.

"Nothing mate," he replies, with a harsh tone to his voice. It's clearly not nothing.

"Come on buddy, talk to me," I reply, keeping my tone soft. I reluctantly let go of Cassie, and look down at her to make sure she is ok, before I turn back to Nat.

"You're just going to let them keep us up here, huh? Olive is down there mate. We should be down there too, we should be looking for her! You know I am right!" he says, his voice now raised.

"Nat, seriously, did you not hear what Cassie just said?" I ask him, as he suddenly looks down at Cassie as if he just realised she was there, and I try to keep my voice even, "Not only that but don't you dare question my loyalty to Olive. Ever. She is my sister. MY responsibility."

Nat shrinks away from me as he senses the anger building up inside me, before turning and walking to the other side of the road. Cassie looks up at me and gives me a smile, before touching my arm and turning to go to talk to Nat. I know she will talk some sense into him and try to calm him down, but tensions are high at the moment and for good reason. Nat and I have had several fights in the past, but usually about far less serious matters. But in the back of my mind, I've always suspected that he had a bit of a crush on Olive, although he had never acted on it.

"Excuse me, Jake?" an officer says to me, tapping me on my shoulder.

"Yeah?" I reply, turning round to face him. "What's up?"

"The CI asked me to tell you that two of the Armed Response Unit were already on their way here, they're going to come and talk to you. Just waiting for them to show up. I'll send them over to you when they get here. Don't go too far." he tells me, before going back to talk to the other police officers.

"What was that about?" Cassie calls over to me, as she walks back over. I try to look for Nat but he has seemingly walked off. Noticing me looking, Cassie adds; "Don't worry, he has gone to clear his head. He'll be back in a minute. It wasn't really about you. Promise."

"No, I know. Thank you for talking to him." I say to her. I give her a little smile and nudge her with my shoulder in what I hoped came across as a playful gesture. No matter what was going on, Cassie had always been able to keep me grounded, keep me stable.

"Well, he is my boyfriend, plus I hate seeing you guys fight," she says, smiling back at me. "So what did he say?"

"That other Unit he mentioned? They have a couple of guys on their way here. They're going to come find me to talk about Olive," I tell her. "Did you want to go grab Nat?"

"No. I think I'll wait with you," she replies, looking up at me to check, "If that's Ok?"

"Of course. Thank you." I say to her, and I put my arm round her shoulders and she reciprocates by putting her arm around my waist. We stand like that for a few minutes, just enjoying the relative quiet, given the day we have had so far. Even with the chaos going on around us, we were in a little bubble. "Thank you, Cassie. You're always there for me. Even now."

"Always Jake. Best friends, remember?" she tells me.

"Hardly likely to forget." I reply, and for a moment, I try to ignore the dread that is threatening to burst out from inside me.

Another few minutes pass, when I see a couple of officers walking towards us. They are both over six foot tall, broad shoulders, probably mid to late twenties. They are both wearing Kevlar vests and helmets, with their Heckler & Koch MP5SF's held across their chests. No real question that these are the two officers from the Armed Response Unit.

"Jake, I presume?" the one on the left says, and I nod back at him. "Hi there, my name is Sergeant Harry Stephens, and this is Sergeant Adam Froom. We understand that you have some information for us about the attack here?"

"Hi guys. Yeah I do, I guess. This is my, err, well this is Cassie," I tell them, stumbling over the words, "and we have another guy walking around called Nat, he'll be back soon."

"Hi Jake, Cassie. Let's go talk over there, it'll be a bit quieter." Adam says.

We follow them to the other side of the road, away from the group of Met officers still standing outside the now closed off tube entrance while trying to organise their next steps.

"So tell us what you know, and then we will try to answer any questions you have," Harry says to me. "As long we can actually answer them, of course."

I appreciate their honesty, and they seem like nice enough guys, so I launch into the full story of our day, where we were that morning and how we ended up here searching for Olive, before going on to the eye witness reports that seem to indicate that she had been taken down into the Underground as a hostage. Saying it all out loud made it suddenly feel very surreal, like none of this could actually be happening.

"That is quite the story there Jake. I'm sorry," Adam says, and I can see that he is being genuine. "If my sister had been taken, I'd be trying to get down there too. Honest, I would."

"Same for me mate," Harry tells me. "Listen, that Met CS told us that you had demanded to go down into the station. But you have to understand Jake, we can't just let anyone go down there."

"I know that, but I can't just stand here and do nothing. Can I?" I ask him.

"No, you can't. Listen, come with us back to the temporary base we have set up near Monument station. It's literally just round the corner, but it is where we are coordinating all our operations from, we'll talk to the CO about you staying there when we do go down, and then you can be kept up to date of everything as it happens. Well, shortly after it happens." Harry says to us.

"That seems fair, but will you at least ask if I can come with you? Because you know I will." I reply, and look down at Cassie and tell her; "plus I know you'll be safer at that base, than anywhere else in London right now."

"Probably True. I'll run and find Nat, where shall I meet you?" Cassie asks the two officers.

"Don't worry, I'll come with you and bring you both back to the jeep," Adam tells her.

I watch Cassie and Adam set off down the road to look for Nat. And although I know she effectively has her own personal bodyguard, I feel a slight pang in my heart knowing that for the next few minutes, I have absolutely no control over her safety.

"Come on Jake, let's go," Harry says. "Have you got any other questions for me?"

"Just one actually. Have you actually seen one of these things in the flesh yet?" I ask him.

"Not yet. But given all the reports coming in, we've got really itchy trigger fingers right now. These things have the upper hand, and we are desperate to fight back," he tells me.

I climb in the back seat of the jeep behind Harry, before turning to look out the window and find myself scanning all the faces in the crowd for Cassie, Nat or our new ally, Adam. A few minutes pass before I can finally see Adam's head bobbing along the top of the crowd, shortly followed by Cassie as they break through into the open ground. But where is Nat?

As Cassie approaches the jeep, I open the car door to get out, and hear Harry doing the same. That is when I notice Cassie is crying.

"Cassie, sweetheart, what's wrong? What's happened?" I ask her, but she just buries her head into my chest and wraps both her arms round me, and I put my arms round her shoulders and hold on to her tightly, before looking up to meet Adams gaze.

"It would seem that your friend thought it would be a great idea to find a way through the side entrance into Bank station," Adam tells me flatly.

"What the hell is he thinking? He is going to get…" I start to say out loud, before quickly stopping the sentence short. Cassie doesn't need to hear the end of that sentence right now. I know she is probably already thinking it, so I give her a squeeze and kiss the top of her head in a vain attempt to comfort her.

"Let's get back to base, they should have the camera feed up and running so we can try to track him down while we locate where these things have taken your sister," Harry says.

I nod to him, and then help Cassie into the back of the jeep. I put her seatbelt on and then run round the jeep to climb in next to her and close the door. I put my arm back round her shoulders and pull her closer to me, and she takes my other hand in hers. Harry starts the engine and the jeep lurches forward as we begin the short trip to Monument station.

"We'll get through this Cassie, we all will. I need you to trust me, just for a little longer," I whisper to her.

Chapter Eight

Despite being the middle of the day on a usually busy weekday, our journey takes barely a minute. The only cars I can see on the road are the emergency services, although I feel a pang of heartache when I realise the majority of the vehicles are ambulances and paramedic vehicles.

Up ahead, I can see a line of chain link fence, with several blocks of concrete siren across the area ahead of it. Harry slows the jeep, aiming for the soldiers standing at the gap in the fencing and lowers his window.

"Hey, we're here to see the commander. Got some civilians with us, can you radio it through to command." Harry instructs the soldiers.

"Sure, head up and park on the right," the guard responds, and I see him lift the radio to his mouth as we drive through.

I look down at Cassie, and I realise just how tired she looks now, drained of her usual energy and positivity. It hurts to see her like this, to see her so vulnerable, so I squeeze her hand to try and remind her that I am still here.

"Right here we go guys," Harry says back to us as he reverses the jeep into a gap by one of the larger tents. "Jake, Cassie, we will take you through to command. It's the big vehicle over there in the centre. The boss should be in there, so we will explain why you are here and then get you settled in to one of the med tents while we plan our next move."

"I'll drop our gear into the armoury, I'll catch you guys up in command." Adam tells Harry, before jumping out the jeep and collecting their gear from the boot.

I retract my arm reluctantly from Cassie, and open the door to the jeep, before turning back to help Cassie with her seatbelt. She is fumbling with the button as I lean over to eject the buckle and take her hand to lead her from the vehicle.

"Hey you," I say to her once we are both out.

"Hi," she replies, and I can hear the strain in her voice. "I'm sorry. I'm still here."

"I know you are," I tell her, raising a hand to her chin and looking into her eyes, "So am I. Always."

She nods at me, but I can sense that she is still lost in her thoughts. As we walk round the back of the jeep, I take a moment to look around the area and can see hundreds of men and women standing around the area, all clad in Kevlar and carrying various weapons, radios and equipment.

The base, as they had called it, had not existed an hour or two ago. The chain link fences had been hastily erected to create an outer boundary to the numerous tents that had been put up around the large structure in the centre. Now that I have a moment, I can see that it isn't a structure as much as a large lorry cab, with a purpose-built trailer that was clearly acting as the command centre for the base.

Harry leads us towards the back of the trailer, and jumps forward to hold open the door so we can climb up inside. As I look around the cramped space, I can see rows of monitors on both sides with various images from across London on every screen, with at least two or three people gathered at each one. Harry leads us towards the back of the trailer, where an older man is leaning over a table that has a map of London on one half and a map of the Underground on the other.

"Sir, I have the civilians that have some information from the attacks at Bank. This is Jake Shepherd and Cassie Hollings" Harry formally addresses the man in charge, as he stands to attention. As he had been relatively informal with us, I had almost forgotten he was still an officer with superiors.

"Thanks Sergeant." the man says to Harry, giving him a nod before turning to us. "My name is Commander James Franks. While I don't mean to be blunt here, time is a luxury we frankly don't have. I was told you had some information on the attack that might be useful?"

"I think useful may be the wrong word to be fair," I tell him, wincing at the choice of words. "But we do have some information that is important to us, at least."

"Information is information. Fire away," the Captain states, looking up from his maps to watch us.

I take a deep breathe, before launching into the same story I had told Harry and Adam not long ago. I hesitate before I get to the point about Olive and her potential kidnap, taking another deep breath before I carry on.

"These attacks. They all happened within minutes of each other, didn't they? Straight after the warning? But nothing since. They had the element of surprise, but then didn't use it." I state, trying to sound convincing.

"You know, I had thought the same thing." he replies, and his honesty takes me by surprise, "But I can't work out why."

"To be honest, I don't know why either. But after going in that conference centre, it's pretty clear that these things are clearly very organised. They killed hundreds of people without taking a single casualty. It was a massacre. It was brutal," I tell him, letting the disgust and anxiety show in my voice. "But the strangest thing was that they took a hostage with them when they left."

"That seems to be the general consensus," he tells me flatly, looking back down at the maps on the table.

"That is why we are here," I state to the top of his head, causing him to look back up at me. "The girl they took? I think it was my sister, Olive."

"Are you sure it was here?" He asks me, a quizzical look passing over him as he looks at me and then Cassie.

"Not entirely sure, no." I admit to the man, "But I searched the building that was attacked and I couldn't find her in there. Not in the body bags and not among the bodies still being searched."

"While I don't want to take away any hope, you also need to be prepared to face that it might not have been her," he tells me, standing up straight and pinching his nose.

I am vaguely aware of nodding at him as I look down at the maps strewn across the table.

"Can you tell me what you know about her so far," I ask him desperately. "Any sightings? Anything at all?"

"Well, no, and not because I don't want to, but frankly, we don't know. Hell, until this afternoon, we had no idea that orcs even existed, let alone that we would be hunting them!" he says, shaking his head in disbelief. "We have been trying to track the orcs' movements, both on the streets and the Underground, but it isn't easy. They are keeping to the shadows where possible, and destroying any cameras they spot. Right now, we can only definitively say where they are not."

"I wish I could stand here all day and share ideas with you, but we have more to worry about than one girl. I'm sorry, that is just how it is," he tells me, and while I know he isn't intentionally trying to be harsh, I can't help but feel like I've been sucker punched. "Sergeant, can you escort our guests to the medical tent, so we can check them over."

"Of course, sir," Harry tells him, and I note the twinge of disappointment in his voice as we watch the commander turn back to his maps and his plans.

I nod slowly, desperately trying and failing to not picture Olive being carried or dragged through the dark and dirty Underground tunnels, as I follow Harry out of the command centre. Once we are all outside, Cassie looks up at me and then rests her head on my arm. She knows there is nothing she can say that will make this better, so instead resorts to the basic human contact which we both crave in times of need.

Harry leads us slowly to one of the tents over to one side, with a large red cross blazoned across the entry flap, signalling that this is one of the medical tents.

"I know that wasn't what you wanted to hear, and I am sorry, truly I am," Harry tries to explain. "If that was my sister down there, I would be doing everything I could to try and save her."

"I know, it's not your fault, or his," I reply, nodding back towards the command vehicle. "I just feel so helpless, not even knowing where she is, you know?"

"Listen, Jake, if I hear anything about your sister, I'll come find you, ok?" Harry offers.

I am about to ask him what's next for him, when I hear the sound of a horn go off in the distance, followed by another just behind us. Within seconds, there are horns being blown all around the base. We all look at each other with the same wild, fearful look.

"Shit. They're here," Harry says, a blank look on his face. "We're surrounded."

Chapter Nine (Shadow War)

"We're surrounded!" An elf to my left shouts, as I cut down an orc that had made for me.

"Knights, to me! Form up! Shield wall!" I holler, trying to focus the elves around me. They may have saved my life, but now I needed to take charge if we are all to survive.

All around me the knights begin to line up, carefully positioning themselves so that roughly half the elves were in a large circle, while the remaining elves cut down any orcs trying to penetrate the ring of elves. As one, the elves all pull the shields off their backs, using their strength to push the orcish horde back before plunging the pointed bottoms into the ground, each shield slightly overlapping the next and held firmly in place by the ground under our feet and the elves at their back. Once each shield is in place, I take stock of our makeshift safe zone and take a moment to breath before I need to make our next move.

"My Prince, we stand with you. What are your orders?" asks one of the knights from behind me, and despite the perilous situation, a smile creeps onto my face.

"Captain Petr. I should have known you would be here," I say to him. Petr is one of my oldest friends, and one of few that I trust implicitly.

"My life for yours, always," says Petr, as he lifts his helm from his head revealing a matching smile on his face.

"Not today, old friend," I tell him, clasping my hand on his shoulder. "I mean to live, as you should too."

"That would be my preference, my Prince," confirms Petr. "So how do you plan to make that happen?"

All around the wall, orcs attempt to climb up and over the shields only to be met with either the blades of the elves stood within or arrows from the archers still watching over us from atop the city walls.

Closing my eyes for a moment, I focus the Light within me to dissipate my helm into the aether. While all elves have the Light within them, most cannot wield it at will like I can. Like my father can. The tales tell that my father is as old as the world itself; and upon seeing the sun rise, he took its Light into himself and so was the Shadow of the night born. It was nonsense of course, but it made for a good children's story. I had even told it to my children when they were younger, the thought of them bringing me back from my memories.

Looking back up at the castle to focus on my family, it was clear what the plan would be. Turning back to face Petr, I take a deep breath before sharing my thoughts.

"We are of no use like this, in fact we are more of a hindrance; between our cavalry having to avoid us and our archers having to give us attention they can ill afford." I tell Petr and the two Officers that were listening nearby. "We need to make our way back to our infantry, so we can rejoin our forces and help protect the city."

"I agree, my Prince," Petr states, before offering his own advice. "Should we attempt the pincer?"

"The orcs are likely moving against the city now, so the majority of the orcs ahead of our position will likely have their backs to us." I say, talking myself into Petr's plan more than trying to explain the reasoning to the elves around me. "That should allow us to make steady progress, largely unimpeded by their main force."

"I will signal the archers to thin the horde ahead of us," Petr tells me, before turning away to make arm signals back at the wall while I carry on explaining the "pincer" to the two Officers still present.

"

We will peel open the front of the shield wall, half of the elves inside will then charge out and cut down any orcs immediately ahead of us," I state, talking quickly but trying to keep my voice level and clear above the sounds of battle raging all around us. "The remaining elves will then file out of each side and plant their shields to become the new front of the shield wall."

"Once the front of the circle is secure." Petr effortlessly takes over, having finished relaying our plan to the archers. "Those at the rear of the wall will then fall back inside the circle, ensuring that the shield wall stays sealed at all times. The archers will cover the front and back as needed."

"The front and back of the shield wall will never be open at the same time," I add, "so that we can give our entire focus to each side in turn."

The two officers both nod, before turning away to ensure all the knights are aware of the plan and ready to put it into action. The elves closest to me all begin to readjust their shields, ensuring the straps are tight on their arms, before drawing their swords and moving towards the front of the circle. I look over to Petr, who nods to confirm that he is ready before placing his helm back on his head.

Following his example, I focus my Light to reform my own helm back into place. While I can't see it, I can always feel my eyes begin to shine even brighter than usual when using the Light; the green taking on an almost luminous hue. A look that had been described as intimidating the first time Petr had seen it, back when we trained together in our youth.

Like my father, mother and brother, I was able to pull my entire suit of armour and all my various weapons from the aether, and push it back there, on demand. It had taken decades of hard work and practise, starting with smaller objects like a cup or dagger, before working up to my armour. Over time, I had stored hundreds of weapons in the aether, waiting to be called back, along with the hundreds of items I had sent there and not been able to recall. Now it had become second nature, I was confident enough in my own abilities to pass this knowledge onto my sons, although they were still learning the basics.

"Be ready my brothers, for as soon as the arrows fall, we must be ready to move." I tell them, and draw both sabres from my hips, twirling them at my sides as I step towards the front of the shield wall. I might be able to call my weapons from the aether, but sometimes it was easier to just carry them on me. "I will lead each charge out of the shield wall."

We all stand there; tense, ready and waiting. Within moments, the first arrows hit their mark and I see the elves ahead of me lift their shields and push forwards, the motion resembling the opening of the large gates on the city walls. I charge through the gap, cutting down the two orcs in front of me and spinning to block a third, who then falls to Petr's blade as he catches up to me. Another twenty knights come through after us and together we fight off the orcs that have spotted the opening and have turned towards us..

"Shields, now!" I shout, and within seconds, the remaining elves charge past us to place their shields into the ground and our wall is once again continuously connected.

I turn to the back of the circle, to see that the rear most elves had lifted their shields so they could peel inwardly while keeping the gap as small as possible. Any orcs that had tried to push through the wall had fallen to our archers' perfect aim. We are safe again. We had made progress, but not much. Every step we take will be hard fought. I see Petr raise his hand again.

The arrows land, Petr and I burst forth to fight those orcs around us. Again, the knights swarm us and plant their shields into the ground. Forward we go, foot by foot, the minutes draining away.

"My Prince, we are making progress," Petr says to me after the tenth push. "But I fear it is too slow."

"I know, Petr," I tell him, looking back up at the castle.

I can see that the archers are now having to engage much closer to the city walls, but I can no longer see the cavalry making their runs and realise I hadn't heard the sound of their hooves in some time. If they have had to retreat to support our infantry, then the orcs are already too close to our walls.

"Petr, we need to make more ground," I tell him. "Put more elves into the shield wall, let's try to take more ground each time."

"Are you sure, my friend?" Petr asks me, concern in his voice. I can appreciate his apprehension, while the progress is slow, it is also safe. Any attempt to speed it up may put us in more danger.

"I am." I tell him, a smirk forming on my lips. "Between us both, we can hold off the orcs. I have faith in you, old friend."

"I may be old, my Prince, but I have kept you alive this long," Petr calls back, the tenseness in his voice gone.

"You heard the Prince!." Petr shouts to our group, and I can see him smiling under his helmet. "We are all to push forward as far as possible this time."

Once again the front of the shield wall opens up, and I charge forward with Petr to meet the orcs waiting for us. I bring my right sabre across to cut down the orc on my left, before spinning back round and cutting the head of another orc on my right. Just beyond I see Petr pulling his sword out of the chest of an orc, but there is another orc is directly behind him that he hasn't seen. Knowing any warning would not give him time to react, I toss my sabre at the orc and it slides cleanly through its armour, lodging itself in the orc's chest as it falls to the ground.

Petr doesn't look back as he turns to cut down another orc, we both know that we do not have time for sentimentality. I turn in time to parry an orc that had run across, and then use my free hand to pull his helm up as I draw my blade back across the orc's throat. The elves now surge past us, enclosing us both within the shield wall.

Looking around, I can see that we have stretched ourselves this time, taking almost twice the ground as before. I'm feeling pleased with the progress as Petr claps me on the shoulder and nods to me before going to supervise the movement of the rear of the wall.

I sheathe my sabre and then walk over to the dead orc to pull the blade from its chest before it joins its twin in its sheath on my other hip. I go to take a step towards my friend, when my attention is drawn to the elves on my left as they suddenly buckle and tumble backwards, followed by a number of orcs holding what looks like a tree trunk being used as a battering ram.

Instinctively, I lift my right hand on the hilt of my great sword, lifting it off my back and holding it vertically in both hands, blade pointing towards the sky. I close my eyes, and picture my wife, my sons and my daughter clearly in my mind. I am here for them. For their safety, and their futures.

I feel the Light surging inside me and when I open my eyes, I can feel them burning the brightest green. Suddenly, a bright white light starts to emanate from within my armour, moving up through my shoulders and along my arms. As it reaches my hands, it moves into the great sword, the light swirling around the hilt and covering the entire blade.

I lunge forward, swinging the blade back behind me and as I start to descend, I bring the great sword down in a flash. As it connects with the earth, the energy circling the blade surges forward in an explosion of Light, transforming into a shower of small white darts that surge forward in a wave, cutting through everything stood in their way.

As one, the knights all pick up their shields and rush to close the gap. Petr walks over to me and puts his hand on my arm. I had put as much power into the attack as I had dared, without weakening myself in the process. The Light was powerful but it was not infinite, although it would regenerate over time.

"That certainly worked, my Prince," he says to me, concern clearly in his voice.

"I know, but the orcs will have seen that," I tell him, the same concern echoed in mine.

"What do you think they will do?" Petr asks me.

I am about to answer when I hear horns being blown in the distance, with more being blown from just outside the shield wall. As I look around, I notice that the knights are no longer bracing against their shields, and some of them have even stepped back slightly.

I risk standing up on my tip toes, to look out over the wall, and I can see that the orcs have fallen back by about twenty paces. As I spin round the circle, I am forced to stop as there is now a wide channel running all the way back to the rearguard of the orc army.

I stand there with Petr and watch as a group of ten extremely large orcs, all clad in dark plate armour adorned with bones, make their way down the newly formed channel. My attack may have stopped the orcs from breaching our position, but it had also brought us the unwanted attention of the orc leaders.

Chapter Ten

The horns are sounding all around us now and I can see everyone panicking, trying to get to where they need to be. Whatever they happened to be carrying has been discarded and is now laying scattered on the floor, the wind blowing papers all around.

"I've got to get you two inside!" Harry shouts to us over the noise of the horns. "Over there!"

Harry leads us over to one of the darkened tents in the furthest corner of the base. He pulls his handgun from the holster and disappears inside for a moment.

"Get in here, quick." Harry says through the door, and we follow him in. He doesn't need to tell us twice.

Once we are inside, I can see that it is some form of medical tent, and more importantly, it is currently unoccupied. A sad thought crosses my mind that while an empty medical centre is usually a good thing, meaning no-one is injured, in this instance it likely means that no-one has survived an attack yet.

"Just try to hide, ok?" he asks us, "I'm going to find Adam, then we will come back and get you once this is all over. For now, just stay out of sight."

I grab Cassie's hand and pull her over to the corner nearest the entrance. I push her down into the corner, and then crouch down to position myself right in front of her.

I lean forward slightly and pull one of the cots a bit closer to us, trying to obscure the line of sight from the doorway.

As we are crouched there, I feel Cassie let go of my hand and thread her arms round me, and I rest my left hand on hers.

"I'm so scared Jake. They're everywhere. They're coming. Aren't they?" Cassie whispers to me, her voice trembling as much as she is.

"I'm scared too sweetheart, but Harry and Adam are coming back for us," I tell her, sounding as firm as I can manage. "And in the meantime, I won't let anything happen to you."

We sit there, huddled together in the corner, listening to the carnage outside. Gunshots, screams, roars, more horns. Several wayward bullets come through the fabric of the tent, missing us, but causing Cassie to squeal and squeeze me tighter. There is no way to know who is in control out there, and I'm not about to go check. The lights begin to flicker within the tent, before giving out entirely and leaving us in the now darkened tent, the only light coming through the murky plastic window panel.

Suddenly the tent flap is ripped open, and I watch as an orc steps through the opening. It takes a few steps forwards and looks around the room, but the room falls back into darkness as the flap settles. I feel Cassie tense up behind me, and I reluctantly peel her hands off my chest and thread them back under my arms.

I keep an eye on the entrance for a few more moments, I don't want another one to come through and see what I'm about to do. I creep forward, keeping as low as I can, while trying not to make a sound.

As I get to the edge of the cot, I see the orc turn away from me, so I step forward and straighten up, walking up slowly behind it. Approaching slightly to its left, I jump as high as I can and drive my right foot down as hard as possible on its left knee, and feel it buckle under the impact. The orc roars with pain as it goes down hard on the now broken leg, and I drive my left fist into the side of its head, although it isn't a particularly hard punch, it was enough to knock the orc onto its side and stop the roaring for a moment. As the orc tries to get back onto its knees, I lean over and grab the back of its head and force it down onto the side of the cabinet next to us and it crumples onto its back, sprawled out and unconscious.

I stand up to take a deep breath, but the sudden brightness in the room forces me to turn to the door flap, and I can see another orc now standing there. Seeing its comrade lying on the floor, the orc draws its sword and starts to march towards me.

"Oh, you shouldn't have done that boy. Not that it matters, you are too weak to kill us without your precious weapons." The orc snarls at me with its harsh voice, "And that is the beauty of a sword, it never fails to kill."

At the mention of a sword, I lean down and grab the sword from the orc lying in front of me, and tug it out from its sheath. Weighing up the blade, I tentatively hold it out in front of me, pointing it at the orc.

"I'm counting on it." I tell it.

The orc lunges at me, swinging the sword across my body but I manage to parry and move past it so that I am between the orc and Cassie. It comes at me again, swinging from left to right to left again, and the best I can do is to move backwards and try to block each swing. The orc is almost chuckling now, seemingly enjoying the messy exchange. I try to fight back, swinging the blade clumsily at its shoulder, before bringing it back to block another of its swings, but I am met with a backhanded slap by the orcs offhand and find myself tumbling sidewards. I should have seen that coming, but now the orc is only feet away from Cassie. I have to fight the urge to look at her. It hasn't seen her yet, so it's all I can do to not give away her hiding spot.

The orc takes a step forward, raising its sword again to strike so I stand my ground and raise my sword to meet the blow. There is a loud clang as the two blades meet in front of us. The orc is only a few feet from me, and I can see the darkness of its skin, the emptiness of the orc's eyes and the rank odour coming from its armour. I push the sword away and step back before swinging my sword down in a wide diagonal arc, which is easily parried. I take another step back, this time swinging the sword at a horizontal level, but again it is parried. Instead of stepping back this time, I pull the sword round straight behind me and swing it down over my head, which takes the orc by surprise and forces it to move to the side to avoid my blade.

I quickly straighten up, and bring the sword back up between us. That is when I notice the orc is smiling, but not at me, he has seen Cassie.

"Now I know why you fight so hard, boy." It says excitedly. "I'm going to enjoy my time with her."

It lifts his sword to attack, but it never comes. Instead I hear two loud cracks, and see its body jerk backwards awkwardly, before slumping to the floor. I turn back round to look at Cassie, who is as shocked as I am, and then to the door where I see Harry and Adam come through, Harry with his MP5SF held up to his face. I drop the sword and look over to Cassie with relief.

"Sorry it took so long, we had to fight our way to the armoury." Harry tells me.

"Here, put these on, then we have to get out here." Adam says, throwing a Kevlar vest to me, and then passing one to Cassie.

I quickly put mine on as I walk over to Cassie, then help her get into hers and turn her to face me so I can help tighten up the straps for her. She looks up at me, and I can see that she has questions for me, but she doesn't say anything as she wraps her arms round me to steal a quick cuddle which I reciprocate gladly.

I turn to see Harry walk over to the orc he had shot and pull out his handgun, putting a bullet into its head.

"Better to be safe than sorry." he says to me, knowing I was watching.

Adam goes to look at the first orc, kicking the body before leaning down to check for signs of life.

"Well, this one is already dead," Adam says, sounding surprised. "Let's go."

"Where are we going?" I ask them.

"Away from here, but we need to be fast. The base is lost, they're mainly attacking through the front gate now, so we will try to sneak out the back. Follow me." Harry says, heading to the back of the tent.

I take Cassie's hand and follow them through to the back of the tent, but I stop at the first orc, I let go of Cassie's hand for a moment and bend down to undo the belt around its waist. Sliding it out from underneath its heavy body, I stand back up and tie the orcs belt round my waist, then step forwards to retrieve the sword I had dropped from the floor, sliding it back into the sheath.

I walk back over to Cassie and smile at her, taking her hand in mine again and follow her back to the others, who are now cutting a slit in back of the tent for us to escape from. Harry goes through first, followed by Cassie, then me and finally Adam joins us outside.

"Adam, we need to get through this fence too. From memory, there is an alleyway on the other side of here, so we can escape down there and then try to get our bearings," Harry tells him.

Adam nods and walks over to the fence, resting his submachine gun on its strap across his chest and pulls out a pair of wire cutters from his pack. He starts cutting the links in the fence one by one, so I crouch down with Cassie to keep out of sight, while Harry stands near the corner to keep watch.

"Ready. I'm going through now, count to ten and follow," Adam whispers urgently back to me, disappearing through the hole.

I step forward and get ready to hold the gap open for Cassie. Eight, nine, ten. I pull the two sections of fence apart, and Cassie climbs through. Harry walks over to me and does the same for me. As I climb through, I see that he was right, we are now in a long alleyway, with the tall buildings on each side providing some cover from any orcs that may be waiting to breach the camp. I turn round and hold the fence apart for Harry to climb through.

"We've got to keep moving, come on," Harry says, starting to move down the alley.

Harry goes first, then Cassie and I follow, with Adam right behind.

At the end of the alleyway, we can see that we are clear of the commotion going on behind us in the camp. We run down the edge of the path, sticking close to the buildings lining the road. As we go round a corner, Harry points to a cafe just down the road, and Adam nods. We all move off together and make our way inside.

"Let's go upstairs, it'll be easier to defend, if it comes to that," Harry explains. "I'll go check it out, wait here."

Harry disappears upstairs, but moments later we get the all clear from him. I let Cassie go first, and follow her up the stairs to find it completely deserted. Much like the rest of London. We all take a seat, away from the windows, and I notice that Harry and Adam take care to sit facing the stairs.

"What happened?" I ask them.

"After I left you, I went to look for Adam but I couldn't find him in the comms tent so I went to the armoury instead," Harry tells me.

"I was going to go there, but when the attack happened, I ran straight to the command tent to see the boss. He gave us these maps and told me to get 'those bloody civilians' and to get us all out," Adam explains to Harry, before turning to me. "He also told me that they had just got word from the team monitoring the tubes that they think your little sister is being held near Westminster, and they last saw your friend on the monitors. Apparently, he managed to follow them most of the way there. He marked it all on the map for us."

I look at the two of them and let out a massive sigh, and Cassie grabs my hand.

"They're both ok Jake. That's good news," Cassie says to me and I'm glad to see the spark back in her eyes. I need her, just as much as she needs me.

"It is. I know it is. Thank you," I say to them all, and I mean it.

"We know what you're thinking, Jake," Harry says.

"And we are coming with you," Adam tells me, smiling.

Chapter Eleven

Adam takes his pack off his back and pulls out the maps that the commander had given him. I help Harry clear the table of cups, saving the condiments to hold the corners of the maps once Adam has rolled them out.

I see Cassie lean forward and rest her elbows on the edge of the detailed map of the Underground, and watch as she traces the Jubilee line, looking for the mark that indicates where they last saw Nat on the cameras. I know I shouldn't feel jealous, so I try not to think about it and drop my own pack to the floor as I grab a chair, ready to look for the mark that would show me where they thought Olive was being kept.

I can see Harry is looking at a hybrid satellite map of London, when he marks a large red cross on the nearby camp to reflect its new status.

"I'm sorry guys, about the camp, and all those people. Do you know what happened?" I ask them, although I'm not sure that I want the answer.

"No idea. The commander said that the enemy activity had gone quiet, which concerned him. I guess his intuition was right." Adam told me, with sadness in his voice. "I hope he made it out. Last I saw him, he was making his way to the gate to help hold them back."

"Stubborn fool. He should have gotten out when he could. He was a good CO," Harry remarks. "He could have helped elsewhere."

"It's too late for that, so let's just focus on what we can do, yeah?" Adam says to Harry.

I look back down at the map, still trying to find the mark for Olive, but I can't see anything obvious. Turning my head to look at Cassie, I can see that she is just staring at the map, her eyes completely glossed over.

"Cassie, sweetheart, have you found anything yet?" I ask her. I reach out and touch her hand, which breaks her from her thoughts and makes her look at me.

"Hey. No, nothing yet," she replies, forcing a smile.

"I'll help you look," I tell her, before turning to Adam, "You said they thought they had found him, do you know roughly where?"

"They last saw him hiding out in a service tunnel, about half way down the Jubilee line from Green Park, heading towards Westminster," Adam tells us, leaning over to the map and pointing at a mark. "I think it was about there."

Cassie leans right forward and studies the little green mark. Eventually, she lets out a little sigh and sits back up straight, before putting on a smile and looking over at Adam.

"What about Olive?" she asks him, "You said they had taken her somewhere?"

"Looks like these things have set up some little bases of their own. There are a few we have managed to locate so far, one up near Wembley, another in Greenwich, we think there may be one near Camden but it isn't confirmed. But the one we think that they took her to is in Westminster," he explains. "It isn't the biggest one, that is the good news. But there are more orcs coming in all the time. Which is kinda the bad news."

"You said you're coming with us. It would be super helpful right now, if you had a plan to go with that offer," I say to them with a smile.

"Working on it," Harry tells me, still staring at his map. He hasn't looked up from it in a while.

"I'm going to check the bar for drinks or food. I haven't eaten all day," I say to the group, and notice Cassie rolling her eyes at me.

"You really can't look after yourself, can you?" she says, smiling. "I'll come help, and force feed you if necessary"

I give her a gentle nudge as she tries to stand up, and get a poke in the ribs in return. I need to try and keep this version of Cassie with me. I've seen her upset, scared and horrified all in one day, it could take its toll on her before this is all over, and I can't let that happen.

We walk behind the bar and I start to check through the fridges for fresh drinks while Cassie looks through the cupboards for snacks. I find some water, orange and apple juices. I collect them up just as Cassie pops up with some crisps, nuts and olives as her haul. She suddenly looks horrified with herself, and I just smile at her.

"It's fine, sweetheart. We will get the real one back soon enough," I tell her.

"I'm sorry." she says back.

"I've told you before, you never have to apologise to me. You know that," I say to her, smiling, "Come on, let's go eat, drink and be morbidly merry."

We head back to sit down at the table, laying the drinks and snacks out on the spare parts of the maps that don't have any markers on them. Harry and Adam have been talking in hushed voices for the last few minutes, presumably coming up with a plan, but have quietened down now. Adam grabs an orange juice and some crisps, Harry just takes a water.

"Any ideas yet?" I ask them.

"Ideas, yeah, plenty. A plan?" Harry says warily, "Not so much. The green markers are your sister and your friend. All these red markers are suspected enemy bases and the blue markers are sites that have already been attacked. Not entirely sure what the yellow marks are, but they're all further north so we will deal with that later."

"There isn't going to be an easy way to do this." Adam confirms. "I think we are just going to have go down there, take it slowly, quietly, carefully, and hope we find your friend."

"He might have more information for us. Something we don't know," Harry continues. "Then we can decide how to move on to Westminster and find your sister."

I nod to them both and look at Cassie. She looks lost in concentration, but meets my eyes and smiles back at me.

"I hate to go all motherly on you, but let's eat and drink first. Somehow, I think we shouldn't be going anywhere on empty stomachs." Cassie says to us all.

"She's a keeper mate," Adam says to me, with a wink.

"That she is," I tell him, but she isn't mine to keep.

Chapter Twelve

After we have finished drinking and eating, we all start to pack away our things. Adam rolls up the maps and puts them back in his pack, while the rest of us share out the remaining water across the four of us. I help Cassie put her backpack on over her Kevlar jacket, making sure all the straps are still tight enough, before tending to my own pack and ensuring my newly acquired belt was still tied securely around my waist and the sword sitting comfortably on my hip.

Harry walks over to me while looking in his pack, and as he gets to me he pulls a handgun and belt holster, holding it out to me.

"I think you should take this. Just in case. If anything happens to us, at least you can protect yourself, and Cassie," Harry says to me. "It's a Glock 26, nine rounds in the magazine plus one in the chamber, so you don't need to rack the slide before you fire."

I nod and take the gun, and mull over what Harry told me. I guess racking the slide is what the heroes do in the movies when they pull the sliding mechanism back to load the gun every single time they get into a gunfight.

It feels strange in my hand, almost wrong somehow. I know he is right, but I don't know if I like having it. I slide the holster onto my belt, the gun now positioned on my right hip, with the sword still on my left. I look over at Cassie and realise that whatever feelings I may have about guns, if it would save her life then I would use it without hesitation.

"Right then. Let's get moving," Adam says to us, and heads for the stairs.

We all follow him downstairs and back outside. The streets are now eerily calm and quiet after the loudness that was present only minutes ago, echoing over the rooftops from the attack on the camp. The orcs must have left now, and I can't help but think about exactly what it was they left behind.

The walk from Bank to Charing Cross is fairly uneventful, after everything else that has happened today. Police cars come flying past us at one point, on the way to the scene of another attack, or away from one, but otherwise we don't see anyone around. Whether it is man or monster.

Ignoring the grand building that houses Charing Cross in front of us, we walk down towards Embankment station which is the first destination of our makeshift plan, as Harry knows some of the officers guarding the gate there. The plan hinges on Harry convincing him to let us through, so we hang back to let him do the talking. Once Harry disappears from sight, I see Adam turn to look back up the hill, offering me a brief moment of privacy with Cassie.

"Hey you. How are you holding up?" I ask her, speaking softly.

"I'm ok darling. Honestly," she tells me. "It's good to be trying to do something. You know?"

"Yeah, I know what you mean," I tell her, smiling. "Thank you for coming with me Cassie, I know its selfish, but I am glad you are here with me."

"I'm glad, Jake. I'm always here," she says, smiling back at me. "But I need you more. You saved me earlier, you risked everything to save me. Thank you."

I pull her into a cuddle and hold on to her tightly.

"Best friends, Cassie. You know I wouldn't let anything happen to you," I tell her, resting my chin on the top of her head.

"I know you wouldn't, I could see it in your eyes earlier when that orc attacked us. You didn't even hesitate, you just did it. But I have to ask Jake…" she says to me. "How?"

"I'll do anything to protect you. All I could think about was making sure you were safe," I tell her. "Plus I am the biggest geek you know, and I think Star Wars taught me that every stick is a light sabre, so I have had a lot of practise over the years."

"Such a dork," She tells me, with a small laugh.

I see Adam turn around and he smiles at me. He still thinks we are together, I'll correct him at some point. Probably. He then looks up past me, and I let go of Cassie slightly so I can turn to look and I see Harry wave us over. I give Cassie a quick squeeze before reluctantly letting go and we all walk over to where Harry is waiting.

"My guy will let us down there. He owes me a favour, plus he wants someone to go and teach them a lesson," Harry explains. "So this is your last chance, if you want to walk away, now is the time."

"I'm coming. That's my little sister down there," I tell him adamantly.

"Me too. She is basically family to me as well, and we need to go save Nat from whatever stupid situation he has gotten himself into now." Cassie says dejectedly. "Plus I'll feel much safer having you three with me than being holed up alone."

"I'm not even going to dignify that with an answer," Adam tells Harry. "Let's go."

We all follow Harry round the corner and his friend nods to us, and raises the gate to the tube station. We all duck under and watch the gate come back down behind us. We all silently look at each other, acknowledging that we are now on our own in enemy territory.

Harry leads the way down the unnervingly stationary escalators, taking us down to the platform for the Circle line. I remember back to earlier when the first police officers told us that the trains had been stopped and evacuated as soon as the orcs first came down here, but I see Harry looking at the live rail, trying to work out if the power was cut.

"Apparently, they turned off the electricity as well, but I would rather be safe than sorry," Harry says, jumping carefully down onto the tracks. He takes a chewing gum out of his pocket, removes the foil wrapper and puts the gum in his mouth. Screwing the foil into a ball, he drops it onto the live rail and watches as it harmlessly rolls of the side.

"We're good," he confirms, obviously relieved.

I lower Cassie down to Harry, who takes her and puts her safely down on the ground, then jump down behind her with Adam following up behind me.

"We're gonna head west down this tunnel for about half a mile, then there should be a service tunnel that will take us to the Jubilee line, where we can start the search for your friend." Adam explains. "The tunnel should keep us far enough away from the orcs gathering up ahead, but keep your eyes open. Even if you only think you see something, stop and tell us."

We all move as slowly and quietly down the tunnel as we can, and unsurprisingly no-one talks. I reach over and take Cassie's hand in the dark, and feel her squeeze it tightly. I know her better than anyone, but even I wouldn't try to guess what is going through her mind right now.

I see Harry stop and duck down, so we all drop down to our knees instinctively. Has he seen something? After a few minutes, he slowly stands back up.

"False alarm, let's keep moving. The service door should be just up here on the right," Harry tells us.

As we are walking along the tunnel, I spot a door and lean forward to tap Harry on the shoulder as he is already started to pass it. He turns to look at me with a puzzled look, so I nod to the door. He climbs up to the platform with the door and tries to open it but it is stuck shut.

"Adam, give me a hand, will you?" He whispers down.

Adam and Harry both try to open the twisting lock, but it doesn't give an inch. I am looking forward to making sure nothing is coming towards us, and I know Cassie is keeping an eye on the tunnel back where we just came from.

"Once more," Harry whispers again.

This time, I see them both throw their entire weight behind the handle. For a moment, nothing happens, then I see the handle suddenly give way, and relief fills me as it slides down to open the door. That feeling of relief is short lived as the last two inches of the movement create a loud squealing, grinding noise that travels right down the tunnel in every direction. We all just stare at each other, waiting to see if there is a reaction.

We don't have to wait long. Roars come from the tunnel ahead of us, and then the sound of hundreds of footsteps running towards us. I grab Cassie and practically throw her up to the platform, where Harry and Adam grab her arms and pull her inside the door. I see Harry lift his MP5SF and point it down the tunnel, ready to engage, while Adam offers his hand down to help me up.

I pile inside the door to find Cassie hunched over and shaking again. I put my arm round her in an effort to comfort her. Turning back, I see Harry and Adam forcing the door closed and trying to pull the lock back up but it is stuck again. I let go of Cassie and go to help them. As we are trying to pull it up, the first of the orcs start banging and crashing against the heavy steel door. On the third try, the handle moves back into the lock position and all three of us hold it there, struggling against the orcs on the other side who are now trying to open it again.

"Cassie, can you find something we can jam under the handle?" Adam asks her.

"Umm, ok, I'll have a look," she says, snapping out of her daze.

She walks a little further away and out of sight due to the curve of the tunnel, and I have to fight the urge to go looking for her, but she returns almost straight away with a sturdy metal bar. She hands it to Adam, who positions it under the handle and we all tentatively step away, ready to grab the handle again if the pole doesn't work,. Luckily it seems to hold. For now.

"Let's go, now, we need to get out of this service tunnel otherwise they could trap us in from the other end," Harry says urgently.

We move as quickly as we can down the long thin tunnel, Harry up front, then Cassie, me and Adam all in single file. The tunnel is dark, with the exception of some red emergency lights every fifty or so yards apart.

Eventually we reach the end of the tunnel, and find a door much like the one we had just come through. Harry walks up to the door and reaches out for the handle when we are startled by a voice in the dark behind us.

"I wouldn't go out there, if I were you mate," says the mystery voice, but I know that voice very well, and watch as Nat steps out of the shadows.

Chapter Thirteen

We all stand there, staring at Nat. He looks terrible, he has a cut above his eye and looks like he has been hit in the face more than once, his chin has scrapes on it and there's a bruise forming on his left cheek. I look over to Cassie, who is frozen to the spot.

"Nat, what the hell happened to you?" I ask him, stepping over to pull him into a hug.

"I don't know what I was thinking. I'm sorry," he tells me, letting go and stepping back. "I just wanted to do something, you know? All that standing around. I was going mad."

I look at him and nod, I know that feeling. I wanted to come down here myself, but I couldn't leave Cassie alone. Cassie. I turn round to look at her and she is looking straight at Nat, tears falling down her face.

"Nat. What. The. Hell!" she shouts at him, taking a step forward and hitting him on the chest. "I thought you were dead! Dead!"

Nat pulls her into his arms, trying to console her but I can see it isn't working as she tries to push herself away from him.

"I'm sorry Cassie. I had to do something. I just…" he tries to explain, as she pulls free of him and backs off, shaking her head.

"I'm sorry to break up this little reunion guys, but we really should think about moving," Harry says to us, before turning to face Nat. "Nat was it? I am Harry, and this is Adam. We are here to help get Jake's sister back."

"Then I am with you. 100%. What's the plan?" Nat asks him as if he was already part of our rag tag rescue team.

"Right now? To get the hell away from here," Harry tells him, "We attracted the attention of some orcs getting in here but we managed to lock the door behind us. You said we shouldn't open this one either, why?"

"I've heard noises on the other side. Like they are running back and forward out there," Nat says. "But I haven't heard anything in the last ten, fifteen minutes maybe."

"Well, we know for a fact that there are orcs back that way, so we need to risk it. We need to get out of this tunnel, and the one on the other side of the door leads to where they are keeping Olive," Adam interjects.

"Agreed. I'll go out first with Jake. Nat, Cassie, come through next and Adam will come through last, securing the door again," Harry tells us. "Jake, might want to draw your gun."

I put my hand on the Glock, and pull it out of the holster. It still feels strange to hold it, and when I look up I see Nat looking at me, trying to work out why I even have a gun in the first place. I nod at Nat, and look over to Cassie who has managed to fight off the tears but still looks angry. I don't blame her, I had been trying to understand what Nat was thinking when he ran off and left her, to no avail. I smile at Cassie and then turn to walk up behind Harry, putting my hand on his shoulder to let him know that I am ready.

Harry pulls down on the handle, which thankfully moves far more silently than last time. He slowly and carefully pulls the door inwards, wide enough for him to slip through with his MP5SF held up in his right hand, aiming it down the right side of the tunnel. I follow him straight through with my gun held up in front of me, but aiming to the left to avoid any potential crossfire. I can't help but grin briefly, I guess all those hours spent on the Playstation are finally paying off.

As I climb down from the raised platform, I see Harry turn around and kneel down to stare down the tunnel in the direction of Westminster station. I follow his gaze, crouching down myself, but I don't know why as it is too dark to make anything out.

I can hear Nat climb down from the platform, and when I look back, I see him help Cassie down but as soon as her feet hit the floor, she lets go and walks away from him. Lastly, Adam appears through the door and closes it behind him. He locks the door again, before joining us down on the lower level.

"Let's drop back a bit, see if we can find somewhere to hide and talk properly," Adam says, and Harry nods his agreement.

"Adam, lead the way. I'll hang back and cover us," Harry tells him.

Adam turns and starts to walk back, with Cassie and Nat close behind him. I hesitate to turn away from the station, I know Olive is down there somewhere, but eventually I turn and start to walk back behind them, and ahead of me I can see Nat take Cassie's hand but this time she doesn't let go. I walk in silence for a few moments watching the two of them together, the sight of them irritates me a little which takes me by surprise as it never has before, not like this anyway. As we come round a bend, I'm startled by a noise from behind me.

I turn round to see Harry jogging up behind me, and as he approaches, I realise he looks worried.

"Adam, wait up," he says softly, and I see Adam, Nat and Cassie all stop and turn to us.

"What is it?" Adam calls back, trying to keep his voice low.

"I can hear noises coming from the tunnel. I think they're on the move. You need to go, now," Harry tells him.

"What about you?" Adam asks.

"I'll hang back, lay down cover fire if needed and then fall back," he replies, "Don't worry, I'm no hero. I'll run when I need to."

"You bloody better! Don't fall behind," Adam tells his friend firmly.

Adam leads the way down the tunnel, and I continue to follow Nat and Cassie down the tunnel, who are still hand in hand. About two hundred yards further down the tunnel, Adam stops at a raised platform and climbs up. He tentatively tests the handle on the door, which opens quietly enough and leads to a small room filled with pipes, dials and a ladder leading back to the surface, hopefully.

"Right guys, we are going up here. I'll go first, Cassie follow me up, then Nat. Jake, come up last, ok? But leave the door open, so Harry knows we went this way," Adam tells us, before disappearing up the ladder.

Cassie puts her hand on the ladder, but turns to me before she climbs up and looks at me, her eyes full of concern. She really does know me better than anyone.

"Remember your promise Jake," she tells me, and I do… I'll always find her.

"Of course," I say to her, "I'll see you soon."

She climbs up, and I see Nat turn and look straight at me.

"Thank you for being there for her mate, when I couldn't be," he says to me, and I throw him an incredulous look which makes Nat shrink back.

I watch Nat start to climb up the ladder, when I hear gunshots coming from the tunnel. I duck back out the doorway, but I can't see Harry, he must still be further down.

"Nat, get up that ladder!" I shout up to him, "Get Cassie to safety! I'll wait for Harry. Don't worry, I will be right behind you."

"Are you nuts? Get up here, he'll be fine," Nat shouts down. He doesn't know these guys, but I do and they're part of our group now.

"Get Cassie out of here and stick with Adam, we will find you!" I shout back up, and seeing him continue to climb up, I shut the door.

I jump down from the platform and move down the tunnel towards the gunfire. As I come round the corner, I can see Harry's silhouette each time the submachine gun fires, as well as the ten or so orcs in front of him. I bring the Glock back up in front of me and pick out a shape to the right of Harry, trying to line up his chest in the little sights notched in the top. I take a deep breath, and then let it out, squeezing the trigger.

The bang is followed immediately by the jerking recoil of the gun which throws it up higher than I was expecting, but not overly so. I refocus on the target and see that it hadn't gone down. My shot missing it by quite a bit.

"What the hell are you doing here Jake?" Harry calls back to me, as he shoots the orc that I had missed. "You were meant to be getting out of here with Adam."

I move up next to him, and pick out another target. Inhale, exhale, squeeze, shoot. I knew to compensate for the recoil this time, so I hit my target square in the chest. Taking aim again, I go through the motions; inhale, exhale, squeeze, shoot and watch as another orc hits the floor. Next to me, Harry takes another shot and then lets his submachine gun drop down to his waist as he pulls out the magazine, quickly replacing it with another from his belt.

"It didn't feel right leaving you behind," I say to him. "Plus this is keeping Cassie safe. They managed to get up to the surface, I'll show you the door. Come on."

We stand and look down the tunnel to make sure there are no other orcs immediately behind us, before turning back and running back towards the door.

"You're a pretty good shot, Jake," he tells me, as we run back. "I'm impressed."

"Thanks, I think," I reply sourly, being a good shot was coming in handy but it wasn't something I was ever expecting to master. "The door is just up here."

I climb up the platform and open the door. I put the gun back in the holster, and look back at Harry to make sure he is ready, before climbing up the ladder. At the top, I peek over the lip of the ladder and see that the room is empty and I feel a pang of sadness that Cassie wasn't here.

I climb out of the hole, and crouch down to help Harry up. Once he is off the ladder, we take a moment to listen down the hole to make sure we hadn't been followed.

"Where did they go?" Harry asks me.

"I don't know, I never got up the ladder. I came straight for you when I heard the shots," I tell him.

Harry looks around the room and nods at the door on the opposite side.

"Looks like they busted the lock to get out the door," Harry states, heading over to the door.

I follow him over and he eases open the door so that we can lean out to look down the street. The entire area outside is devoid of life, but I pull out my gun again as we step outside. After Harry shuts the door, we both straighten up, looking down the street, and I can see Harry trying to think about where Adam would have taken them to hide and wait. After a few moments, Harry starts to move off down the road and I follow him.

As we get to a corner, Harry stops and looks down the side road. He turns back to me and mouths, "I can see them," back to me. I creep forward until I am next to him and look round the corner, just below where his head is. In the distance, I can see Adam, Cassie and Nat crouched down behind a dumpster.

Harry takes off round the corner, moving towards them in a crouched jog and I follow right behind him. Adam sees us coming, and gives Cassie a nudge and points at us. I see her smile and relief washes over me.

"Took your time?" Adam mocks Harry.

"Someone had to do the hard work," Harry smiles back at him, hitting him on the arm.

Cassie jumps up and wraps her arms round me.

"I knew you'd come back," she whispers in my ear.

"Always," I whisper back.

I let go of her, turning to Nat and hugging him too. He may be an idiot, but he is my idiot.

"Let's get off the street. We need somewhere to camp up. We are going to need to rethink our plan, get some rest and try again in the morning," Harry tells us, and I see Nat tense up at this suggestion, obviously against the idea of waiting.

"I agree, we all need to rest," I say in support of Harry, which only fuels Nat's unease.

"I saw a B&B just up ahead. There weren't any lights on, we can try to get in and stay there tonight," Adam tells us.

Adam leads the way down the alleyway, and across the road to the building. He climbs over the low wall, and peers in through the window for a minute before heading back over.

"Looks empty. I'll go round back and find a way in. Keep an eye on the front door," Adam whispers.

We all move up to the doorway, and crouch down to stay out of sight. The sun is coming down now, and given the orcs choice of hideout underground, it's a safe guess that they have a preference for the dark. Who knows what will happen when night falls?

After a minute or two, we can hear the locks clicking behind the large red door and it opens to a smiling Adam, clearly pleased with himself.

"Welcome to Castle Froom," he smirks while putting on an overly upper class British accent. "I do hope you enjoy your stay."

Chapter Fourteen

I follow Adam into the hallway, and look in the first door to the right where there is a large reception room but as initially expected, everything looks abandoned.

"I'm just going to check the other floors quickly," Adam tells us, making his way to the stairs. "Make sure we actually are alone."

I dump my pack on the floor by the stairs and walk through past the sitting room, into the kitchen at the back. In the far corner is the back door, now with a broken pane of glass where Adam had let himself in. The kitchen is fairly large, lots of cupboards, with a larder and a large fridge in the corner. I walk over and open the door, pleasantly surprised by how well stocked it is. I make a mental note of the supplies as they will definitely be useful tomorrow, but more importantly we can get a proper meal tonight. With that thought, my stomach begins to grumble as I realise that other than the snacks earlier, I haven't really eaten today and now that we have the chance to stop and rest; I am starving.

Cassie walks in behind me, followed by Nat. She smiles at me, and walks over to the sink to wash her hands. Nat just starts looking through the cupboards, taking out a box of cereal and eating it straight from the box. Looking at the pair of them, you'd never know the world was ending outside as I had watched them do the exact same in my kitchen at home a hundred times.

"Where is Harry?" I ask him.

"Waiting by the front door. Doing his lone wolf sentry thing," Nat replies nonchalantly.

I poke my head round the doorway and see him stood by the front door, peering out the little window at the road outside. The street lights have come on now it is getting darker. He glances back when he hears Adam coming back downstairs, and spots me looking at him so gives me a smile and a nod, which I reciprocate before going back to exploring the fridge.

After a minute or so, Harry and Adam join us in the kitchen.

"What's the food situation like?" Harry asks us.

"The fridge looks pretty good, there's some chicken, eggs, milk, cheese, all kinds of other random bits," I tell him, the appreciation in my voice giving away my hunger.

"There is some pasta over here, and rice too," Cassie calls over.

"And Nat has his cereal," Adam laughs. "I suggest we make some proper food for the rest of us though. But please, please, don't let Harry cook."

"I'll do it, don't worry," Cassie says, rolling her eyes at him.

"We should all wait upstairs," Harry says, looking back at the front door.

"Easier to defend?" I ask him, and he nods. "I'll stay downstairs with Cassie while she cooks, then we will bring the food up."

I wait for Nat to argue, wanting to stay and talk to Cassie but he just nods and heads for the door. I watch him leave, and try to work out how he can walk away from Cassie so easily, time and time again.

"Sure, see you guys soon," Harry says, "Shout if you need us. I'll be at the top of the stairs."

As if he could sense my thoughts, I watch Nat walk over to Cassie and kiss her on the cheek, before heading upstairs with Harry and Adam. I pull myself up to sit on the worktop, and look over to Cassie, who has started to pour the pasta into a pan.

"You ok Cassie?" I ask her.

"I'll be ok. It was a shock, seeing him. I honestly thought he was dead," she replies, her voice breaking slightly.

I jump down and walk over to her to pull her into my arms. She just cuddles me back, not needing to say another word. After a minute or so she pulls back and let's go, turning back to the pasta.

"Thanks, Jake," she says. "Can you pass me the chicken from the fridge?"

I go and get the chicken for her, grabbing the milk as well. I slide the packet of chicken across the counter and walk over to the kettle, flicking the switch. I search the nearby cupboards to find a couple of mugs and teabags so I can make us both a cup of tea. Next to me, I can see Cassie reluctantly cutting up the raw chicken and smile to myself, she has never liked touching raw meat.

I pour the water into the mugs and swirl the tea bag around with a spoon, before adding the milk. I can't be bothered to find a bin, so I skillfully fling the tea bags into the sink using the teaspoon and I'm almost positive I caught Cassie rolling her eyes at me. I put the tea down next to her, but when she looks up at me I can see that the smile on her face has reached her eyes. This is the first time today that she has nearly looked like her normal self.

Cassie has the pasta on boil and the now diced chicken is frying away in the pan with some random pesto sauce that we found in a cupboard.

"You didn't have to offer to stay down here with me, you know," she says to me.

"Yes, I did," I tell her. "You probably wanted to be alone, or in silence with our new commando friends. But if I hadn't offered, then Nat would have." I pause. At least I assumed he would have at the time, but after he said nothing and walked away, I'm not so sure. I continue; "At least with me, you know that you can just be you and not even have to talk if you don't want to."

"Sometimes it scares me how well you know me," she says to me, laughing a little now. "You pest."

"Can't argue that one, but at least I am your pest." I wink in response, and laugh a little.

She walks over and leans on me, so I put my arms around her shoulders while she watches the food. After a few minutes, she goes back over and starts to look through the cupboards for the plates so I go and get the knives and forks from the cutlery drawer I found earlier during my mission to make tea.

Cassie splits the chicken up five ways on the plates, although one portion is definitely smaller than the others, and the pasta is divided up equally along with the leftover sauce in the pan. I grab three of the plates and carry them upstairs while Cassie follows me with the other two.

We find the others in the first bedroom we come to, and I hand out the plates and pass out the cutlery with my now free hand. We all just sit on whatever surface looks reasonably comfortable. Harry is on the windowsill overlooking the front of the house, Adam now on the floor by the door so he can watch the stairs. Cassie joins Nat on the bed so I sit down on the floor opposite. We all eat in silence, just enjoying the food. Cassie is a good cook, even in unfamiliar territory and under even stranger conditions.

"That was great, thanks Cassie," Adam says, as he shoves the last mouthful into his mouth.

"Good job Cassie," echoes Harry. "Definitely filled a hole!"

"Always does," I tell her, and Nat just nods along.

"Glad you liked it," Cassie says, smiling. "And that I could finally contribute. I've felt pretty useless so far."

"I think you have a bigger impact than you realise," Adam says to her, getting a confused look from her in response, but I know what he is getting at so I just smile to myself.

Adam collects up the plates and takes them downstairs to the kitchen for us. When he gets back, we are all just laid out, making the most of the peace and quiet. It is the most relaxed I have felt all day, considering the circumstances. Although deep down I still feel restless and need to find Olive, remembering her face fills me with a sadness and longing. I need to find her.

"What is the plan of action now then?" I ask the group.

"Might be better to discuss it in the morning. We will all be rested, fed and ready to go. Plus the plan will be fresh in our minds when we leave," Adam suggests. "Just everyone think through their own ideas, and any information that may be useful, so we can brainstorm in the morning."

"But for now. We should get some rest," Harry says to the window, and I realise that he hasn't looked in at us the whole time. "We will set up a rota to take watch, changing every 2 hours. I'll go first."

"I'll take second," I tell him.

"Third then," Adam says. "I'm going to take the room upstairs. There are another two rooms up there if you want them?"

"Sure, sounds good," I reply.

"We will stay here, I think," Nat tells us.

I smile at Cassie and lean over to give her a cuddle, then clasp Nat's shoulder and say goodnight to the group. I follow Adam and Harry out the room, where Harry goes to sit on top of the stairs so he can see the front door and I follow Adam up to the second floor. He takes the room on the left and I head right.

The room is fairly standard, nothing special, just a double bed and dresser table, cupboard and en-suite bathroom. I sit on the bed and pull my boots off, stretching my feet out. It feels good to be sitting down. I contemplate going into the en-suite to have a wash, but decide to set an alarm for two hours and just put my head down. I realise

I haven't used my phone since I messaged Cassie earlier this afternoon, so luckily the battery hasn't drained entirely but it won't last that much longer. But then once I have Olive back, everyone I need will be with me.

After what feels like seconds after my head hits the pillow, I hear my phone alarm going off quietly beside me so I sit up and stretch before turning it off. I lean over to retrieve my boots, pulling them back on and tying the laces. I slowly stand up and go back downstairs, where I find Harry sitting on the stairs in the exact same spot I left him. I tap him on the shoulder and he stands up, suddenly looking very tired.

"Nothing much happened, hopefully it'll stay that way," he whispers to me, so I smile and sit down in his spot.

I hear Harry walking up the stairs, but he catches his boot on the last step and falls over, cursing loudly.

"You ok?" I call up to him.

"Yeah, just a bit too tired. My bad," he calls down.

I hear Harry close one of the doors at the top, and I settle in to my watch. I need to try and stay awake, so I think through the events of the entire day, all the little details and everything I have seen. Trying to keep it sharp and focused in my mind, ready for the morning.

About ten minutes later, I hear the door open closest to me and I look up to see Cassie looking down at me. She silently comes down the stairs to sit with me.

"Hey you," I say to her, smiling.

"Hi," Cassie says, smiling sleepily at me.

"Can't sleep?" I ask her.

"Oh no, I was out of it, but Harry woke me up with his cursing. So I thought I would just come say hi and make sure you're ok," she replies.

"Job done, now go back to sleep. You're going to need it," I tell her, and she leans over to kiss me on the cheek before going back up the stairs.

"Night Jake," she whispers down.

"Night sweetheart," I whisper back.

About a minute later, I can hear Nat talking. He must have woken up too. Although I know I shouldn't, being about four feet away means I can't really help but listen to their whispered conversation.

"Cassie," he says to her, "I need to talk to you."

"About what?" she replies, still sounding sleepy.

"To explain. You know, why I left," he tells her, sounding a little nervous.

"Ok... Well, this should be interesting," she says, and I can hear a defensiveness in her voice. Cassie tends to get a little sarcastic when she feels the need to protect herself. "Please enlighten me."

"When we got to that conference suite, all I could think about was finding Olive. I mean, I know that was why we were there, but I wanted to be in there helping Jake. But he shut me out," he explains. "That really annoyed me, I already felt helpless and now I couldn't even do that. Then he just gave up at the barrier when that policeman wouldn't let him through. What's worse is that he then sent you over to try and talk to me about it. Didn't even come and do it himself."

"Hang on Nat. That's not really fair. He didn't shut you out, he asked you to stay outside with me, because I am your girlfriend. Plus he didn't give up on her, he decided to find another way. And lastly, for what it's worth, he didn't tell me to come and talk to you, I did that. My choice. As your girlfriend," she tells him, the sleepiness now totally gone from her voice.

"Whatever, all that doesn't really matter," Nat says, dismissing her comments entirely. "The thing is, I haven't been able to stop thinking about Olive all day. Whether she is safe. Whether she is hurt. Whether she is even still alive. It is driving me crazy."

"Tell me something Nat, at what point today, did you stop to think about me? About whether I was ok? Whether I was hurt? Or if I was alive," she asks, her voice breaking at the end.

"It's different. You were fine," he says, with a hint of annoyance in his voice. "And you were with Jake."

"You didn't know that though, did you?" she demands.

"Well no, but, I did. He wouldn't leave you, would he? It's not who he is," he tries to explain.

"No it isn't. But apparently it is who you are, Nat…" she says, and it sounds like she is crying now.

"Well maybe you are with the wrong one then Cassie," he says, his comment dripping with venom.

Then there is just silence. I have no way of seeing Cassie, of reading her response or seeing in her eyes what she is thinking and I am suddenly aware that I am holding my breath. I realise that her response to Nat's comment matters to me more than it should. But before I have the chance to process that thought, I hear Cassie talking again.

"You are my boyfriend. You're meant to put me first. I'm meant to be your priority," she says to him, crying now.

"I'm sorry Cassie. I know that, I do, but in the grand scheme of things today, well, you weren't the one in mortal danger," he says flatly.

"Well, Nat. Let me make this easy for you," she says, the harshness now back in full. "From now on, you won't have to worry about me like that ever again." I listen to her get out of bed. She walks out the room, not even looking in my direction and heads to the other bedroom, slamming the door behind her.

I sit there alone in the dark. All I want to do is go and comfort Cassie, I could still see her face as she left the room, tears streaming down her face. Nat just broke her heart. But then I realise that I also want to go and see Nat, but for an entirely different reason; I want to punch him in the face. Instead, I sit there alone in the dark with my thoughts. Watching. Waiting.

Chapter Fifteen

I wake up the next morning, feeling tired and confused. The sun is just starting to come up outside, but it is still dark outside. Adam had relieved me about four hours ago, but despite my best efforts I couldn't stay asleep for more than a few minutes. I had lain there for hours, going over the argument I'd overheard on the stairs. I had always known that Nat had a crush on Olive, but he had chosen Cassie. I know he really likes her, he always has done, and I remember when he came to talk to me about asking her out on a date.

"Jake, can I ask you something?" he had asked me, when we went to get a coffee one day at work.

"I think you just did," I replied sarcastically. "But go ahead, I'll let you ask another."

"Ha ha ha, funny guy," he smirked at me. "But this is serious."

"I can do serious. Sometimes," I told him. "Spit it out."

"I was thinking, and wondering, about whether I should ask out Cassie?" he said, taking me by surprise. "You know I like her, and I think she likes me. You're her friend, what do you think?"

"Wow, mate," I had replied, still slightly shocked. "She is a lovely girl, and you know I think the world of her. She is my best friend, after all."

"I know mate. I'm serious about this. I really like her," he told me.

"You better be. Me and you? We are friends and I love you like a brother, but you break her heart, I *will* break your face," I remember telling him with a smile, but I was only half joking and I think he knew it.

I sit up in bed, and stretch my arms up. My left shoulder is still sore from an incident years ago, although I always told Olive it is my body giving up in old age, which would always get an eye roll from her. I have been going to physiotherapy for years now but it still twinges from time to time, especially if I don't get enough rest.

I get out of bed, and make my way downstairs, stopping on the first floor landing to look at Cassie's closed door. I hope she is ok. Nat's doors is wide open, and the room is empty. The others must be downstairs already. I resist the urge to knock for Cassie, opting to let her get as much rest as possible, if she even slept at all, and head down to the kitchen.

I find Harry and Adam looking over one of the maps on the kitchen counter, and Nat eating cereal from the box again. I walk over to the kettle and turn it on, I'm not sure I am ready to talk to Nat yet.

"Anyone for tea?" I ask the room.

"We've got one already, thanks though," Adam says.

"I'm good," Nat tells me, not looking up from his box of cereal which is somehow the most fascinating thing in the world right now.

Are you? I think to myself. How? But it is not my place. I need to speak to Cassie first, before I take out my anger on Nat.

I hear Cassie coming down the stairs, and get another mug out to make her a cup of tea as well.

"Morning," Cassie says solemnly, walking into the kitchen.

"Hey you," I say to her, turning to give her a smile, but she doesn't meet my gaze.

"Hey Cassie, sleep ok?" Adam calls over, and Harry gives her a little wave.

"Not too bad, all things considered," she says, but I know she doesn't mean the orcs.

"I'm making you a tea, do you want anything to eat?" I ask her.

"No thanks, I'm not hungry," Cassie replies robotically, before adding, "But thanks for the tea."

I finish brewing the tea, throwing the bags in the sink to join the ones from last night. I hand the mug to Cassie, who has taken a seat at the table in the opposite corner of the room to Nat. I can see she is hurting, all I want to do is hold her and tell her she isn't alone but now isn't the time nor the place.

I sit down opposite her at the table, and try to make eye contact with her but she is just staring down at her hands, picking at her nails. I can just about see her face, and even at this angle I can see that she had been crying and probably hasn't slept at all. I slide my hand forward towards hers, but she pulls it back into her lap. I can sense her closing up on me.

"Jake, we need to go through the plan," Adam tells me, looking up briefly to meet my gaze.

I get up from the table, and rest my hand on Cassie's shoulder briefly as I walk past. At least she doesn't shy away from it. Sitting down on the stool next to Adam, I look over the maps and can see that they have been making notes on it. There are a few arrows marked near Westminster that I don't remember being there yesterday.

Nat walks over to join us, taking a seat the other side of Adam. I see Cassie get up from the table but she just stands near to Harry, being careful to keep her face down, looking only at the map.

"Nat. Can you tell us what you saw while you down there?" Harry asks him.

"Sure. Well, when I got down there, I could hear them moving about, so I crept down the tunnel as quietly as I could. The live rail was still on at that point, so I had to be really careful," Nat explains to us. "I followed the sounds of their voices for what felt like miles. It got a bit tricky at Bond Street, as they changed over to the Jubilee line, but I managed to stick with them."

"You did a good job Nat, consider me impressed," Adam tells him. "What happened after that?"

"Thanks. After we got onto the Jubilee, I started to get as close to the station as I could. I managed to crawl up to about twenty feet away at one point and I could hear those orcs talking."

"What did they say?" Harry asks, looking up for the first time.

"They were talking about the station, how it was secure. All entrances covered, and more orcs on the way. That sort of thing. But then they mentioned the girl that they had brought back from the attack. Olive. They said that she had been taken for a reason. Something about her being touched by some sort of light?" he says. "I tried to listen to more, but then one of the orcs saw me, so I ran away."

"Is that what happened to your face?" I ask him, trying to keep my voice level. I'm angry at him, but he's still my friend.

"The orc that chased me, he caught up with me and tackled me to the floor. He hit me a couple of times in the face, and the chest. I saw him pull a knife so I kicked out at him and he fell backwards. I started to walk backwards, and he lunged at me with the knife to give me what will be a lovely scar on my forehead, almost as good as yours Jake," he says, pointing up to the cut above his eye but his smile fades when I don't smile back.

"How did you get out of that one?" Adam asks, his voice full of curiosity.

"I managed to push him away and then I kicked out at him. His armour touched the live rail and fried him. I don't think I'll ever forget that smell. It was like what I assume a farm would smell like if you set the whole place on fire," he says, turning his nose up at the thought.

"You were really lucky," Harry says.

"I know. It was at that point that I realised how stupid I had been. So I ran and hid in that tunnel and stayed there until you found me," Nat says, his voice now full of fear as he was clearly replaying it all in his head.

"So it seems like the station is full of orcs, and they have all the entrances covered," Adam says offhandedly, his mind clearly whirring away at a plan. "I think the tunnels may still be the best bet. We can stay on the tracks as long as possible and work our way into the station, then go from there once we can see how many we are dealing with."

"How much ammo do we have left?" Harry asks.

"Plenty. I filled my pack up with as many boxes as I could at the base," he replies. "And I haven't fired a shot yet, so we have only used what you two heroes fired yesterday."

"Well, none of their armour is thick enough to withstand the MP5SF's, I was able to shoot them in the head and chest. They went down easy enough," Harry explains.

"I hit two of them with the handgun. They both went down with chest shots," I confirm, wincing slightly at the memory.

"We have our two MP5's, and I've got a spare Glock for Nat." Adam says. "And one for Cassie too," he says, looking over to her; "If you are going to want one?'

"No thanks. I don't think I would be able to use it," Cassie says, without looking up.

"Are you sure you want to come with us?" I ask her.

"I can't stay here alone, Jake," she says, sighing. "And I won't ask any of you to stay here with me. We all need to go, together."

I reach over and put my hand on her shoulder, squeezing it gently, and she looks up enough for me to see her smile a little.

"You aren't alone Cassie. I'll be right there with you, every step of the way. I won't let you get hurt," I tell her, hoping she knows I don't just mean when we get down in the tunnels.

"Thank you Jake," she says, looking at me for the first time today. "I'm going to go see if there is anything on the news."

I watch Cassie walk through to the sitting room and hear the TV turn on. Adam and Harry have gone back to staring at the map, while Nat just sits there distractedly eating his cereal.

"Err, Jake! You might want to come and see this!" Cassie shouts from the other room, and we all run through to see what is wrong.

On the TV, there is the same orc from yesterday, standing in the same studio with a portal open behind him. It is the orc Warchief, Gro'alk.

"I had warned you that war was coming, and you will know now that this was no idle threat," the Warchief states. "In one of our raids, we found a girl who is now of great interest to us."

Another orc steps through the portal, holding a a much smaller person in front of him with what looks like a sack over her head.

"This girl has been touched by the Light. It flows through her. It is disgusting," Gro'alk says grimacing, and then rips the hood off the girl's head. "The last race to have had the Light were the elves, and they are long dead. Our Shadow God saw to that last time we came to your world."

"We want to know how this came to be? Who gave her this Light? And why?" Gro'alk continues. "Someone out there is responsible for this abomination."

"We expect your response within the hour, you can find us at the Underground place you know as Westminster," he states. "If we do not hear from you, the girl will die. Followed very quickly by the rest of your pathetic kind."

We all stand there in silence. Harry and Adam don't quite realise the importance of what we are seeing on the screen. But Cassie, Nat and I are stood there transfixed, because we know, without any shadow of a doubt, that the girl they captured was Olive.

Chapter Sixteen (Shadow War)

I stand in the centre of the shield wall, Petr at my side, both of us watching this new threat march towards our little group. These orcs are far larger than those that surround us on all sides, and remind me of the orc that had knocked me from Moonwalker not long before. Not just in size, but their armour is also thicker and darker than the grunts' standard gear, and like the mace wielding orc, they too have trophies hanging from their armour. Before turning away, I note that they each carry different weapons, ranging from great swords to maces.

"Do you have a plan, my Prince?" Petr asks me as I look into the eyes of my oldest friend, and despite his usual optimism, I can see the concern clearly etched into the strong features of his face.

"Kill them before they kill us," I tell him, in a somber attempt to lighten the mood.

"While I admire the simplicity of it, my friend, I feel like it may need a little more work," Petr says, laughing a little, his face softening slightly.

He has been my second in command for almost as long as I have been General, and given the circumstances, I could not wish for a better warrior at my side. I had trained him, mentored him and ultimately befriended him, and I would never deny that he is a skilled swordsman, a born leader and a loyal friend. The elves stood around us may be part of my father's army and under my command, but I know that they chose to follow Petr into the middle of the orc army in order to protect me, not that I was going to complain. They had saved my life.

"I am working on it, Petr, but initially I intend to meet with them, and attempt to parley. I would not ask you to join me, old friend," I tell him, putting my hand on his shoulder. "But I expect you will anyway."

"My life for yours," Petr tells me, tilting his head slightly. "Always."

I take a moment to look at the elf before me, thinking about how he has grown over the centuries, before slowly forcing myself to look back at the approaching orcs. They were nearly upon us, so I signal for Petr to move towards the front of the shield wall, and two of the Elves peel their shields back, allowing us to step through into the dead zone beyond.

"May the Light protect you, my prince," one of the elves says to us as we pass, and I nod back to him, trying to hide the apprehension and anxiety that is threatening to overwhelm me.

We slowly walk forward to meet them, and I note that they have stopped just shy of the arrow shafts that are dotted about the ground. They are out of range of our archers. Clearly, they are more intelligent than our scholars had initially guessed. Looking down the line of ours, I can see that their weapons are all unique in design, unlike the more uniformly crude blades the orcs usually carry. In total I can see that they have two great axes, a large mace, several great swords, two lances, a two-handed Warhammer and finally an orc with dual broadswords. This will certainly be an interesting fight, should it come to that, and I find myself smiling at the thought.

"So you are the Lightbearer, little elf?" say the middle orc, stepping forwards as he did. He must be the leader.

"I am," I tell him, stepping forward to match his movement. "Although the Light flows through all elves."

"Some more brightly than others." He smirks at me, before adding. "Little prince."

"You are well informed," I tell him. "Consider me impressed."

"I consider you dead, little prince," the orc spits at me. "Just like the rest of your pitiful race."

All around us the orcs start to shout and cheer at the comment. I glance back at our group, wanting to check they are remaining vigilant to any sudden attack from the main force. Whatever happens to me, or Petr, I don't want them to fall. They can still make it back to the city.

"And yet here we still stand, orc," I exclaim, lifting my arm up to indicate the elves behind me.

"Not for long, not for long," the orc says, will stepping back in line with his fellow orcs.

"What do you hope to achieve here, orc?" I ask them all, hoping to keep them talking.

"For you to die, little princeling," another of the orcs shouts, to more cheers from the orc army. "For you all to die."

"The elves are a race of peace," I tell him, my voice flat and calm, "we value life above all else."

"Bah! Peace? With such a grand army! You do not know peace!" the new orc spits at me, stepping forward towards me. "Either that or you do not know your King."

"Our army exists only to protect the world and all those in it, and to fight those who challenge that peace," I tell him firmly. "Never have we started a war, not with the orcs nor any other sentient race that has ever lived."

"It matters not what you say, Princeling," he tells me. "By the end of this day, your city will fall, and so will you."

"If I am to die today," I tell him, drawing my great sword from its brace on my back, "Then so be it. But I will not die quietly, nor easily. My fight, and even my death, will be remembered."

"Your death will be forgotten, as will your race," the orc says, laughing.

"History is written by the victor, orc," I tell him, smiling back at him. "So probably best not to get too ahead of yourselves."

"I could say the same to you, little princeling," the orc spits at me.

I laugh at his retort, and pushing the point of my great sword into the earth, I offer him a dramatic bow, before refocusing my helm back onto my head.

"I am both a Prince and General of Lor'ahan," I explain to the orc. "If I am to die today orc, I would ask the name of the orc that intends to grant me that death."

"My name?" The orc snarls at me, although I can see the smile on its lips. "My name is Gro'alk, Warchief of the Dark Bloods, and soon to be the Slayer of Princes."

"Very well," I reply, pulling my great sword from the earth and bringing it up to rest on my shoulder.

"I am going to enjoy killing you, little princeling," he tells me. "I will be treated as a great hero, when I deliver your head to the Shadow God."

"I can't wait to meet him," I mutter under my breath, and I hear Petr chuckle.

I see Petr draw his twin sabres out of the corner of my eye, and I turn to watch him take up a defensive position to my right. As we stand there, five of the orcs unsheathe their weapons and step forward eagerly to engage us. I can see that we are against a great axe, a lance, two great swords and the mace. Curiously, the orc known as Gro'alk does not move.

"Petr, you can fall back to the wall," I tell him, hoping he will listen, despite knowing that he will not.

"Not a chance," he says flatly. "I will take the two on the right."

"Very well, my friend," I tell him, a feeling of intense gratitude washes over me. I really could not have asked for a more loyal friend. "For the Light, and for our families."

"And for you, my prince," Petr replies, before moving off to the right side of the incoming orcs.

Ahead of me, the two right most orcs move towards Petr, leaving me with the three orcs carrying the great axe, the lance and one of the great swords to fight. As soon as they are in range, I lean forward and swing the great sword off my shoulder, turning my body in a circular motion to force my blade into a spinning attack that catches the three orcs off guard, knocking the one with the lance down to the floor as he clumsily attempts to parry the swing with the shaft of his weapon.

I regain my balance, and using the momentum of the swing to bring my blade downwards against the handle of the great axe, where upon impact I immediately turn and thrust my blade at the third orc, who parries it away with his own blade. I spin the blade out of its new unintended arc to swing it back towards the great axe, parrying one of his own attempted swings. I can see the great sword coming in and step back to avoid the attack, kicking the blade once it safely hits the ground I was occupying moments before, and take the opportunity to punch the orc with my left hand while it's unbalanced.

The lancer has now regained its footing and is rejoining the fight, so I swing my blade at the great axe forcing him to stop his current move so that it can parry it, before using the sudden stop in momentum to twist my body in the other direction and bring my blade back up over my head, before slamming my blade straight down into the lancers helm, cleaving him from head to navel.

My heart skips a beat as I realise my blade has become wedged in his plated chest armour, so instead of pulling the blade free, I push the blade back so the tip is in the ground and vault over the orc's corpse to avoid the great sword now swinging down towards me. Once I land, I use the new angle to wrench my sword free and back up a few steps to take stock of the situation, the great sword coming to a rest on my shoulder once again.

In the distance, I can see Petr fighting the two Warchiefs. Using his twin blades to deftly parry their attacks while continuing to keep a fair distance from them. He is fighting uncharacteristically defensive, and the sight fills me with a sense of dread as I watch my friend battling the two orcs. I have to trust in his abilities as I force myself to focus on the two orcs ahead of me.

One of the orcs lunges forward, thrusting his great sword at me, so I spin to my left to avoid the strike, before bringing my own blade into a downward blow against the great axe, hitting the weapon in the centre of the handle, breaking it in two. Seeing the confusion on the orc's face, I decide to press the advantage and thrust my blade straight into its chest. Fearing a repeat of the last orc, I quickly turn away from him, using the motion to pull my blade from its chest and face the last remaining orc.

Just beyond the orc's shoulder, I can see that Petr has managed to kill the orc that was wielding the mace, and is now fighting the other great sword much more aggressively. A smile forms on my lips as I realise that I should not have doubted him.

The Warchief suddenly charges at me, tearing my attention away from my friend as it wildly swings its blade in sloppy arcs that I can easily parry as I step back to match the pace of the orc. At the end of his charge, I spin to his left, holding the great sword flat against my back to stop any potential attacks from the orc while my back is turned towards it. I realise that the orc's charge had caused it to lose balance, and was still turned away from me so I quickly swing my blade up to cut the orc in a powerful upwards strike. I watch as my blade easily cuts through the armour, and as I bring the blade round to its usual resting position, the orc falls to its knees. Dead. The wound may not have been deep, but it would have completely severed its entire spine.

I turn to see Petr slide next to his remaining orc, cutting the backs of its legs and forcing the orc to kneel, before spinning back up onto his feet and taking off its head without his blades even stopping. Their movement so fluid, more like an extension of the elf wielding them than just a mere weapon.

"So who is next?" I ask the orcs, as Petr walks over to join me.

They all draw their weapons, which I take as an adequate answer to my question.

"Same again?" Petr asks, between the deep breaths.

"Good luck, my brother," I tell him, nodding at my friend. "If I don't see you after, then I will see you in the Eternal Forest."

"I will see you after, my prince," Petr states confidently, punching me on the arm as he moves to intercept the orcs.

I am disappointed, and concerned to see Gro'alk and his hammer go towards Petr, I was hoping to have the chance to fight him myself. This time I have a great axe, another lancer and the orc with the two broadswords.

I readjust the great sword on my shoulder, flexing my arm slightly to alleviate some of the tension that had built up from carrying it, all while trying to pick out which orc to engage first. Mal would always advocate attacking the strongest first, saying it will weaken the enemy, more but Petr always chose the fastest as it would slow down the pace of the battle, allowing you to keep better control of the flow.

I make a snap decision that the broadswords need to fall first, as much as I love my brother, he is gone and Petr is here, so I decide his advice could arguably be more reliable.

I swing my blade towards the lancer, who clumsily parries the attack, so I spin it back towards the great axe and he jumps back out of the way, leaving me temporarily alone with the broadswords. Using this small window, I lunge forward thrusting my sword at him. He parries the attack, but needs to use both swords given the size of my weapon and the sheer strength I put into the attack. I immediately pull my blade back and swing it down, forcing him to parry it again to the side, I then push the flat of the blade against him and spin away from him, turning my blade as I do, slicing his arm and causing him to drop one of his swords.

I use the aftermath of that swing to attack the lancer again, the strength of the blow knocking him back. I block a swing from the great axe, and move back to get a better view of all the orcs standing around me. In the background I can see Petr fighting Gro'alk and the other orc with its great sword.

I am about to start my next attack when I glance over to see Gro'alk dummy a swing of his hammer, but just before it starts to drop down, the orc thrusts it straight into Petr's face, staggering him. Before I can even react, I see the other orc thrust his sword straight into Petr's back, his sabres falling from his hands as he brings his arms up to grasp at the blade now sticking out of his chest.

I can hear someone screaming, it is a deep guttural noise, and it takes me a moment to realise that it is coming from me.

The orcs all start to charge at me, weapons raised. For a moment, I just stare at my friend as he feebly tries to push the blade out of his chest. The orcs are almost on me before I regain my senses, and without hesitation, I lift my great sword up and as I plunge the blade downwards, I feel an overwhelming burning sensation pulsating out from my heart as the Light erupts down my arms and into my blade.

As the tip of the blade connects with the earth, a shockwave blasts outwards, knocking the orcs into the air and I watch as the Light engulfs their dark forms. I turn away from the orcs, my attention elsewhere, although I faintly register that their screams are quickly silenced once the Light has finished incinerating them from within their armour.

Ahead of me, Gro'alk and the orc that had impaled Petr are getting to their feet, the shockwave having knocked them over. I pull my great sword from the ground and lunging forward, I swing it over my head and let go, throwing it straight at the second orc. I take a fleeting moment of satisfaction as the fear registers on the orc's face, before watching as the blade cuts him clean into two and jams itself into the ground a few feet behind the orc that was now cleaved in two.

I pull my sabres from their sheaths as I turn to face Gro'alk and Petr, who is now kneeling on the ground and looking up at the orc, one hand still holding the blade sticking out of his chest, the other having now fallen to his side.

"We shall meet again, little princeling," he says to me, before turning and walking back towards the channel. As he does, the orcs all around us start to storm forwards.

"Coward!" I scream at his back.

"Call me what you like, elf," the orc taunts me, adding as he turns away; "But knowing the pain you must be feeling now is far more pleasing to me than your death. For now at least."

I run to Petr and drop my blades next to him, putting my hand on the blade through his chest, I can hear him trying to talk.

"Lea… Leave it, my Prince," he stammers. "I am done."

"Petr" I say to him, "I'm sorry, my friend."

"My life for yours," he whispers, and I feel him collapse into my arms.

"I will meet you again in the Eternal Forest, old friend," I whisper back him, as tears fall down my cheeks.

As the orcs approach, the Royal Knights that had been watching from the nearby safety shield wall surge forwards and close in around me, planting their shields into the ground, recreating the shield wall around Petr. Around me.

I sit there, holding the lifeless body of my best friend in my arms, with the sounds of orc war horns ringing once again in my ears.

Chapter Seventeen

I am stood, rooted to the spot, in a state of shock, while we had all assumed that the girl that was taken hostage was Olive, we now have irrefutable proof that it was her. No, that it is her, but more importantly that she is still alive. A wave of relief washes over me as I take in the news.

"Jake, it's Olive. It's really her!" Cassie says, turning to look at me, and I can see the hope in her eyes.

Looking down at her, I realise that this is the first time she has properly looked at me since last night, so I make an effort to focus on her for a moment, and smile back at her. For the first time since this all started, I let myself hope. Olive and Cassie aren't lost to me. Not yet at least. I take a deep breath.

"Yes it is, and she doesn't look hurt," I say out loud to the group, turning back to the screen, and to Olive.

"That's Olive?" Adam asks me, before adding; "She is a very pretty girl."

"Tad inappropriate," Harry tells him, giving him a non-so gentle nudge in the arm.

I look over and smile at their little exchange. I've known them, what? A day? But I am truly grateful they are here and honestly, I don't feel like we would have all got this far without them. I also can't shake the feeling that I'll not only need them to get Olive back, but to keep our little group safe once we do.

"Well, I'll be sure to introduce you properly once we get her back," I tell him, and I see Nat wince out of the corner of my eye. "But for now, it seems we now only have an hour to make that happen."

Out of the corner of my eye, I can see Nat begin fidgeting. He doesn't know that I overheard the argument with Cassie, and I wonder whether he suspects that I know about his feelings for Olive. It is the one thing he has never been talkative about, for good reason. I told him once that I would break his face if he hurt Cassie, and I still haven't ruled that out after last night, but he must wonder what would happen if he ever hurt Olive. I find myself clenching my jaw as I wonder that too. It wouldn't be pretty, that's for damn sure.

"What is it?" Cassie asks me, seeing the stern look on my face.

"Just thinking about Olive," I tell her, which is partially true.

"You're right, Jake. If we are going to do anything, it has to be now," Harry says solemnly. "Get your stuff together guys, we leave in five."

"Harry, we still need to talk about the plan?" Adam questions him.

"We are going to have to talk and walk, mate," Harry explains, "With a healthy dose of improvisation sprinkled on top of the whole thing."

We all charge up the stairs to gather our bits together. My pack is still in my room, the contents all safely inside since I hadn't bothered to unpack anything last night. I was too drained after my turn taking my watch, and then listening to, and processing, the argument between Cassie and Nat. Shaking away that line of thought, I throw the pack over my shoulder and pick up the sword from the dresser table, tying the belt back around my waist and clipping the gun holster back onto my right hip.

On my way out the door, I catch sight of myself in the mirrored wardrobes. Disheveled would be an understatement. I have two days growth on my face, dark circles under my eyes and a layer of dirt covering it all. My short dark hair is still in its usual wavy style, the fringe flicked up. But the whole right side is sticking out at odd angles where I obviously slept on it.

I attempt to flatten my hair down a bit as I make my way downstairs. I can see Nat down by the front door talking to Adam. I stop at the landing and can see Cassie in her room, meticulously going through her bag to make sure it is all there. I walk over and tap on the door to let her know I'm here, and she looks over but then looks back down at her pack sheepishly once she realises it is me.

"Cassie, are you ok sweetheart?" I ask her.

"I'm fine," she replies, I instantly know that she is, in fact, not fine.

"No, you're not," I tell her, taking a few steps towards her.

"Ok, no I'm not, but I will be. I just need a bit of time," she explains, "Got a lot going on in my head at the moment. I'm sorry."

"Cassie, you know I am always here for you," I try to tell her, "About anything, anytime, anywhere."

"I know Jake, but this is something I need to try and work out by myself." She says, her voice breaking a little at the end.

"Ok, Cassie, I get it," I say, "But you know where I am if you need me."

I take the last few steps towards her and wrap my arms around her from behind, and I feel her relax into them and she brings her hands up and rests them on my forearms.

"I know you are Jake. I know," she says, squeezing my arms and letting go.

"I'll see you downstairs, ok?" I say to her, before begrudgingly leaving the room.

Once I get down to the ground floor, I find Adam clipping a holster to Nat's belt while Nat holds the handgun out in front of him, tilted slightly like some sort of gangster, and I hear Harry walk out of the kitchen, laughing at his pose.

"You'll never hit anything like that," Harry tells Nat. "You're going to want to hold it straight, or I'd rather you didn't hold it at all."

"Like this?" Nat asks, straightening the gun.

"That's more like it, but use both hands," Adam corrects him, lifting Nat's other hand to support the base of the gun.

Nat stands there for a few seconds, getting a feel for it, before putting the gun back in the holster and turning to me with a big smile on his face. I'm not sure if it's because he finally has a gun, or that we are finally doing something to get Olive back. I know how he feels on that front, this is the closest we've been, but I'm not ready to forgive him for what he has done to Cassie in the process.

"Let's go guys, and girl," Harry says, opening the front door. "We will head back to the same entrance and head in from that direction. At least we know it, and it will double as an escape route if it comes to that. Try to focus and remember the route there, if we get split up, this is our safe house, ok?"

We all file out the door and down the steps to the road below. Harry looks up and down the road, before stepping out and we all follow him back towards the entrance to the tunnels below. A few minutes later, I'm helping Adam open the door that we had come out of yesterday. Harry had done a bit too good of a job of jamming it shut, so it took some effort to get it open as quietly as possible. We all gather into the room and close the door again, and we all look at each other in the dimly lit room. Looking at the hole in front of me, it seems like a lifetime ago that we were climbing out after I went back for Harry. I follow Harry down, followed by Cassie, Nat and Adam. We stop in the small room at the base of the ladder, while Harry pushes the door open slowly to see out into the tunnel.

"Looks clear," Harry whispers, before moving through the door and dropping to the tracks below. I quickly follow him down, and can hear the others doing the same. I can barely hear Adam slowly closing the door behind us.

We walk through the darkness in single file, still in the same order as we came down the ladder, and I feel better knowing that Cassie is directly behind me. Harry slows down as we reach a corner, and as I catch up to him, I can see why. There is a light flickering from the tunnel ahead.

"Well, best guess is that since the power is still out, they have lit fires to provide them with some light down here," Harry whispers back to me, and I nod back in agreement. Seems logical.

He starts to edge slowly forward, moving slowly round the bend. I motion for Cassie and the others to stay back, as I follow him forwards. As I get closer to where Harry has stopped again, I can just make out where the tunnel opens up into the station ahead.

About halfway down the left platform, I can see a fire burning with two orcs standing around it, their backs to us. From where we are crouched, the other platform appears to be clear. Harry turns back to face me, and motions for us to fall back to the others.

"Adam, there are two sentries on the platform ahead," Harry explains, "we will go ahead and take them down quietly," Harry explains. "Jake, you come to the edge of the platform and cover us, and keep an eye on the other side."

"The rest of you will then join us up on the platform on our signal." Adam nods along in agreement. Quickly followed by the rest of us.

"Be careful, Jake," Cassie whispers up to me, and I turn back and reach out to squeeze her hand. I'm pleasantly surprised when she squeezes back.

I see them crawl off down the tracks, keeping tight to the left-hand wall in order to keep out of the line of sight of the orcs, in case they turn round. Once they are ten feet short of the orcs, I push up to where the platform starts, and then turn my attention to the other platform. The two barrels are burning brightly, throwing shadows all over the station.

I see Harry turn back and look at me, so I lean out and chance a quick peak over the edge of the platform at the two orcs above. They both still have their backs to us, so I give him a thumbs up. I see Harry lean his MP5 against the wall and draw a knife from his belt, before climbing quietly up to the platform, quickly followed by Adam. They move silently up behind the unsuspecting orcs and watch as they both bury their knives into their necks while reaching their spare hand round to cover their mouths to limit any potential noise. Once both orcs are laying on the ground, Harry waves back to me, and I repeat the signal down to the others. I wait for them to reach me, before we all move up to where they are on the platform.

"So far, so good," Nat says to Adam, as he helps him up to the platform.

"Let's not get ahead of ourselves," Harry says, taking a knee and offering his hand down to me.

Instead of taking it, I turn to Cassie and unceremoniously lift her up to Harry, getting a small squeak in surprise from her in the process. As Harry pulls her up to the platform, I retrieve their submachine guns and pass them back up.

Adam starts to roll the orc bodies to the edge, and Harry jumps down to help me lower the orcs down to the tracks, hoping that it will keep them hidden in case any more of them happen to come down here. I pull myself up to the platform and stand next to Cassie, as we both enjoy the warmth of the fire for a few moments.

Adam motions for us to move forward, so we all form up behind Harry again at the archway that acts as an exit to the main station beyond. We are about to move through, when Harry stops and raises his finger to his lips. There are voices coming from the other side of the arch.

"Gro'alk is obsessed with that girl," one of the orc says.

"He says she has Light inside her," says the other.

"No one has the Light anymore," the first one exclaims. "It died with the elves!"

"But how do we know the elves are dead?" he says, "We only have *His* word for it." Harry looks at Adam, and they both share a curious look at the orcs exchange.

"Careful now orcling, that kind of talk will get you killed," says a third orc.

"By who? You?" spits the first.

"The Shadow God does not tolerate traitors!" says the third orc again, and I hear him draw his sword. "I'll do what needs to be done."

We are all frozen, listening to the orcs, and there is the distinct sound of two more swords being drawn from their sheaths. Within seconds, the three orcs are all fighting. The sound of it is impossibly loud in the enclosed space of the station, and while it means less for us to deal with… I find myself desperately hoping it doesn't draw more of them down here.

"Wait until I tell Gro'alk about this," chuckles the third orc, his voice growing fainter as he walks away.

We wait a few more moments, before Harry leans forward to look through into the room beyond. He quickly pulls back and motions for us all to move through. As soon as we enter the large room, I can see the two dead orcs on the floor. Harry shakes his head at the sight of their butchered bodies, and Adam sighs. I purposefully position myself between the bodies and Cassie, to break her line of sight of it and save her from the brutality of it.

Harry leads us on towards the escalators ahead, and crouches down behind the right most steps, which provides us some cover.

"Well that was certainly interesting," he whispers, a flicker of a smile on his lips.

"I don't think we will be lucky enough to have them all kill each other," I tell him.

"No, but why are they so obsessed with Olive?" he asks me. "What is this Light they keep talking about?"

"Maybe we can ask the next orc we come across?" Adam replies, laughing a little, and I am glad he fielded that question.

"I'll leave that to you," he says, moving round to climb the escalators.

I follow Harry up the stationary escalator steps, taking them one at a time, all while making sure my sword doesn't knock on the steps or the sides. At the top, Harry stops again and holds his hand out for us to stop. There are more voices ahead.

"Warchief, I thought you should know that I have killed two traitors that dared question your judgement of the girl, and even the word of the Shadow God," I hear the orc say.

"Grah! Traitorous cowards!" Gro'alk spits. "Make sure that their bodies are burnt. They do not deserve to be given the death rites."

"Very good, Warchief." the orc says, "I will burn them myself."

"No, not you. Send others to do it. I want them to see what happens to traitors and cowards," Gro'alk demands, "And I want you to watch the girl. Your reward for your loyalty, orc."

"Yes, Warchief. My blade is yours to command," the orc says.

"She is through there, go and gather others that you trust and replace those guarding her now," Gro'alk says.

"Yes, Warchief," the orc tells him, clearly feeling pleased with his sudden change in circumstance. "At once."

Harry looks round, with a big smile on his face and I smile right back. This is our chance.

"We need to get in there before that orc gets back with more," Harry whispers. "We will come back this way, get back down to the platform and out through the tunnels."

"I'll stay here with Cassie and Nat" Adam says from behind me, "Call if you two need back up, otherwise I will cover the escape route."

Harry nods to me and I nod back. He peaks his head out over the top of the escalator and gives me a thumbs up to say the coast is clear, so I look back at Cassie, she is too far back to reach and hold, so I just offer her a smile, before I head off after Harry.

Just as I stand up, I hear a scuffle behind me and turn to see Nat struggling away from Adam, who is trying to hold onto him. I give him a stern look and try to motion for him to stop, but he breaks free of Adam and pushes past Cassie, knocking her into the side of the escalator.

Nat comes marching up to me, looking ready to join us, but he looks mildly surprised when I push him back.

"What the hell are you doing?" I whisper angrily to him.

"I am not sitting on my arse, knowing Olive is right there!" he says, a little louder than he should have.

"Shhh, you idiot!" I whisper. "This is not the time for heroics. Go back to Cassie. Now."

"If you are that worried about Cassie, you go back and sit with her. I'm going after Olive. You remember her right, she's your sister?" he asks me.

I turn to look at Harry, who is just staring at us, trying to work out what the hell Nat is doing. I smile at Harry, and then turn back to Nat, and punch him straight in the face, who crumples backwards onto the floor, clutching his bleeding nose with a look somewhere between confusion and shock on his face.

He made a noise when he hit the ground, but luckily not enough to draw any attention. I can hear Adam trying to pull him back to the escalator, but I am already moving back to Harry. Olive has to be my priority for now, Nat can look after himself.

"He probably deserved that, just maybe not right now," Harry says, smirking.

"Oh, he definitely did," I tell him. "plus it stopped him making more of a scene."

"Agreed," Harry whispers to me as he carries on.

We walk up to the short tunnel leading to the Eastbound Jubilee line, and can hear a few different voices coming through. From what we can make out, they are talking about the war, the spoils that they are going to enjoy and whether the Warchief would let them keep the girl once the hour was up. I tense up at the last part and draw my gun. Harry looks at me and nods, bringing his gun up to his shoulder.

"Time to go loud, and go home," he whispers to me, standing up straight with a determined look on his face.

We both jump round the corner, finding seven orcs in front of us. At first, they don't quite realise what is about to happen, but they quickly catch on as we both open fire on them, dropping the closest three before they even had the chance to draw their weapons.

I line up the orc closest to me and squeeze the trigger, completely forgetting the breathing bit and subsequently missing the orc entirely. I start to blindly shoot at the orc, and one of the bullets hits it in the stomach, but worryingly the orc doesn't go down. I am aware of Harry's shots going off and see another orc drop behind the one now approaching me, sword drawn.

I put the gun back in its holster and draw my own sword, somehow feeling much more comfortable about this choice of weapon. The orc smiles at me and lunges, but I easily parry the blade to my left and pull my sword back into a swipe of my own which connects with his shoulder as he moves past me.

I am now on the other side of him, standing between him and Harry. The orc runs at me again, so I parry the swing to my right this time and continue to spin the blade, twisting my body with the momentum, bringing the sword right round to slice the orc's head off in one clean motion.

As the orc collapses to the floor, I see Harry lower his gun behind him and tilt his head to look at me with a puzzled look on his face.

"I missed," I said, shrugging my shoulders and sheathing the sword. "Twice."

Just beyond him, I can see a small figure curled up with a black sack over their head. Without thinking, I run straight over, sliding the last two feet on my knees, before pulling the sack off her head, and looking into Olive's green eyes for the first time since yesterday morning.

"Jake," Olive whimpers. "You're here? You came for me."

I pull her into my arms and feel her start to cry into my shoulder, which immediately sets me off as well.

"Come on, let's get you up," Harry says, lifting us both up so we are standing.

Harry bends down to cut the ropes binding her ankles, and then her wrists, allowing her to finally cuddle me back.

"We really have to go. That ruckus will have definitely been heard by every living thing down here," Harry says firmly.

Olive is a bit unsteady on her feet, so I put her arm round my shoulder and practically carry her towards the archway. As we approach, I can hear gunshots from beyond when two orcs come charging through. Harry quickly drops them both with his MP5. I reluctantly let go of Olive's arm and help her to steady herself, before I pull the handgun from its holster and replace the magazine with a fresh one. I take Olive's hand in mine and then lead her through the archway, following after Harry.

I can see hundreds of orcs running down the stairs to our right, with Adam providing covering fire from his position on our left. Harry fires a few times at the surging crowd, who carries on regardless of how many orcs fall from both Harry and Adam's submachine guns. He looks back at me and holds up three fingers. I mentally count down with him as he curls back each finger, and on three we all step out to make the run across to the others.

Almost immediately, I hear a grunt from Harry beside me and I pull us all back into the cover of the archway. I quickly check Olive, who's unhurt, but when I look at Harry, I can see that he has an arrow sticking out of his left shoulder.

"Ah shit!" Harry shouts. "They really hurt."

He reaches up and snaps the shaft of the arrow, leaving just the tip in his shoulder.

"We aren't going to make it over," Harry tells me, although I already knew it.

"I know," I say, looking over at where Adam and Nat are firing at the orcs, with Cassie just below them. "We will have get out through this tunnel and meet them back at the house. You going to be ok to run?"

"I'll be fine," Harry says, grimacing.

I reluctantly let go of Olive's hand and hold my own up to my mouth.

"Adam!" I shout, getting his attention. "Get out of here, we'll meet you at the house!"

I see him nod, and after firing off a few more shots at the orcs, I see him turning to usher Cassie and Nat down the escalators. I see Cassie looking over at me, fear clearly etched on her face as she turns away, and I watch as her head drops down out of view and then turn to follow Harry back onto the platform, he jumps down to the tracks with a grunt, and after helping Olive make the drop, I jump down to join them.

Harry looks up and down the tracks, trying to work out which way we should run.

"We should go that way," Harry says, running off down the tracks to the far end of the platform.

Olive goes next, and I follow up from behind, glancing behind me to check we aren't been followed. As we near the end of the platform, an arrow goes flying past my head, luckily missing all of us. I turn and lift my gun, but I can only see two orcs on the platform giving chase. Does that mean all those orcs are chasing the others?

I fire back a couple of pot shots at the orcs, causing them to duck away from the edge of the platform and then I run into the tunnel, and back into the darkness, to follow Harry and Olive.

Chapter Eighteen

I run down the tunnel, away from the roars of the orcs swarming onto the platform behind us, and can see Olive just ahead of me. As I catch up to her, I can see how frail and weak she is, probably through exhaustion, hunger or dehydration, I can't be sure which.

"Come on, little one," I say to her, grabbing her hand in the dark, "Just a little further."

We keep running, and can still hear the noises of the orcs behind us, clearly not willing to give up the chase that easily. We stole their prized hostage, after all. Ahead of me, I see Harry slow down and adjust his gun, before stopping and turning to face us.

"I'll hold them here, give you two time to escape," he says to us.

"No you bloody won't," I tell him, grabbing his shirt with my other hand and pulling him along with us. "You aren't dying alone down here. Not after everything we've been through, so don't you dare."

Harry doesn't fight my grip and just runs along with us, much to my relief. I can't carry them both.

"Fine. Then we need to find a way out of here," he says, "And soon. My shoulder is killing me."

"And I can't keep running Jake. I'm exhausted," Olive says, her voice sounding strained.

"Come here, you," I say to her, before grabbing her and hoisting her onto my back, she hooks her arms round my neck and I loop my arms under her legs. I shuffle a few times, making sure I have a good grip and then we set off again. Harry is clearly struggling to keep up the pace, but he doesn't complain or try to stop.

"Jakey, over there!" Olive exclaims, and I see a door just ahead.

Harry runs up to the door and tries to open the lock but struggles to do it one handed, so I put Olive down and push him to one side. Luckily the bar gives on my second attempt. I pull open the door and let Harry through first so he can clear the room, and then push Olive ahead of me before closing the door behind us and slowly lowering the bar back down to lock it again. Within seconds, we hear hundreds of footsteps rushing past the other side of the door, but their pace doesn't falter and I feel the tension in the little room dissipate as we realise they hadn't seen us.

I turn around and see Harry slumped on the floor, clutching his shoulder, the arrow still protruding from the wound and blood now soaked into his jacket. I make my way over to him, stopping as I pass Olive to give her a kiss on the forehead, and then kneel down to look at his wound.

"It's not good, Jake," Harry tells me, his breath sounding laboured. "But I'll be ok for a bit."

"Let me see? We have a bit of time." I reassure him calmly.

He relaxes his arm, allowing me to peel the Kevlar vest back off his shoulder and over the bit of shaft still attached to the arrow head. Underneath, his shirt is drenched with blood. I take the pack off my back and open it up, looking for something to use to dress the wound, but all I have is a spare pair of socks from my gym kit. Luckily, they're clean. I separate them and roll them up, putting one on each side of the arrow shaft.

"Here, apply pressure to these," I tell him, and he lifts his other arm up to hold them in place, but I can see the effort it requires to do so. He is clearly in a lot of pain.

I take out the rest of my gym kit, a running jersey and tracksuit bottoms. Not the best first aid kit in the world, but it'll have to do. I use the jersey to wrap around his shoulder, and secure it under his armpit so that he can let go of the makeshift bandages, and then pull the Kevlar vest back over the top to hold the whole thing in place. He doesn't make a sound the whole time, but I can see him wincing from the movement.

"Put your arm in here," I say, gesturing to the leg of the tracksuit bottoms. "You are about to get a very fetching Spurs themed sling."

"Oh Jake, and we were getting on so well," he tells me with a smile. "Now I wish I'd stayed in the tunnel."

"Bloody stubborn Gooner," I say to him, laughing a little now.

While I have never really been one to engage in the more serious side of the rivalry between the Arsenal and Spurs football fans, I welcome the light-hearted banter and change of pace given our current circumstances.

I tie the ends of the two legs together around his neck and sit back to admire my handiwork. It looks ridiculous, but it'll do, and hopefully it's more comfortable than before.

"Thanks mate," Harry says to me. "For saving me."

"I think we are pretty even on that front Harry," I tell him, clapping him gently on his good shoulder.

"I'm going to try and rest for a bit, while we wait for this to calm down," Harry says to us both, "But I'm not giving up, honestly. We still need to find Adam, Cassie and well, I assume you want to see Nat again, but I'm not entirely sure after what happened."

"Take your time mate, we are safe here for now," I say, and turn to Olive, who has sat down on the other side of the little room we are currently hiding in.

The sight of her sitting there, actually sitting there, brings tears to my eyes. I quickly close the gap between us and sink down next to her, pulling her into my arms.

"Olive," I say to her, tilting my head to look at her. "I…"

"You don't have to say anything," she interjects. "You came for me. I knew you would."

I pull her in closer as she shuffles her body towards me, burying her head into my neck and resting her legs against mine. For the first time since yesterday, I feel myself relax. I found her. She's here. She's safe.

Chapter Nineteen

The feeling of ease and relaxation lasts about twenty seconds, as my thoughts turn back to Cassie. I feel the familiar sense of fear and panic rising up inside me, as I think about the last time I saw her. It had been about fifteen minutes since I watched her run away from the hundreds of orcs who were in pursuit, and away from me.

"What is it Jakey?" Olive asks, feeling me tense up.

"Just thinking about Cassie," I tell her, trying to hide the panic I was feeling.

"What happened?" She asks. "And I don't just mean back there, I want to know everything."

"Where to start, little one," I say to her, knowing full well that she is only asking me right now to distract me from my thoughts about Cassie.

"Allow me to kick things off," Harry tells me, shifting awkwardly so he is facing us. "About 2pm yesterday, what we now know are orcs, literally turned up in the BBC newsroom and gave a rather vague warning about war, mass destruction and other horrible sounding threats."

"I was with Nat at the time, we saw it live," I carry on. "We tried to get hold of you, but it went to voicemail so we rushed over to find Cassie, and then went to look for you at Bank."

"Oh Jake," she whimpers. "It was horrible. We were all sat there listening to the lecture, when they came bursting in. They didn't talk, or ask anyone anything, they just started slaughtering everyone. There was so much blood, and screaming, and, and…"

"I know, I went in there to look for you," I tell her, cutting her off from reliving that moment. "I saw what they did."

"I was in the back row, and I tried to hide," she admits, her voice breaking at the memory.

"Olive, it's ok," I tell her, "You don't have to do this now."

"No, it's fine. I'm fine," she says, psyching herself up. "One of them found me and dragged me out with the others, he was about to kill me when another one of them stopped him. I was co confused, I didn't know what to do."

"What happened Olive?" I ask her, my curiosity getting the better of me. "What did they say?"

"One of those things, they kept asking me how I got it? Where I got it?" she explains. "But I didn't know what they were on about. I couldn't answer them. I was so scared."

I feel her lean away from me, and watch as she tucks her knees up under her chin.

"After they had finished… with everyone else," she says, tears forming in her eyes, "They dragged me outside and down into the tube. We walked for ages, it was so dark, I had no idea where we were, until we got to Westminster."

"We had heard they took someone in the attack, a small girl with red hair," I tell her, reaching out to hold her hand. "We assumed, well more hoped, it was you."

"It was. Obviously," she says with a small smile and a slight shrug of her shoulders. "Once we got there, I was taken to that bigger one. The others called him the Warchief?"

"That would probably be Gro'alk. It's the same orc that gave the message on TV," Harry confirms.

"Ok. Yeah, him," she says. "He told me that I had something called the Light inside me, but I didn't know what that meant."

"You obviously heard the second message that went out," Harry says. "He mentioned the Light that time too, but we didn't know what it meant either."

I sit there nodding as the two of them talk, taking in all that Olive had said, and trying to retain all the important points.

"He kept asking me about my family, about my friends," Olive carries on. "I told him that my parents had died when I was younger, along with my brother in an accident. About how I had been on my own since then as all my family was dead."

"Oh, Olive," I say to her, squeezing her hand, remembering how painful it had been the first time she told me.

"I didn't tell him about you Jake," she says, smiling at me.

"That's not what I was worried about, little one," I tell her. "You just shouldn't have had to go through any of that."

"He was obsessed with the Light," she continues, squeezing my hand as she talks. "I didn't understand. I tried to tell him I didn't know anything. He explained that it was an old power, but that was lost when the elves were all killed and shouldn't exist anymore. I tried to explain that elves and orcs only exist in books and movies but they wouldn't listen."

"Apparently that Warchief was there when the elves all died," Olive explained. "Well, all except one, and that their Shadow God, whoever, whatever that is, had hunted that last one for thousands of years but he had eventually been killed as well. Apparently, there isn't meant to be any more Light left. Except for what's inside me."

"This whole situation seems so far-fetched," Harry laughs. "Yesterday I woke up worrying about terrorists, today I am talking about orcs and elves like they've always been a thing."

"You're not wrong, Harry." I tell him, and turn back to Olive. "Did he say anything else? About you, or the Light, or their plans? Anything at all?"

"No, just kept asking the same questions. Over and over." she says.

"OK, OK, don't worry, it doesn't matter right now," I say to her. "That bit is over with now, you're here and we're back together."

We all sit there in silence, thinking about what Olive had told us, but it doesn't take long for my thoughts to turn back to Cassie. The image of her scared face as she ran away replaying in my mind over and over again.

Chapter Twenty

Pulling myself away from the thoughts of Cassie, I turn to look at Olive and notice that she is starting to shake now, however it is far from cold in here. I get up and go over to my pack. I search through the pockets, pulling out a bottle of water and throw it over to her.

"You need to drink," I tell her. "I'll try and find you some food, although it'll only be junk, we haven't had much chance to go shopping."

I hear her open the water while I go back into my bag. All I manage to find is a packet of Skittles, some crisps and another bottle of water. As I walk back over to her, I watch her drain the last of the first bottle so I hand the second one to her, along with the snacks.

"Skittles?" she asks me, with a laugh. "Really pushing the boat out there, Jakey."

"You'll appreciate the sugar high in a minute," I reply, smiling back at her.

"Only for about ten minutes," she says, rolling her eyes.

"Better make those ten minutes count then," I say, looking back over at Harry.

"And then we should try to make our way out of here," he agrees. "Find a way back up so we can contact Adam and the others."

We wait for Olive to eat her Skittles and drink the remaining water, and Harry drinks some of his own as well, before packing up our bits. I pull Olive up to her feet and then walk over to help Harry stand up. He still looks weak, but is adamant that he can walk despite the pain.

I walk over to the door and push my ear against the cold metal, straining to hear any movement or noises the other side. After a minute or so, I turn to the others and shrug, I can't hear any orcs but that doesn't mean they're not waiting. Although, given our experiences so far, they seem far more likely to attack the door than wait us out.

Gripping the handle firmly, I pull it slowly to avoid any unnecessary noise, and the door gives easily enough. I peer out into the darkness, and can't see any signs of the orcs, so open the door a little more and motion for the others to follow me.

I carefully jump down to the rails and, with Olive's help from up top, lower Harry down to me before catching Olive when she jumps down. We crouch in the darkness, all of us listening for any noises from down the tunnel but the only noise is the laboured breathing coming from Harry. We really need to get him out of here.

We move down the tunnel side by side now, with Harry in the middle of me and Olive, in case he needs to use us for support. We walk at a fairly slow pace, so it takes us nearly fifteen minutes to walk up towards Green Park station. Luckily the walk goes without incident, and the station itself seems to be free of any orc presence at the moment. I can't help but wonder if they passed through here during their search for us, and if so, are they due to come back?

I climb up onto the platform, so I can pull Harry up by his good arm and Olive surprises me by jumping up by herself. I can't help but smile at her sudden burst of energy, the Skittles obviously worked, but the smile earns me a punch on the arm.

"Welcome back," I tell her.

"Thanks," she replies. "Now we just need to find the rest of our little family, don't we?"

"Yeah, about that," I tell her as we climb up for the first set of escalators. "It might not be such a happy family anymore."

"What? Why?" she asks, concern in her voice now.

"Nat and Cassie kind of broke up," I explain. "Or rather, Cassie broke up with him, because of something he did."

"What?" She gasps, stopping to look at me as we reach the top of the escalator.

"It's a long story, but the short version is; Nat left to find you on his own. We saved him. He told Cassie that finding you was more important than protecting her," I tell her, although I'm not sure why I am.

"He is such a bloody idiot. Cassie is literally the best thing that's ever happened to him," she exclaims, with a perplexed look on her face. "And I'm just your sister. He knows you'll come get me."

"While I don't agree that you are 'just' my sister," I reply, "I do agree that he is a complete and utter asshat for hurting Cassie."

Behind me I hear Harry start to laugh a little louder than he should.

"Jake Shepherd," she says flatly. "What did you do?"

"Well, I didn't not punch him," I say sheepishly. "And it definitely wasn't right on his nose."

"Jake!" she says, hitting me on the arm again. But much, much harder. "I can't believe you actually followed through on your threat."

"How do you know about that?" I ask her.

"Nat told me after he came to me to talk about asking Cassie out," Olive replies.

"He asked you too?" I say, confused.

"He felt that he needed to, as she is my best friend and unofficial big sister," she says, rolling her eyes at that, reminding me again of Cassie.

As we come into the main station lobby upstairs, I can see all the gates are closed exactly as I expected. We walk through the now open ticket barriers when we hear a voice call out from behind the furthest gate.

"Stop right there!" the voice says, at least it sounds human. "Who are you and what are you doing in there?"

Harry steps forward, holding up his gun sideways, in an attempt to show that we weren't a threat.

"I am Sergeant Harry Stephens, Armed Response Unit, Met Police," Harry tells them. "We were performing an undercover recon mission just north of here, but got split up from the rest of our team."

The lie flows confidently from his lips, even I was convinced for a moment until I remember that I'm not a police officer, and neither is Olive. And worse, we look nothing like police officers. We all stand there, waiting for the officer ahead of us to pass his own judgement.

"Ok, Sergeant," he says, "Get over here, I'll open the gate but you've got to be quick. We heard a lot of movement down there not long ago."

Once we are all through and the gate is securely locked again, we follow the officer round the corner to find the rest of the officers who are stationed here. There are about fifteen of them, ranging from early twenties through to late forties, maybe early fifties. I'm not sure what the Met expect any of them to do if the orcs came out of the station in force, they don't even have a gun between them.

"You're hurt," our first officer says, matter of factly.

"I'll be fine," Harry tries to tell him.

"No you won't mate," I interject, and ask the officer; "Where is the nearest hospital?"

"The closest one that is still open would be St Thomas', I reckon," one of the other officers tells us.

"Any chance of a lift?" I ask, and desperately hope the answer is yes.

"Sure, our cars are just down the road. I'll go get it and come back for you," the overly helpful officer replies.

I can't tell if he is just happy to be doing something, or for the chance to get away from the potential danger of the station for a bit. I watch him walk off and then pull my phone out of my pocket. 8% battery left. I try to call Cassie but I get her voicemail. Is she still underground? Or has she run out of battery? I feel the panic rising again and try to swallow it down. She is still alive, she must be, I can feel it.

"Cassie, it's Jake. We made it out, we are headed to St Thomas' hospital to get Harry looked at. I'll come for you. I promise," I leave on her voicemail.

Less than a minute later, the police car pulls up next to us. I open the front passenger door and help Harry into the seat, before jumping in the back with Olive.

None of us talk during the ride over. I just sit in the back seat staring out the window in the direction of Westminster hoping to catch a glimpse of Cassie, but I feel Olive take my hand in hers and squeeze, so I turn to her and give her a smile.

"We'll find her, Jake," she tells me. "Together. Like you both found me."

I just nod at her. I know if I try to talk, I'll break and I can't do that right now. I need to be strong for Olive, and for Cassie. The thought of losing the ones I love is my single greatest fear. It always has been.

When we pull up to the main entrance, I can see that the hospital is surrounded by armed police and soldiers in their combat gear, it would appear they aren't taking any chances now that the army are here. I wonder how many other places have been hit since the attacks yesterday, civilian or otherwise. There is far more smoke in the distance now, so I would bet it is quite a few.

I climb out of the car, and help Harry get out of his seat. He is getting weaker by the minute. As we stand up, two nurses run over to us with a wheelchair and I help him to sit back down.

"He is police, we went to the Underground and he took an arrow to the shoulder," I explain to the nurses, keeping the lie intact. "I tried to control the bleeding, but he'll probably have lost a lot of blood."

"Thanks, we'll take it from here," the male nurse says.

"What about you two? Both ok?" The female nurse asks.

"We are both unhurt, just tired, hungry and dehydrated," I explain, nodding at Olive.

"Ok, follow us inside," she tells us. "I'll get someone to come check you over."

I say my thanks to the officer that drove us over, and wish him luck, then we both follow the nurses pushing Harry inside. As we walk into reception, I pull out my phone and try Cassie again. Voicemail. I take a deep breath and remind myself that she has Adam with her, she will be fine. For now.

The nurses have taken Harry into one of the trauma rooms and have started to remove his vest and clothing, but as I make my way over to talk to him, a nurse comes up to me and Olive, gesturing for us to follow her.

"Harry, I'll come find you in a bit." I shout over to him, and see him nod weakly back.

Olive and I follow the nurse into one of the other side rooms.

"I was asked to give you both the once over, anything I should be aware of?" she asks.

"No, I am fine," I tell her, "But Olive here has been deprived of water and food for the last 24 hours."

"Yes, of course. Well that explains your colour," she gasps, taking a second glance at Olive. "Wait. You're the girl, from the video? Aren't you?"

I look at Olive and Olive looks back at me. The cats out the bag already.

"I'll take that as a yes, the nurse says, smiling at Olive. "Right, I'll put a saline drip in to get you hydrated again, and some electrolytes to rebalance you and perk you up. You poor little thing," and she gives her a quick hug, which makes me smile as I know it would have made Olive feel incredibly uncomfortable.

I watch her leave the room, and take the seat by the desk to rest my legs. When I look over at my little sister, I can see that she looks exhausted. I could hear in her voice how terrified she must have been as she recounted the story, but I can't imagine what the last 24 hours must have been like for her.

A few minutes later, the nurse returns with the saline drip, catheter and electrolytes, but she isn't alone. There is someone in urban combat fatigues with her.

"Jake Shepherd?" the man asks.

"That's me," I reply tentatively. "And you are?"

"Captain James Franks, British Army," he replies. "And am I safe to assume that you are Olive Shepherd?"

"Safe, and sound," Olive tells him, with her trademark cheeky smile.

"Well, well, well." he says, now grinning. "I would love to know how that happened."

"I'll tell you everything you want to know," I tell him. "On one condition."

165

"Name it," The Captain says, and I smile back at him.

"I need your help to find our friends, and then you need to bring them back here."

Chapter Twenty One

"Her name is Cassie Hollings," I tell Captain Franks, noting the urgency in my voice. "She will be with two others, a guy called Nat Smith and another police officer, Sergeant Adam Froom."

"The obvious questions are; where and why?" he asks me, giving me a curious look.

"The why is easy; they were with us when we rescued Olive, but we got split up on our way out. Cassie is my best friend, and currently the person I care about most in this world, after Olive of course," I tell him, nodding my head at Olive who is perched opposite me. "Nat is a… was a friend, and Adam is Harry's partner and has been through hell and back with us."

"Ok, well that certainly answers the why," He says, nodding along. "So what about the where?"

"Things got a bit noisy once we had found Olive. We had to shoot our way out, basically. The orcs started to charge at us, and we couldn't make it back to the others," I explain, my voice choking at the end. "We had to split up, while also trying to draw off as many orcs as we could."

"That was both brave and stupid," the Captain says, chuckling a little. "Did you have a back-up rendezvous?"

"We did," I explain, feeling pleased that we had at least gotten something right. "The safe house we stayed at last night, we were to all head there if we were found."

"Ok, Jake," he says, taking a note of the location as I explain where it was. "I'll send a unit out to pick them up right now."

"Thank you," I tell him, relieved. "We couldn't get there, not with Harrys injury. They're probably worried sick." If I can't get to her myself, then sending the army seems like a fair compromise.

"Olive, you stay here with the nurse. Rest up," he tells her. "I'll come back down to talk with you, after I have to spoken to Jake."

I throw the Captain a curious look, before following out the room, I give Olive a quick wink as I close the door behind me. We walk in silence down the corridor towards a quieter part of the hospital, but I keep track of the turns so I can make my way back. Captain Franks motions to a door on our right, before opening it up to check inside. Moments later, he invites me to join him inside.

"Take a seat, Jake," he tells me. "We should talk."

I take the seat opposite him, and can't help but feel a sense of anxiety. He is just the right level of pleasant and encouraging, while still being distant and calculating. I trust him enough to ensure Cassie's safety, if the army can't get her, then I doubt many could. But for some reason, I don't know how much I can trust him with the rest of our story.

"What would you like to know?" I ask him, putting the ball in his court.

"I would like to say everything, but I have a feeling I won't get it." he replies, turning his palms upwards and shrugging. "You don't trust me, and I don't blame you. In all honesty, I certainly don't trust you yet. It is basic human nature."

"I want to trust you, Captain. I do," I tell him, trying to sound sincere. "But the last twenty four hours have been somewhat of an eye opener as to what is and isn't real."

"Couldn't agree more, Jake," he says, and I note the repeated use of my name, probably some form of soft interrogation technique. "But you must understand that my main priority is the continued safety and protection of everyone in this city, and well, to be fair, in the country."

"Of course. I couldn't agree more about that. They all need you," I say, no longer needing to force any sincerity, before correcting myself; "We all you need you. But over the last day, my main priority was getting Olive back, and now it is getting Cassie back to me. Everything I've done, and everything I'm doing, is to ensure those two things happen."

"Then for the time being, can we agree that our interests are aligned?" he asks.

"We can," I reply, nodding.

"Then let us talk openly for a moment," he suggests. "Right now, I am not a Captain, we are just two grown men having a discussion."

"Works for me," I tell him, doubting that's all we are.

"What happened down there? What on earth did you see?" he asks, leaning forward to look closely at me.

I take a deep breath, before launching into the story of how we saw the second message on TV, and then re-entered the tunnels to infiltrate the station. I explain about the setting of fires for light, the sentries posted on the platforms and then the orcs that began fighting between themselves. I finish the story off with the sheer number of the orcs that gave chase once we had rescued Olive. To his credit, he listens attentively throughout and doesn't interrupt, but I can see that the last part of the story visibly shocks him.

"I'm impressed. It would seem that Harry and Adam are a credit to the force for their part in the mission," he says, sounding much more like a Captain than a civilian.

"I agree, they were instrumental in her rescue," I tell him, and make a mental note to properly thank them next time I see them.

"I don't understand why you were all there though. No offence, but what did you all bring to the table?" he asks me, and I can tell that it wasn't meant as a slight.

"Well, I had helped Harry the day before. He had fallen behind to cover our escape and I went back for him," I tell him. "Although you may be right about Nat as he proved to be more of a hindrance than anything, and honestly, I couldn't leave Cassie alone, not that she wanted to be left alone. I guess I selfishly needed to know she was safe."

"Fair enough. That's fair enough," he says, laughing a little. Back to being the civilian.

"You have provided some interesting insights into these orcs, Jake," he tells me, shaking his head. "Their numbers concern me most. We knew that they had a fair amount down there, but what you described is the first eye witness report from within one of their strongholds. So thank you."

"You're welcome. Is there anything you can share with me?" I ask.

"Anything in particular?"

"How many attacks have there been now? What are we doing about it? Are we even prepared?" I reel off.

"We don't know how many, not exactly, more and more seem to happen every hour. There have been about forty attacks in London alone. Interestingly, and horribly, your Olive remains the sole survivor. The majority of the targets have been seemingly random, except for the military bases, which the reason should be obvious," he tells me, dejectedly. "What are we doing about it? The honest answer is; not enough. But that is because we just weren't prepared. How could we be?"

"That was surprisingly honest," I tell him, sighing. "And depressing."

"Hence my desire to talk to you," he says, letting out a big sigh. "We are trying to formulate a plan and all information is useful."

"Yeah I bet," I say, letting my gaze drop to the table.

"The second message," he says. "That orc, the Warchief. He basically said that they picked Olive out for having something called the Light?"

"He did. We saw it too," I reply, looking up to meet his gaze. The civilian has gone, the Captain is back. This is clearly what he wanted to talk about all along. "We asked Olive about it. She has no idea, other than they seemed obsessed with it and kept asking her about it over and over and over again."

"I don't know if you noticed, but if you ignored the disgust in the orcs' voice, then it was almost like they were scared of it," the Captain says, smiling now.

"I thought so too," I tell him. "But why?"

I see the Captain's teeth now as his smile grows, his mind whirring away at the beginnings of a plan. I lean forward in my chair, but before I can say anything his phone starts to ring.

"Excuse me, Jake, I'll be right back," he says, leaving the room.

I sit there in silence, still thinking about that second broadcast of Gro'alk. The tone of his voice and the choice of words. The Captain had a point, he did sound scared. Despite the grim focus, it doesn't take long for my thoughts to turn back to Cassie. I close my eyes and try to picture her climbing up out of the ladder and walking back to the safe house with Adam and Nat. Please be safe, Cassie, please. I know she can't hear me but I desperately wish she could.

Captain Franks opens the door behind me, bringing me back to reality.

"Jake, you have been extremely helpful," he tells me. "Thank you."

"You're welcome. I'm glad I could help," I tell him. "Let me know if there is anything else I can do."

"You kept your end of the deal, Jake," he tells me, smiling. "Now I'll keep mine. The Unit I sent out to get your friends are due back in the next few minutes. I'll have one of my men take you back to the front desk now, so you can be there to greet them."

I practically jump out of my chair to follow him back outside, where a young man dressed in army fatigues salutes the Captain, before turning to lead me back to the front of the hospital. I wave to Olive as we pass her room with a big smile on my face, which she returns along with an enthusiastic wave. She knows why I am smiling. I nod to Harry as I go past, he is looking a little perkier now. I make a mental note to tell Adam where he is.

As we walk outside the hospital, two blacked out Range Rovers come screeching into the ambulance bays and pull up just in front of us. Olive comes running out of the hospital to stand next to me, clearly ignoring all medical advice, based on the expression on the nurse that had followed her out here, but also not wanting to miss their return.

I watch as both passenger side doors open, and see Adam jump out the front and close his door behind him, he gives me a nod as he runs straight into the hospital to find Harry. I only remember to tell him where Harry is once he is already inside. Just behind him, I watch Nat slowly get out the rear door, his face now looking quite sore with two blackening eyes and a very swollen nose.

"Jake, how hard did you hit him?" she asks me, sounding shocked.

"Not as hard as I wanted to, little one,' I reply distractedly.

I'm still watching Nat, who only has eyes for Olive as he hasn't even so much as glanced at me yet, but then he turns and closes his door behind him.

I feel my heart drop out the bottom of my chest and all I can think is:

Where is Cassie?

Chapter Twenty Two

I stand there, frozen, and watch Nat walk towards Olive, his two black eyes giving him a look that would be sinister if it weren't for the purple swollen nose between them. I desperately look over at the second Range Rover that came in, and see several army personnel climb out and head into the hospital.

As I turn back to look at Olive, the panic inside me threatening to consume me, I notice that the driver has only just climbed out of the Range Rover and is now opening the rear passenger door. A few seconds later, I see Cassie walk round the back of the vehicle, her arm tied up in a make shift sling. As soon as she sees me, she runs towards me and I involuntarily launch myself towards her, meeting her half way as I wrap my arms around her. She puts her left arm go round my waist, her head straight into my shoulder and I feel her start to sob.

"Cassie," I say to her, trying not to let my voice break. "I've got you."

"I was so worried about you," she tells me.

"Me? I was fine, sweetheart," I say, laughing a little. "I've been worried about you!"

"Clearly! You sent the army to come find us!" She mumbles, and I can almost hear her smiling as she talks into my shoulder.

"It was the next best thing to coming to get you myself," I tell her, my right hand now stroking her hair. "Come on, lets get you inside."

I reluctantly unwrap my arms from her shoulders, and watch as Cassie gives Olive a big cuddle and they both tear up in each other's arms. They've always been close, like sisters really, and is just another reason why Cassie means so much to me. She is part of my family. While the girls are catching up, Nat just looks off to the distance, purposefully avoiding any eye contact with me. I know I need to apologise to him eventually, but not just yet.

Once the girls finish talking, I take Cassie's hand to lead her inside, noticing that Nat and Olive follow us in as well. Just inside the door, the nurse that was seeing to Olive calls her over to get her drip reconnected and I hear Olive ask her to take a look at Nat's rather bruised face, which again reminds me that I need to talk to him.

I ask one of the nurses in the reception area to take a look at Cassie's arm, and we are led into another side room similar to the one where Olive was earlier. The nurse takes her arm out of the sling and I see Cassie wince from the pain. After examining her arm, the nurse confirms her suspicions that her ulna has a break, but the lack of power for an X-ray means that they'll have to just fit a brace and keep an eye on it. The nurse turns to leave the room, needing to find a brace for Cassie's arm, leaving us alone for the first time since last night.

"Cassie, I can't even explain," I say to her. "I don't have the words. I've been driving myself mad thinking about the last time I saw you. Replaying it over and over. I felt so helpless."

"I hated having to leave you, Jake," she says, frowning at me. "Adam had to literally carry me down the escalators to stop me running over to you."

"Adam did the right thing," I tell her. "Harry got shot by an arrow trying to get across."

"I know, we saw. Is he ok?" she asks, frowning.

"He is in one of the other rooms here, he lost a lot of blood on the way over, but he looked a little better last time I saw him," I tell her. "We can go find him once your arm is sorted, if you want?"

"Yes, please. I'd like to see him," she says. "If that's ok?"

"Of course, it's fine," I say to her. "I need to catch up with Adam too, I owe him a massive thank you for looking after you."

"I'm so glad Olive is ok, and that we're all back together," she says, smiling at me. "We were all so worried when you didn't turn up at the safe house. Even Nat."

"Was he?" I ask, biting my tongue.

"He was, and not just about Olive. He was worried about you too, Jake," she tells me gently, placing her hand on my arm. "He knows he crossed the line at the station. He feels bad about it."

"Cassie. I owe you an apology," I say to her, wincing as I look down at her.

"What for?" she asks looking puzzled.

"I overheard your argument last night. I…" I tell her, hesitating at the end. "I heard it all."

"Oh," she says, looking down and blushing bright red. "Umm, I'm sorry."

"No, Cassie, you have done nothing to apologise for," I tell her. "You said and did all the right things. He was totally in the wrong."

"That's the real reason you hit him isn't it?" she asks me, her eyes filled with curiosity and something else I can't quite place.

"Not gonna lie, Cassie, but it kinda is," I tell her, smiling slightly. "Before he asked you out, I warned him that if he broke your heart, I would break his face. I just never expected to actually have to do it."

"Jake!" her eyes so wide, I have to look away out of fear of what she might be thinking. Then I hear her laughing, "You really are a pest," she tells me. "But you are my pest, so thank you, for always looking out for me."

"Always Cassie," I tell her. "Even if it's not in the most conventional ways. You're my best friend, and I love you dearly. You know that."

"I do know, Jake, and you're mine," she says, smiling. "Love you too…"

Cassie's eyes find mine, and I feel my breath catch in my throat and I force myself to not look away. We had said it to each other before, many times, but always in the context of being friends and loving each other's friendship, companionship and our close connection. I've never let her see the romantic nature of those feelings, despite them being there for as long as I can remember. I wouldn't be able to handle the rejection.

"What happened to your arm?" I ask her, trying to subtly change the subject.

"It's nothing really, but we couldn't lose the orcs before we reached the ladder, so we carried on until we got to Waterloo," she explains. "Then as we were climbing up onto the platform, an orc came out of nowhere and Adam knocked him back off the platform, but he caught me as he fell, and I landed awkwardly on my arm."

My look of shock must have been more obvious than I intended, as Cassie quickly adds; "Don't worry! Adam took care of the orc before he could do anything else."

"I definitely need to go thank Adam, after the nurse sorts out your arm," I tell her, pulling her into a tight cuddle.

Seconds later, the nurse comes back into the room carrying a selection of arm braces for Cassie to choose from.

"Oooh, I'll have the red one please!" she says excitedly.

The nurse injects a local anaesthetic into Cassie's arm, and then carefully slides the brace over her arm and secures the straps down to keep the bone steady. I remember when they used to just give you a cast and send you on your way only for all your friends to draw all over it, usually of an obscene and inappropriate nature. Times really have changed.

"Here are some pain killers, but they are quite strong so take them only when needed," the nurse tells Cassie.

"Thank you," Cassie replies, putting the foil strip of tablets in her pocket.

I get up and take Cassie's good hand in mine, then lead her back out into the busy hallways of the hospital. We walk back round towards the reception so that I can trace my steps back to where I last saw Harry. It doesn't take us long to find the right room.

Inside, I can see Harry laying on the bed with tubes in his arm giving him a saline drip and also a blood transfusion. He has started to regain his colour now, which is a good sign. Adam is sitting on a chair next to the bed, talking to Harry, but he stops when he sees us outside and gestures for us to come in.

"Hey Adam, good to see you mate," I tell him, holding out my hand to shake his.

"Think we are past that, aren't we now?" he says, getting up and giving me a man hug which I reciprocate gladly.

I owe this man a lot. He kept Cassie safe. After I let go of him, Cassie walks over and gives him a cuddle too.

"Thank you Adam, for taking care of Cassie," I tell him.

"I know how much she means to you, Jake," he says to me. "And it was the least I could do for you, since I knew you would be taking care of Harry."

"Of course, I did. After everything you've both done for us," I say to him, leaving the rest unsaid.

"He told me what you did for him, before they knocked him out. Thank you, Jake," he tells me. "He's like a brother to me."

I look over at Harry, who is laying there unconscious from all of the pain medication. I'm glad he is here, and getting looked after, but at the same time, it hurts to see him like this. He's been such an instrumental part of our group, and a strong leader for us all.

"I hope he gets better quickly mate. It'll drive him mad being stuck in here with everything going on," I say to Adam.

"He'll be fine. I'll make sure he is," he tells me. "But what's next for you guys?"

"Not sure, to be honest. I had only really thought about getting us all back together, I never got round to working out what to do once we all were," I say, surprising myself at the lack of forethought on the matter. There is so much more to do.

"Maybe just take the time to rest, while you can," he says, frowning now. "We don't know what will happen tomorrow."

"That's true. Good plan," I tell him. "Also, you might want to catch up with a Captain Franks? He is in charge round here, and he will probably appreciate any information you can give him."

"Thanks Jake. I'll find him later," he says. "Don't leave without saying goodbye, ok?"

"Wouldn't dream of it," I tell him, and give him another man hug before we leave the room to find Olive and Nat.

Chapter Twenty Three

After leaving Adam and Harry, I walk with Cassie through the hallways of the hospital. It's such a strange atmosphere, the hospital is heaving with people, but it isn't busy? It seems like every doctor, nurse, police officer and now the army have come here to serve their public duty. There just isn't any public to serve, everyone is either hiding at home or fleeing the city, or already dead.

We are nearly back at reception, when I have the uncontrollable urge to stop and pull Cassie into my arms, it takes all of two seconds to actually do it, and I feel her melt into my shoulder. The feeling of her body against mine, it feels like home.

"I'm never going to complain about cuddles, Jake," she tells me, her voice muffled as she has buried her face into my chest. "But is there a particular reason for this one?"

"Didn't realise I needed a reason," I say to her, smiling. "But if I need one, then let's put this up to making up for lost time."

"Good enough for me," she agrees, and I feel her snuggle in a little bit harder.

I rest my chin on the top of her head and spot Olive talking to Nat in the room on the other side of the waiting area ahead. Olive is quiet by nature, but can be a boisterous little thing when she gets going, and she is very animated right now. I try to picture the conversation in my head, but after everything that Nat has said and done in the last 24 hours, it could be anything. I'll deal with that in a minute, right now it's Cassie's time and she deserves my undivided attention.

"How are you, Cassie?" I ask her, resting my hand on her head and stroking her hair gently. "Honestly."

"I'm getting there. It was just a shock," she explains. "After everything that has happened, I thought that I could at least rely on him, you know?"

"I know, sweetheart," I tell her. "To be honest, so did I."

"What is worse though, is that I knew," she says, and I hear her voice break.

"What do you mean?" I ask, tensing up, concern clearly etched in my voice.

"How he feels about Olive," she tells me, pulling back a bit so she can look up at me. "I've always known. He'd told me, a long time ago, but he also said that he would never act on his feelings because of his friendship with you."

"Oh, Cassie," I say to her, shaking my head softly. "Then why?"

"He is a good guy, Jake. We were good together, and I know he cared about me, and I think he did love me," she tells me. "Just not enough, I guess, in the end."

"That's not good enough though," I tell her, sighing. "He chose you, Cassie."

"I think it's quite clear that when it came down to it, he chose Olive," she says, looking away from me.

"Then he is even more of an asshat that I thought he was," I tell her, lifting her chin up so I can look into her eyes. "Because he should have chosen you. Every single time."

I kiss her on the forehead and pull her back into my arms, squeezing her as tightly as I can. I want her to feel safe, and loved, and wanted. Because she is, even if she doesn't know just how much.

"Jake. Don't ever leave me," she says, her voice catching at the end. "I can't lose you too."

"I'll won't leave you, not if I have a choice," I tell her. "But if we ever get split up, I'll always find you. Wherever you are, whatever it takes."

I feel her squeeze me before pulling away, looking up at me with tears in her eyes but a smile on her lips.

"Let's go find Olive. She needs you too," she tells me with a poke in the ribs, and I smile back at her.

"Yeah ok, I guess you're right," I tell her. "And maybe after all this new information, I should punch Nat again."

That earns me another poke in the ribs, after which I catch Cassie's hand, and walk with her over to Olive's room. I knock on the closed door and hear her shout to come in. As I open the door, I spot Olive sitting on the bed and get a big beaming smile from her. She has definitely perked up since we arrived earlier, and it warms my heart to see her back to being a bit more like her usual self.

I look over to Nat, who doesn't look any better than he did outside, his eyes are still darkening by the minute. He takes his phone out, but it quickly goes back in his pocket, presumably dead, and walks across the room away from us, taking the seat in the corner while preoccupying himself with a poster on the miracle of child birth.

"Hey little one," I say to Olive, who jumps down from bed.

"Jakey!" she almost squeals at me, throwing her arms round me.

"What have they been giving you?" I say, laughing at her sudden hyper mood.

"A little bit of everything, I think," she explains, a curious look on her face as she looks up at the ceiling in a mock thinking pose.

"It's good to have you back," I tell her, before pulling her back in for another cuddle.

"I feel good, Jake. Happy. We have our family back together. What more could a girl want?" she asks me, while stretching her arms out to point out our little family.

I look over at the top of Nat's head, and can think of a few things that Olive may want. I have always tried to be there for her, as her friend, and her brother, and her protector. But what if that isn't what she wants? Or ultimately what she even needs?

"Cassie," I say, turning to her. "Can you give me a minute with Olive?"

"Of course," she says, smiling. "I'll be outside."

"Nat," I say to him, trying to keep my voice friendly.

"I'm going," he says abruptly, not even looking up.

I watch them both leave the room, and see Cassie take a seat just outside the room while Nat walks further afield. Turning back to Olive, I can see the curious glint she gets in her eye when she is trying to work out what is in my mind. She knows me very well, but she can't read me quite like Cassie can.

"How are you, little one?" I ask her.

"You didn't kick them out to ask me that," she says, smirking slightly. Maybe she can read me better than I thought.

"No, but we will get to that," I tell her. "Right now, I just want to know you're ok."

"I'm fine Jakey. Honestly," she tells me. "A little tired, but alive and here. That's what counts, right?"

I put my hand on the side of her head, stroking her hair down to her shoulder where I rest my hand.

"I've been worrying about you for so long now, it's hard to turn it off, you know," I tell her. We both know I don't just mean since yesterday.

"Jake Shepherd. You have been there for me, every single day, for the last twelve years of my life. When I had no one else," she says to me. "You are the one person I trust with everything. My life, my heart, my everything. When I didn't think I would trust anyone ever again, there you were."

"Olive," I say, "I love you, you know that."

"And I love you too, Jake," she tells me, smiling. "Now, for the love of all things, just say what you came in here to say to me."

"I told you why Cassie broke up with Nat," I say to her.

"You did, and I have told him how much of an idiot he was for doing what he did," she tells me.

"What did he say to that?" I ask her, intrigued.

"He said he did it because of how he feels for me, not because of how he feels about Cassie," she says, looking down at the floor. "I saw it in his eyes Jake."

"I can't tell you what to do," I say to her. "And I wouldn't dream of doing it neither."

"But you are worried about me?" she asks.

"Of course, always. He hurt Cassie. Badly. I won't sit by and watch him hurt you too," I say to her firmly. "You know I won't, and he will get more than black eyes if he ever did."

"I know Jakey. I do know that," she says, putting her hand on my arm. "You love Cassie, and you love me. I wouldn't expect any less, not from you."

"What about Cassie?" I ask her.

"It's not like I am jumping into his arms right now, Jake," she says, rolling her eyes at me. "It is purely a let's see what happens kind of thing, plus I wouldn't dream of doing anything without talking to Cassie, because that's not even a choice. Cassie comes first. For both of us."

"Just be careful, Olive," I say to her. "I can't forgive him yet, nor can I trust him. It'll come back, in time, I'm sure, but until then I can't make the right judgement call here."

"I'd make the same choice as you, Jakey," she says to me. "Every time. I love her too."

Chapter Twenty Four

"Ah Jake, just the man I was looking for," Captain Franks says to me as I walk out of Olive's room. "Is Olive here too? I would like a word with you both, privately if I can."

"Hi. Yeah, she is in her room," I tell him. "We can talk in there."

"That'll work nicely," he says to me, before looking down at Cassie. "You must be the young lady I have heard about, it is a pleasure to meet you at last Miss Hollings."

"Hello," Cassie says, looking at me with a puzzled look.

"Forgive me, I am Captain James Franks. I'm the one that Jake here convinced to send the army out to find you," he tells her with a smile.

"Oh! Hello Captain. Thank you so much," she says, relieved and clearly embarrassed. "We are so grateful for your help."

"No need to thank me, just glad we got you back in one piece," he says, and claps me on the shoulder. "Shall we go in and talk to Olive?"

"Yes of course, after you," I tell him, and give Cassie a smile before I follow him in.

"Hello again Olive," he says to her. "Pleased to see you are looking much better now."

I am starting to like Captain Franks, he seems like a personable guy, but the jury is still out on whether I trust him yet. Time will tell.

"Hello Captain," Olive says, trying to sound as formal as she can given her hyperactive state.

"Listen, I wanted to talk to you both. Well, I wanted to run something by you actually," he explains. "We have a plan, you see, but we are going to need your help to make it happen."

"I told you before, I'm happy to help Captain," I tell him. "If I can."

"Actually Jake, it is Olive's help that we need," he says, taking us both by surprise.

"Oh?" Olive says, sitting up straighter.

"I had an interesting conversation with Jake earlier, and it got me to thinking about our next move," he says. "You see, it would seem that these orcs are scared of whatever this Light is. It's probably that fact alone that kept you alive."

I see Olive's smile falter a fraction, before she puts the mask back on. Something she has been doing for most of her life.

"We would like to try and capitalise on this new information, and use it as a weapon against them," he carries on. "They don't know how much we know about the Light."

"Which is precisely nothing. You know nothing about it," I tell him flatly, my disdain for this plan already showing.

"No, you're right. We don't," he replies. "But they don't know that. Not yet."

"So you are bluffing?" I ask him, puzzled. "Your plan is to bluff them?"

"Well, in a nutshell, yes," the Captain explains, and I catch a hint of mischief in his eyes. "The long version is that we would like to hold a press conference, fully televised and projected throughout the country on the emergency broadcast frequency. That will ensure that it plays on every TV in every home, shop window and office building. We will also arrange for it to be played over the tube station tannoy systems and any large outdoor speakers we can get access to at short notice. Maximum coverage."

"What's the message?" I ask, not even attempting to hide my obvious unease.

"Firstly, we want to announce that Olive was rescued successfully and without incident by a small number of highly trained individuals. Basically, this part of the message is to show the orcs that we were able to retaliate, that we aren't weak, as well as to give the people hope," he tells us animatedly. "Secondly, we want the orcs to know that we have the Light back, and that we will now use it against them. All in all, we want the orcs to think we are strong, we are ready, and that we are coming for them."

"That is one hell of a bluff," I tell him, unsure of how I feel about this plan.

"Yes, it is," he says. "Its main purpose is to buy us more time. The more time we have, the better prepared we will be the next time they come for us."

"Well, I don't disagree with you," I tell him. "But that is a lot to ask of Olive. Making her the face of this bluff. What if they come back for her?"

"Then we will be ready. We will arrange for security to be at a maximum. We would protect her, and you and your friends," he explains, nodding to Cassie sat just outside the door.

"They'll be expecting that," I say, trying to process the plan in my head. "Remember that I've seen them take out an entire base of armed police in a matter of minutes."

"No offence to the police Jake, but we are the army. We are slightly better equipped to deal with this," he explains. "We will protect her."

I stand there for a moment, going over everything that Captain Franks has told us.

"Can you give me a moment with Olive?" I ask him.

"Of course, Jake," he replies, walking to the door. "I would say take your time, but to be candid, we just don't have it."

After Captain Franks closes the door. I just stand in silence, staring at the floor and try to process what we had just heard. I look up at Olive, who is watching me intently.

"Tell me your thoughts, Jake?" she asks.

"Ok, cards on the table? I am seriously concerned," I explain to her, that concern clearly etched in my voice. "Because it involves putting you in a lot of danger. I've only just got you back."

"I know, Jake," she says to me. "I'm scared too. But if I can do something, anything, then I have to do it? Wouldn't you?"

I knew at that point that there was no way I could argue with her, because if the roles were reversed, I wouldn't think twice about doing everything in my power to help.

"Of course, I would. You know that," I say to her. "And I am proud of you for wanting to help. I really am."

"I'm not strong like you Jake, I can't fire a gun, or use a sword," she says, looking at me with a sense of awe. "I can't protect you like you've protected me. But I can do this."

"Then I'm with you, Olive. I'll be at your side the whole time," I tell her.

I open the door and call Captain Franks back in, and also ask Cassie and Nat to join us, much to their surprise. Nat is the last one through the door and I watch him close it behind him.

"Captain. Firstly, I want you to know that we are supportive of your plan. It seems like a fairly decent plan, given the circumstances," I say to him. "And probably more importantly, Olive wants to help."

"I can't thank you both enough for agreeing to this," Captain Franks says, sounding relieved.

"There are some conditions though," I tell him.

"I honestly expected nothing less from you, Jake," he says, smiling now.

"I want to be there. The whole time. No exceptions," I tell him. "And I want to know the entire plan. Every detail, including security."

"Understood, and agreed," he confirms without hesitation, and I expect he predicted these requests.

"I also want your word that Cassie and Nat will be protected during the entire thing," I carry on. "And lastly, I want Harry and Adam to be reassigned to your Unit."

"You have my word. Miss Hollings and Mr Smith will both be under the same level of protection as yourself and Olive," he tells me firmly. "And I will do what I can about the two Sergeants in the other room, but it may be above my pay grade. Plus one of them is currently injured, so his reassignment will have to wait."

"Given the situation, I doubt you'll get many objections," I say to him, "but I understand your point about Harry."

"Then I accept your terms, Jake," he says to me, holding out his hand. "Thank you."

"I am trusting you with my family," I tell him, taking his hand. "Don't let me down."

Chapter Twenty Five (Shadow War)

"My Prince. What are your orders?" one of the knights calls out to me, although I don't answer. I am still kneeling, holding Petr in my arms.

I carefully pull the sword from his chest and lay him on the floor, crossing his arms over his chest before laying a discarded shield over his body. He deserves better, but there is nothing more I can do for him now. Tearing myself away from my grief, I stand up and look at the knights still stood around me.

"My knights, my brothers. You have fought with honour, and secured your place in the Eternal Forest!" I shout to them. "We are surrounded, but we are not beaten. Not yet."

All around me, the knights lift their swords and lances to cheer. A jovial noise in a sea of screams and roars, just the other side of the shield wall. Our little moment of jubilation is disturbed by the rumble of trumpets from atop the cities wall. The repeated chorus can only mean one thing, they are calling for all remaining elves to come to the main city gates. That means that the infantry posted outside are becoming overwhelmed by the orc army.

"The orcs may have been dealt a blow with the loss of so many of their leaders, although it came at too great a cost," I say, and I can hear the strain in my voice. "The orcs are advancing on our city now, but I fear that their numbers are too great for those defending its walls. I know you are tired, I know you are grieving, I ask you now my brothers, to fight with me back to the city walls where we can mount a new defence."

"We will follow you, Prince," the knights call out. "For the King, and for Captain Petr."

"Thank you my brothers," I tell them, looking down at my old friend one last time.

I pull my great sword from the ground and put it back onto its brace on my back, before retrieving my sabres from the floor and sheathing them.

"Knights. We make for the city, to provide our support to the Wolf Gate. We will follow the same strategy as before, but we will fight harder and faster," I tell them. "Open the shield wall, fight through, and only close it if we need to regroup."

"May the Light guide us home," says a knight to my right.

"May the Light give you strength, brother." I say to him, clasping his shoulder.

I unsheathe both sabres simultaneously, twirling them around in front of me before holding them vertically against the backs of my arms.

"Let's go home, brothers!" I shout.

The frontmost elves lift their shields and push outwards, followed by thrusts of their swords to cut down the first few orcs. Most of the orcs ahead of us are racing towards the city now, and fall to our blades with impunity as we move back towards the city. I fight at the front of our circle along with several of the other knights, clearing the path for those in the Shield Wall to drag their shields along the floor in order to follow us, while trying their best to hold the shape and repel the orcs on our flanks and rear.

We progress slowly, but steadily, and find that we do not have to close the shield wall at all on our return journey. Within half an hour, we are in range of the archers upon the City walls, who send up a volley of arrows that fell a large number of orcs ahead of us, allowing us freedom to push forward unopposed. We are making good progress now, and I can see the Wolf Gate clearly ahead of us.

"We are nearly home, brothers!" I shout, taking the head off an orc to my right while impaling another on my left. "I can practically hear the Wolf Gate howling!"

We fight on to the sounds of the elven trumpets and orcish horns. Less than a hundred yards ahead of us, I can see where the orcs are clashing with the elven infantry in front of the Wolf Gate.

"Our brothers need us! One last push, let us join them!" I shout.

I launch forwards, cutting at any orc that turns my way. I swing both sabres to my left to cut down an orc, and spin my right sabre back to parry an attack while thrusting the left sabre into the now disorientated orc's chest, with the right sabre carrying on its motion from the previous parry to decapitate a third orc before bringing them both down into the head of a fourth. All around me the orcs begin to back off, not wanting to engage me any further. I start to run back to our infantry lines, and any orc that dares to come near me doesn't last long against me or my brothers. We are nearly home.

The last few orcs at the front lines ahead of me fall to the combined might of my sabres, my knights and the infantry beyond. The infantry open their shields to absorb our numbers into their own, and I hear cheers and chants from the elves as they realise who has joined them.

"The Prince has returned!" I hear them shout. "Long live the Prince!"

"We will stay and fight with our brothers," one of the knights tells me. "Call on us if you are in need. We will answer."

"May the Light protect you, brothers," I say to them, turning towards the gates.

As I reach the large Wolf Gate, I see the wicket gate open on the right and make my way through to the courtyard beyond. Earlier there were thousands of Royal Knights lined up, ready for battle. Now there are merely pockets of armed civilians and various squires too young to join their knights earlier, all now waiting impatiently for whatever may come through those gates. I look over them, willing them to keep strong, then I turn towards the castle.

As I run through town, I notice that it is far too quiet. I have never known Lor'ahan this still, which is only further exasperated by the deafening noises coming from outside the city. It has always been a city of love and peace and happiness, full of song and dancing. Now all I see are empty streets and empty homes, a lifeless shell. But the walls still stand, we have not lost yet.

As I round the last corner, I see the castle standing strong against the skyline ahead. However, standing just outside the main gate, I am surprised to find my father atop his horse, both him and the steed in their full plate armour, purest white, red and gold as a sign of both the Royal Knights and the Crown's Army. His helmet having been carefully crafted into an intricate wolf's head, whose jaws are currently parted to reveal his face.

"My King," I say, bowing my head.

"My Son. Glad am I to see that you have returned to us!" he says to me, and I can hear the relief, and pride in his voice. "Glad am I to have seen you one more time."

"Father, why are you not in the castle?" I ask him. "Where is mother? And my family?"

"They are still atop the castle, my son," he tells me. "They wait there for you."

"Then come back with me? Let's see them together." I ask him, and I find myself becoming increasingly concerned. My father was not one for rash decisions.

"I cannot come with you. I have something I must do, as do you," my father tells me. "Plus trust in me, one last time."

"Father?" I plead with him.

"Go be with your family, my son. They will explain what needs to be done. I am glad I got to see you, to speak with you," he tells me. "I love you, my dear boy, and I am so proud of everything you are." And with that, he spurs his horse towards the Wolf Gate, with his bodyguards in tow, but not before he calls back to me, "It is time that the Light meets the Shadow."

Chapter Twenty Six

"I'll start to make the arrangements now," Captain Franks tells us. "We are looking to get the announcement out tonight, so I will send a Unit over to bring you over to the TV Studio we will be using in Southbank, once we are ready."

"Sure," I say to him. "We will get our stuff together here, and be ready for your call."

"Thank you, Jake," he says sincerely. "And thank you, Olive. You're a brave young lady, and I am sure your brother is very proud."

"It's the least I can do," Olive says, a hint of fear in her voice. "I'm just happy I can help, in some small way."

"I'll be in touch soon, Captain Franks tells us all, before leaving the room and I watch as we walk through reception and back outside.

I turn back to the others and let out a deep sigh. I can see that Olive is scared, Cassie is concerned and Nat is confused.

"Someone care to explain what the hell is going on?" Nat asks through gritted teeth.

"They want to put out an announcement, confirming that Olive was rescued and that they now have the Light to use as a weapon," I explain to him.

"And can they?" Cassie asks me.

"No. They can't. It's a bluff," I reply. "They are doing it to buy more time before the orcs start to attack again."

"Will it work?" Nat asks.

"Best case scenario, yeah it works and we all get some respite to work out what is going on here before they attack again," I tell him. "Worst case scenario, no, they call our bluff and attack anyway."

"So either way, they're going to attack," Olive says dejectedly, she has already made her decision and doesn't want Cassie or Nat to try and talk her out of it.

"Most likely, yes," I say, echoing her dejected tone.

'I don't like it," Nat says to me, with a glare.

"You don't have to like it, Nat," I tell him, straightening myself up. "You just need to be there to support her when she does it anyway."

I see him open his mouth as if to say something, but he clearly decides against it. Wise choice. I turn to look at Cassie, who is still looking at me with concern.

"What is it Cassie?" I ask her.

"You brought us into the room, so we could hear the plan," she says to me, her eyes full of curiosity. "Why those conditions?"

"Because I am going to be right next to Olive. Every step of the way," I tell her, and with a sideways glance at Nat, "So I need to know that you are safe. Not just probably safe or maybe safe, but you are as safe as physically possible without me being right there beside you."

"Thank you, Jake," she says, and I see the concern fall away, only to be replaced with sadness.

I walk over to Cassie and put my arms round her to pull her into a big cuddle, and lean my mouth down to her ear.

"What is it sweetheart?" I whisper to her.

"I don't want to leave you," she whispers back, her fingers gripping the front of my shirt. "I don't want to lose you."

"I'm not going anywhere, Cassie," I whisper into her ear, before kissing her forehead and moving away.

I walk over and sit next to Olive on the bed, putting my arm round her shoulders and she rests her head on my chest. The mood in the room is somber, at best. Not the happy reunion that I had hoped for yesterday, but at this point, I am just thankful that there is a reunion at all.

"I'm going to go let Adam and Harry know about the plan," I tell them. "I'll be back."

"I'll come with you," Cassie offers.

I give Olive a kiss on the forehead and take my arm off her shoulders, before jumping off the bed and walking towards the door with Cassie, stopping to put my hand on Nat's shoulder and giving him a small smile and a nod. I don't think I will ever forget what he did to Cassie, but it isn't really me who has to forgive him.

Once we are outside, I hear Cassie take a deep breath and sigh.

"Life is never easy, is it?" Cassie says to me.

"No, love," I tell her. "But try to think of it like this; life isn't defined by the hard times or the bad times, but the people we share it with and the memories we make along the way. We might not have had the easiest life, but I can honestly say that despite all that has happened, I have the best people in mine, and some pretty amazing memories to go with them."

"So do I, Jake," she says, smiling up at me. "So do I." She then slips her hand into mine.

We find Adam talking to the still unconscious Harry, same as he was an hour ago. He smiles at us as we walk in, and I greet him with a man hug again. Unlike the Captain, Adam is someone I have come to trust. I wish he would be there later, but I couldn't ask him to leave Harry.

"Are you guys leaving soon?" he asks me.

"Yeah, but not just yet though," I tell him, before explaining the full plan to him just as it was told to us by Captain Franks, followed by the conditions I had set for Olive's co-operation.

"That is quite the plan," Adam says, looking surprised. "When do we leave?"

"We?" I ask him.

"I can't let you go alone. I'm coming with you," he tells us. "And I know Harry would want me to go as well."

"I can't ask you to do this, Adam," I say to him. "You've done enough already, and Harry needs you now."

"Tell you what, come find me when you leave and we will see how Harry is doing. Deal?" Adam says to me, with a hopeful look on his face.

"We will," I tell him. "If that's what you want."

"Thanks mate." He says, now smiling at Cassie. "Now if you don't mind, I was about to tell Harry some really crude jokes so you might want to cover your ears, or bugger off."

"Charming!" Cassie says, laughing a little now as well.

"See you later Adam," I say to him, before looking at Harry as I turn to leave.

I walk back to Olive's room with Cassie, both of us walking much slower than usual to keep our little bubble intact for as long as possible. As we get closer to the room, I see Nat now sitting on the bed talking to Olive, although pleading would be more accurate given the hand gestures.

"He obviously cares about her," Cassie says, and I take her hand to squeeze it.

"Yeah, he does," I say back. "Doesn't he?"

"I'm sorry, Jake," she says to me, and I look at her confused.

"What for?" I ask her.

"Just everything. For all of this with Nat, and now with Olive. It's a real mess," she says, with the sadness back in her voice.

"It's not your fault sweetheart," I tell her, pulling her chin towards me with my hand, so I can look into her eyes. "You're not to blame here. At all!"

"I'm still sorry," she says.

"You're a nightmare, Cassie, you really are," I say to her, and as I look into her eyes, I think briefly about kissing her but I can't, not right now. Her and Nat only broke up last night and I don't even know that she feels the same way, but I can't get what Nat had said to her out of my mind. I realise I have been lingering for a moment too long, so I lean in to kiss her on the cheek and pull her into another cuddle.

Olive spots us outside and waves us in, I think she wants the back up against Nat, whose shoulders drop upon seeing me. He knows the fight is lost now I am there too.

"Jake, tell Nat that this is happening," she demands.

"Sorry Nat. Her mind is made up," I explain to him. "And in case you hadn't ever noticed, she can be a tad stubborn."

"Urgh, fine," he says to no-one in particular, his body language showing total defeat.

I smile at Olive, who smiles back at me, then gets up off the bed and walks over to Cassie to have a cuddle.

About twenty minutes later, I find myself gazing out the room window and see half a dozen soldiers walking through the reception area towards us. Only one steps up to the door and opens it to talk to us, while the others stand just outside the room.

"I have orders to collect Jake Shepherd, Olive Shepherd, Cassie Hollings and Nat Smith," the soldier tells us, very matter of factly.

"All present and correct," I tell him, looking at each of my family in turn.

"Come with us please, we have orders to bring you to the TV Studio for the broadcast. Are you ready?" the soldier asks us sternly.

"As ready as we will ever be," I tell him, turning to the others to say; "Let's grab our stuff and go. I need to make a quick stop on the way though."

"Very well, assume it won't take long?" the solider asks.

"Shouldn't take more than a minute," I tell him.

I help Cassie pick up and put on her backpack over the Kevlar she is still wearing from earlier, then throw mine over my shoulder. Nat picks his up and I see Olive standing there with nothing. Unlike us, she didn't have a backpack.

"You always did travel light," I tease her, trying to cheer her up.

"Little of everything and nothing, me!" she says, smiling as she recalls her childhood motto from when I first met her, and I can't help but laugh at the memory. I hear Cassie let out a little giggle behind me, and even Nat cracks a smile. We are all still ok, I think.

As agreed, I pop into Harry's room as we walk past, to let him know that we are moving out but as soon as I open the door, I can see that it is not good news. Adam has been crying.

"What is it mate?" I ask him.

"They got the blood test results back, it looks like the arrow might have been poisoned," he tells me, his voice raw. "But they have no idea what it is. It's not something they have ever seen before."

"I'm so sorry Adam," I say to him, and I mean it. Harry doesn't deserve this.

"I can't come with you, not yet. But I'll catch up with you, as soon as I can," he tells me.

"Good luck, to both of you," I say to him, giving him one last man hug and leave to catch up with the others.

They had already followed the soldiers down the hallway, so I run to catch them up. I hesitate about telling them about Harry. It wouldn't do them any good to know what is happening, and would only serve to distract them from what is about to happen.

Once I get outside, I notice that they aren't driving the same blacked-out Range Rovers as earlier, but are now driving about in Foxhounds, large armoured vehicles that are used by the British Army when they replaced the old Land Rovers. These ones are all decked out in urban camouflage patterns making them look rather imposing.

We all jump in the back of the first Foxhound, along with the two soldiers in the front. I hear several doors slam behind us, before our convoy sets off for Southbank. Being an armoured vehicle, we have very little in the way of luxuries, or even windows, so it is a very uneventful drive that was luckily quite short.

When we arrive, the soldiers jump out and open the doors for us. I step out into the fading light of the afternoon and can see that Captain Franks was right, the Army really are better equipped. The entire building is surrounded by checkpoints manned by at least ten soldiers each, with large blocks of concrete spread across the paths and roads, and barbed wire spiraling between each block.

At least he is taking the increased security condition seriously.

Maybe I was right to trust him?

Chapter Twenty Seven

We follow the soldiers round the side of the building and I can see the River Thames swirling along beyond the walls. There are a large number of soldiers gathered by the side entrance, all armed and in combat gear, but they pay us no notice as we walk through.

Once we get inside, I am even more surprised to find a whole range of equipment being set up in every bit of available space. There are computers and monitors showing every angle of the interior and exterior, along with what looks like infrared and heat sensors set up at all the entrances.

I'd slowed down to look at the equipment, but ahead of me I notice that the lead soldier has turned back to me and motions for us to follow him, so I pick up the pace to catch up to him. We are led into one of the studios half way down a long corridor, inside it is mostly empty except for the audience seating and a small podium that stands in the middle with a lot of cameras pointed directly at it, along with a fake wood panelled wall in the background which I guessed was an attempt to disguise where we actually were filming this.

"If you can wait here everyone, I'll take Jake up to see the Captain," the soldier says to our group.

I turn to the others and give them a nod before following him up past the seats towards a glass room at the back.

He opens the door, and inside I can see Captain Franks and several other officers stood over a table that is covered in a map of Southbank and what 1 assume are detailed plans of this building.

"Jake, thanks for coming," he says to me, reaching out to shake my hand.

"Of course." I tell him, taking a deep breath, "I can see that you are taking security seriously."

"I gave you my word, Jake. I intend to keep it," he tells me firmly.

"I know. Thank you," I say to him with a smile. "Right, so tell me about the plan."

"Come round this side and I'll talk you through it," he says, motioning to the documents littering the table in front of him.

"So we are here, at Southbank," he says, pointing at the building on the map. "We have set up a one mile perimeter south of the river, with soldiers and transports on every road to ensure that nothing comes near without us knowing about it. There are sentries posted along the river paths, to ensure that nothing comes in from that direction, as well as snipers positioned on the rooftops, giving us 360 degree coverage of the area."

"Now you would have seen the area at the front of the building, where we have set up standard urban defences designed to impede any frontal attack by their infantry and any possible cavalry or artillery they may possess. The blockades and barbed wire should slow down their melee fighters, allowing our soldiers to thin their ranks with our advanced weaponry," he carries on. "Obviously we are not expecting an attack while on air or even shortly after, but in order to ensure the safety of you, your sister and your friends, there are also Foxhounds stationed at every exit, so should we need to evacuate any of you, then we can get you out from any direction."

"You seem to have covered a lot of the bases there," I tell him. "And thank you for thinking of the escape plan. That's comforting to know, although I hope it won't come to that."

"The specifics of the plan are that you and Olive would leave with me and my Unit via the exits on the north or east of the building, while Miss Hollings and Mr Smith would leave with their protection detail to the south or west. All my men are under the strict instructions to ensure the safety of you all, and to rendezvous back at the hospital in the event of an evacuation."

"I understand the logic behind your decision, wanting to split us up to ensure that we have more chance of survival," I say to him, feeling tense. "But I would much rather have us travel together."

"I thought you might say that," he says solemnly. "But we will be keeping the others at a secondary location, away from the main studio floor."

"No, that's not what I had in mind," I tell him firmly. "I get your logic, I do, but I have just got us all back together, so I want Cassie and Nat nearby. I want them in here, in this room, while the announcement goes out."

"Are you sure?" he asks me.

"Positive. I'm not letting Cassie out of my sight," I tell him.

"Very well, I'll have their protective detail stationed in and around this room," he says to me. "I'll get the Unit leader to come down shortly to prepare."

"Thank you," I say to him. "I appreciate it."

"There will be soldiers stationed both inside and outside the studio, covering all potential entrances and exits," he says. "We aren't taking any chances here, Jake."

"It's a good plan, lots of angles covered," I say, feeling slightly apprehensive. "I just hope that you have enough men."

"We will, Jake. If it comes to it, we will," he says to me, before moving on; "I will be giving the announcement personally. Olive will be standing to my right, and I would like you to stand on my left," he says.

"I understand why you need Olive there, given the message you are trying to give, but why me?" I ask him.

"I know you want to be close to her, and you can't get much closer than that," he says.

"Don't take this the wrong way, but I do not want to be involved," I say to him, trying to force a smile. "This is Olive's fight, mine has been, and always will be, more of a behind the scenes type one."

"If that is what you want. I'll arrange for you to stand just behind the cameras then, so you can still be close by," he says, looking disappointed.

"Thank you," I say. "I am sorry. It's just not who I am."

"I understand, Jake," he says. "I appreciate what you are both doing for us. We will accommodate your requests where we can."

"Is there anything else I should know?" I ask him.

"No, that is pretty much the crux of it," he tells me. "Do you have any other questions?"

"Not at the moment," I tell him.

"I'll be in here right up until I give announcement at 18:00 hours. Come find me if you need anything," he says. "My door will always be open for you, Jake."

"Thanks, and good luck," I tell him, turning back towards the door so I can rejoin the others.

I walk down the stairs, and see Olive talking to Nat over on one side of the studio, leaving Cassie sitting alone where I left her a few minutes ago. I walk over to sit on the edge of the seat behind her and lean forward to wrap my arms around her shoulders from behind, resting my chin in the nook of her neck.

"Hey you," I say to her.

"Hello," she says back, lifting her hands to rest on mine. "What's the plan then?"

"They seem to have it all covered, inside and out. I was pretty impressed," I explain to her.

"If you are happy with it, then I am too," she says to me, leaning her head against mine. "I know you wouldn't put Olive in any more danger than we are already in."

"Or you," I say softly. "That was the only bit of the plan I changed. They wanted to keep you somewhere else, so I brought you closer. You'll be in that room at the back with Nat and your own personal army. Right where I can see you."

"Thank you, Jake. I feel better knowing you'll be right there," she says, and I can hear the relief in her voice. "Where will you be, exactly?"

"Down there, behind the cameras so I can be near to Olive," I explain to her. "Captain Franks will be at the podium, with Olive next to him."

"So the only thing standing between us will be the British Army?" she says to me, laughing a little now.

"If that is the only thing standing between us Cassie, then I can live with that," I tell her, and give her a squeeze.

"Me too, Jake," she says, turning her head to kiss me on the cheek.

"I need to talk to Olive and Nat, are you coming?" I ask her.

"No, I'll stay here," she says to me, her lips turning down slightly. She still hasn't forgiven Nat, not that I blame her.

"I'll be back soon," I tell her, as I pull my arms back from around her.

I walk over to Olive and Nat, who are talking and laughing like this is the most normal situation in the world. I realise that this is the first time I have seen Olive truly relaxed since yesterday morning when we left the house. Nat did that. I find myself shaking my head without realising it, damn it Nat, I'm meant to be annoyed at you.

"Hey guys, so here's the plan," I say to them as I approach, and then fill them both in on all the details, including Nat's new place in the room at the top with Cassie.

"Thanks Jake. I'd rather be close by too," he says to me, and I realise that the annoyance towards my friend is slowly dissipating now.

"So I just need to stand there?" Olive asks me.

"No, I think they were planning to make you do a little dance and throw some Light about. Although they might do that bit with CGI, I guess," I say to her, smirking, and totally deserve the punch on the arm, but it was worth it to see her smile.

"Very funny, Jake," she says to me, laughing. "A real comedian."

"Made you laugh, didn't I?" I ask her.

"Yes, you did," she says, punching me again.

"I'll leave you both to it," I say to them. "I'll be over with Cassie, if you need me."

I walk back over to where Cassie is sitting, taking the seat next to her this time and put my arm round her so she can lean into me, putting her hand up onto my chest.

"Can we just stay like this forever?" she sighs.

"One of these days," I tell her, smiling. "I am going to hold on and never let go."

"I'm going to hold you to that," she says, snuggling in a little tighter.

Chapter Twenty Eight

I was sat there with my arm round her shoulders, and she had her head tucked under my chin with her hand resting on my chest.

I remember that it was lunchtime and it was raining outside, so everyone was in the sixth form common room making it far louder than usual. Usually I wouldn't be able to think with all the noise, as I have always preferred the quiet whether it was in my own company or out in nature. On this particular occasion though, I had completely zoned out while I was sat there hiding in the corner with Cassie curled up next to me.

We only had a few more weeks left of school, our final exams were fast approaching, but Cassie's boyfriend had decided that this would be the perfect time to break up with her. Apparently, he had found someone new when he went off to University last year, and he needed to follow his heart, or some crap. All I knew was that he had broken her heart, and now here I was to pick up the pieces.

I'd known Cassie since I'd moved to her school for Sixth Form, and while we knew of each other, it was only as friends of friends up until a few months ago. Her best friend had decided to leave school, so she had found herself feeling a bit lost and confused and alone. I knew that feeling all too well, how crushing it could be, so I had started to talk to her so that she knew she wasn't on her own. Not entirely.

We had become good friends very quickly, Cassie was really easy to talk to. I could talk to her all day, every day and not run out of things to say, and as I quickly found out, she wouldn't stop talking even then. Luckily, I loved listening to her talk, always so enthused in each subject and so emotive with it. I had realised very early on that I'd found someone incredibly special in Cassie, so I opened up to her as much I would allow myself, and slowly she opened up to me too.

Our friendship managed to get me teased at school, although I never took much notice, adults can be rude and offensive but teenagers can be cruel with it. Wasn't like I was planning to stay in touch with any of them, just like I didn't with the boys from my last school. I was nicknamed Friend-Zone, apparently, I had managed to do that to myself, but it didn't matter what anyone thought. I had my best friend, and I was happy. We both were.

But now there I was, three months later, sat in the corner holding an emotional Cassie who had just had her heart broken, and there was nothing I could do to help her other than to hold on tight and remind her that she wasn't alone, and that she would never be alone again. Not if I could help it.

Everyone else was going about their business, no real cares in the world other than who was dating who, or what celebrity was doing what, or if anyone had watched the new episode of whatever rubbish was on TV last night. I wanted to tell them all to shut up and leave us in peace, but I couldn't, and it wasn't their fault anyway. So instead, I just sat there in the corner, trying to hide Cassie away from the world.

"Are you going to class this afternoon?" I asked her.

"I have to, Jake," she said, sounding fed up.

"You don't have to do anything, Cassie," I told her. "If you need space, then you can stay here."

"I don't need space," she said, tapping my chest with her hand. "I just need you."

"I'm not going anywhere sweetheart," I told her, resting my chin on the top of her head. "I'm staying right here, for as long as you need me."

"How does forever sound?" she asked me.

"I can live with that," I had said to her, and I remember kissing the top of her head.

"Just hold on, and never let go," she had told me.

Chapter Twenty Nine

I bring myself back to the present and back to Cassie, who is as still as I am. I want to lift her chin so I can look into her eyes and see what she is thinking, but I'm enjoying the cuddle and I know she is happy where she is, so I decide to stay here for a little longer.

Nat and Olive are still talking over on the other side of the studio, which is now rapidly filling up with camera crew and a fair amount of soldiers. I count at least forty scattered around the room. I watch as two of them approach Nat, who nods at something they said before both he and Olive shake their heads and point over to us. They must be the protective detail assigned to Cassie and Nat, the ones that Captain Franks said would be coming down to check the area. I watch all four of them walk over to us, and notice that the two soldiers are big, bigger even than Nat, and seem to exude a level of confidence that I hope that they can back up.

"Cassie Hollings?" the one on the left asks.

"Yes, that's me," Cassie replies, lifting her head up from my chest.

"Hi Cassie, I'm Cooper, and this is Dan," he says, and Dan gives her a little wave.

"Hello," she says groggily.

"We will be leading the Unit assigned to protect you and Nat here during the announcement," he tells her. "We understood there was a change of plan, so we are here just to get up to speed and recon the area. Nothing to worry about."

"Thanks guys," I tell them.

"You're Jake, I presume?" Cooper asks.

"That's me," I tell him.

"I've heard a lot about you, kid," he tells me. I involuntarily chuckle at his comment. I may not look it, but I am definitely older than he is.

"I expect a lot of it is exaggerated slightly," I tell him, smiling a little. "And I didn't exactly do it alone."

"Maybe so, but for a civilian, it is still pretty impressive," Dan says.

"Thanks," I say, wishing that people weren't taking as much notice of me. I make a mental note to try and shrink back into obscurity once this is all over.

"We're going to check out the room up there, we will come down for you once it is time to get into position," Cooper says, before walking away with Dan who nods at us before turning away.

"Well they're exactly what I thought soldiers would be like," Nat says sarcastically.

"As long as they keep you two safe, they can lick windows as a hobby for all I care," I say absent-mindedly, allowing my humour defence mechanism to kick in, still thinking about the fact that I have a reputation building.

Cassie squeezes my chest with her hand to get my attention, she knew that the remark would be hiding

218

something, and I see her look up at me and frown slightly, her eyes searching mine for the truth. I give her a little smile, and squeeze her shoulder.

"I'll explain later," I say to her quietly, she nods but doesn't look away.

"Are you ready for this, little one?" I ask, turning my attention to Olive. "Not too late to change your mind."

"I'm good, Jakey," she says firmly. "I got this."

"I guess it's nearly time," I say to no one in particular.

Nat and Olive both sit down in the row in front, but none of us are in a talkative mood anymore, so we all just sit there in silence, riding out the calm before the coming torrent.

At 7:30pm, I hear footsteps coming down the stairs from the glass room, which belong to Captain Franks as he comes to stand in front of us.

"We're almost ready," he tells us. "If Miss Hollings and Mr Smith would like to make their way up to the control room at the back, where Corporal Cooper will make sure you are both settled in accordingly."

Cassie takes an audible deep breath and turns to kiss me on the cheek, before getting up to give Olive a cuddle. I lean over the chairs and shake Nat's hand.

"Take it easy mate, I'll see you soon," I tell him.

"Thanks mate. You too," he says back, his eyes watering slightly. "I won't let you down this time."

After Cassie lets go of Olive, I watch as she walks back up to me to put her arms around my waist and squeeze me tightly, so I wrap my arms right around her and give her the biggest cuddle I can muster.

"Try to hold on to this one, until I can give you the next one," I tell her, kissing her forehead.

"I'll try to," she says, giving me one last squeeze.

I reluctantly let her go, and immediately feel like a little piece of me is missing as I watch Cassie and Nat walk up the stairs, and give Cassie a smile as she looks back down at me before disappearing into the room.

"You OK Jakey?" Olive asks behind me.

"Yeah, I think so," I tell her, trying to mask the doubt building inside me.

"At some point, you're really going to have to man up and tell her that you love her," she says, with an incredulous look on her face.

"At some point, you're really going to have to mind your own business," I tell her, smiling slightly as I know that'll never happen.

"Jake. It's been what? Fourteen years?" she asks me.

"That I've known her?" I ask back.

"That you've loved her," she confirms.

"I think it's the same answer to both actually," I tell her, avoiding her gaze.

"She knows, Jake," she says. "Pretty sure everyone knows."

"I can't lose her, little one," I tell her, my voice uneasy.

"You really don't understand women, do you Jakey?" she says, rolling her eyes.

"Do any of us?" Captain Franks says, having walked back over part way through the conversation, and I am glad of the interruption. "But back on topic, we really are almost ready now."

I follow Captain Franks and Olive over to the podium, and watch as he positions her just off to his right, two or three feet behind him. Once he returns to the podium, I step over to her and give her a cuddle.

"I'm proud of you, little one," I tell her, and give her a big smile.

"Thanks Jakey," she says, smiling back.

"Good luck. I'll see you after," I tell her, reaching up to squeeze her arm.

I walk back to Captain Franks, who is going through the index cards with his speech on them, flicking through and mouthing the words.

"Good luck Captain," I say to him. "I hope this works, I really do."

"So do I, Jake," he says, looking up at me. "Just keep quiet and out of sight, then no-one will stop you moving about."

I give him a nod and looking at Olive once more, I turn away to go and stand behind the camera closest to her. I watch her standing there, trying not to fidget. She hates the limelight almost as much as I do, so there is no doubting that she is brave to do this. I know I wouldn't be able to do what she is doing, but that is for a whole different reason.

"We will be going live in 60 seconds!" I hear someone behind me shout.

With a surge of anxiety, I try to come to terms with the fact it's nearly time. I instinctively check the sword moves freely from the sheath on my hip, before remembering to check the handgun is still secure in it holster. Which it is.

"We are live in 10, 9, 8, 7, 6." The same voice calls out, and then I turn to see him counting down the last five seconds on his hand, swiftly followed by little red lights showing up on the cameras. I can't help but think about how every pair of eyes in the country are now on Captain James Franks and Olive Shepherd. My Olive.

"Good evening ladies and gentlemen. My name is Captain James Franks. I am standing here today to provide you with an update on the events that have unfolded over the last 24 hours. I know that many of you will be scared and confused by the news reports," he states, his voice full of confidence. "Yesterday afternoon, an unknown individual broadcasted an unsanctioned message of terror, designed to threaten and intimidate us. We have strong reason to believe that this message was delivered by something that was not human," he continues, although I flinch at his choice of words; "These creatures have made countless attacks across the country, all of which have left no survivors, but during one of their initial attacks here in London, they also took the hostage we were shown in their second unsanctioned broadcast earlier this morning."

"After reviewing the initial eyewitness reports, we discovered that Olive Shepherd was taken from a conference centre near Bank station yesterday afternoon, and I am pleased to say that thanks to the swift actions taken by a small number of brave individuals, Olive was successfully rescued from her captivity shortly afterwards and I am proud to say that Olive is here with me now," he says, turning and holding his arm out to present Olive who is stood there smiling sheepishly at the camera; "Among her rescuers were two London Metropolitan Police Officers and her brother, Jake Shepherd. Their actions undoubtedly saved this young lady's life, and on behalf of the British Army and the Metropolitan Police Force, you have our sincere gratitude for the decisive blow you have struck against this new threat."

"As indicated by the creature, known as Gro'alk, during the second broadcast, Olive Shepherd has something we have come to know as the Light. Upon finding out about this new source of hope, we have taken steps to understand what it is and what power this Light may have. The orcs, as they have called themselves, clearly fear its existence and it is now our sole focus to use this power to drive them back to where they came from. Already, more brave people like Olive are coming forward to offer us their strength in the coming days," he states, and even I almost believe him, his level of confidence unwavering despite how ludicrous it sounds. "I also have a message for the Warchief Gro'alk and his band of orcs. You have to come to our world and threatened our way of life. We do not take these threats lightly, nor will we simply lay down and let you take this world from us. We are here, and we will fight, but more importantly, we will win."

He opens his mouth to continue his speech, but he pauses and stares at something behind me. As I begin to turn round to look at what the Captain is staring at, I hear a strange sound coming from behind me. It sounds almost like the air is being sucked out of the room, that is when I see the swirling grey cloud like substance growing larger and larger in the middle of the room, and that is when I realise that the cloud is making the rushing noise.

"Cut the cameras!" I hear Captain Franks shout behind me as I watch the swirling cloud intensify as it changes shape, morphing into a more solid, but perfectly flat oval shape, before all the noise in the room stops suddenly with a loud crack and I am left stood here, completely shell shocked by the portal that has just opened up in front of me.

Chapter Thirty

All around me, I can hear the soldiers shouting instructions to each other and watch as they begin to take up defensive positions around the edges of the room. There are maybe fifty soldiers inside the studio, all of them pointing their guns at the now fully formed portal ten feet in front of me. Despite the commotion going on all around me, my focus is entirely on the large oval disc, the surface of which is now pulsating with various shades of purple and black, as ripples form on the surface.

"Jake, get away from there!" I hear Captain Franks shout from somewhere behind me.

His voice pulls my attention away from the portal, not because I was concerned for my safety or even his, but it made me remember that stood next to him, was Olive. I am about to call out to her when I see Captain Franks mouth the words 'Oh my God' and I turn back in time to see a stream of orcs charge out of the portal. Gunshots start to ring out from all around me, and the orcs fall easily enough; there are far more guns pointed at the portal than there are orcs coming out of it. The orcs may have the larger numbers, but the army have the better weaponry.

I start to step backwards, towards Olive and the Captain when I hear the now familiar sound of rushing air and I look up at the back of the studio, where a second portal is now forming just outside the room where Cassie and Nat were hiding at the back.

Impulsively, I reach down to put my hand on the hilt of my sword and take a deep breath before pulling it from its sheath.

"This is no time for heroics Jake, we need to get you out of here!" Captain Franks shouts, his voice fill of urgency. "Come on, lad!"

I glance back to look at him, barely registering the confusion, or was it concern, on his face before looking over to Olive. Seeing her stood there, scared, again. My brain screaming, pleading to go to her, but my heart is pulling me away, and I know that I can't leave Cassie. The thought of Cassie, and how scared she must feel, forces me to turn back towards the little room and the second portal forming just outside of it.

I notice movement through the darkened glass moments before the door bursts open and the two soldiers from before, Cooper and Dan, charge out with their guns raised, firing at any orc that gets too close, while the rest of the soldiers begin to file out behind them to form a line in front of the room and take aim at the now formed portal off to the side.

My attention is forced away from Cassie when out of the corner of my eye, I see an orc running at me and I move to instinctively parry its first swing, one that was aimed at my head. Reeling back from the initial attack, I regain my balance and thrust my blade at the orc, forcing it to parry my attack this time. I haven't got time for this. Bringing the blade round to my side, I swing the blade round and bring it down towards the orcs head but again it parries the attack clumsily and I see the orc jerk backwards, a bullet rips through its chest, shot dead by one of the soldiers with Captain Franks, who is still beckoning me to join them at the front of the studio.

I look back up to the glass room and can see that the soldiers are struggling to contain the second wave of orcs from the new portal. Cooper starts to wave his hand at something to his left, and I see four soldiers come out of the room with Nat huddled in the middle. They are bringing him down the steps on the far right, trying to come down on the side furthest from both portals and make their way towards the front of the stage, where Captain Franks and Olive are currently hiding behind the small podium, which has another line of the soldiers in front of it, firing at the first portal. Looking around the room, there are far too few soldiers for the amount of orcs now pouring into the room.

About twenty feet behind Nat's cluster, another four soldiers appear from the room, this time with a far smaller person between them that can only be Cassie and immediately behind them I see Cooper and Dan following them down, in order to provide covering fire against any orc that tries to make an attempt on either group. I duck behind the line of soldiers who are still firing at the first portal and risk a glance, only to see that now the soldiers are having to split their focus between both portals, the orcs superior numbers are giving them the advantage; the combined force from both portals are threatening to overwhelm the soldiers attempting to hold them back.

Their superior technology is counting for little against the unwavering torrent of orcs streaming from the portals.

I turn back to Captain Franks and shout; "Get Nat and Olive out of here. I'm trusting you to do that. I'll get Cassie and come find you!" and I see him nod back at me, a grave look on his face. I take a moment to look at Olive, who is too distracted to see me, as she is staring at Nat, totally focused on him. I'm definitely going to have to apologise to him, even if it is just for her sake.

I turn back to the chaos behind me and run round the last few soldiers, my sword still drawn. Nat is about fifteen feet away when I see a dozen orcs break from the pack in the centre of the room and charge at them. The soldiers are all firing into the orcs that are closest to their own positions, so this new pack goes unchallenged for long enough to get too close to Nat's group and several orcs begin to cut down the two front most soldiers before finally going down from the sustained gunfire from Cooper, or Dan, I couldn't tell which had fired in all the commotion. Not that it mattered.

Nat looks petrified, and I watch as he completely freezes, causing the two soldiers to barge into his frozen form before they become distracted as they try to push him forward. I run forwards to close the gap, and manage to thrust my sword in front of Nat just in time to block a downward strike from an orc who had capitalised on this further distraction to get past the various soldiers firing at the orcs all around them. A second orc drops dead from a well-placed shot by Cooper who is running down the line of steps towards us.

The orc had turned to look at Cooper and I feel the tension between our swords slacken slightly and I pull my sword upwards, forcing the orcs sword up with it. Once my sword is clear of his, I shove him backwards with my left hand while driving my sword through his chest with my right. I pull my sword free, barely registering the orc fall lifelessly to the floor as I turn back to Nat.

"Nat. Are you with me mate?" I ask him, and he looks at me, but his eyes glazed over. "Nat, come on mate. Olive needs you."

"Jake?" he suddenly says, his eyes coming back into focus upon hearing my voice, or more likely on hearing Olives name. "I'm here, I'm sorry, I'm with you."

"Good. Get to Olive, and get her out of here," I tell him, pointing to where the Captain and Olive are hiding behind me. "You do not leave her side for anything or anyone. I'm trusting you to look after her, Nat."

"You have my word, Jake," he states firmly, and I believe him, given that I can see the same stubborn look in his eyes that he had before he went rogue to try and get her back. That and the fact he had pulled his handgun from the holster on his hip.

I watch as he runs past the line of soldiers that are still in position in front of Olive, and I linger just long enough to watch her pull him into a tight hug before I turn back to give Cassie my full and undivided attention. Between Nat, the Captain and what remains of his own personal army, I had to trust that they would keep her safe until I found my way back to them.

Unfortunately, Cassie's group is still a good fifty feet further back, with both Cooper and Dan. It looks like they had come to halt, but now I can see that the orcs from the first portal were actually forcing them to retreat back up the stairs, closer to the second portal. Desperately scanning the room for any sign of support, I feel the hairs on the back of my neck stand on end as I hear a deep gravelly voice erupt from behind me.

"The girl is escaping!" This new voice shouts, and I turn in time to watch as a large orc finishes climbing through the portal, and at first I thought it was Gro'alk, but then I notice that while it is similar in size, and clad in the same dark armour covered in an assortment of bones, this new orc is just another Warchief and not the now infamous one from the recent news reports.

The orcs are still coming out of the two portals in near constant waves, forcing the soldiers who are still in the room to retreat back towards the doorways and the relative safety of the hallways beyond. It's only now that I realise that I can also hear muted gunfire coming from outside the room and I begin to question my decision to let Olive out of my sight. If the building is being attacked from the outside as well, then the safety of their escape has been severely compromised. What have I done?

My concern is cut short when two orcs charge at me, and I parry the first swing to my left and quickly block the second on my right before pushing the left orc away with my spare hand and shoulder barging the one to my right.

I don't have the time to fight them, and the dilemma I have found myself in is threatening to consume me, Olive or Cassie. It's not a choice I ever wanted to make. They are both family. I love them both equally, albeit in very different ways. Somewhere in the building behind me is Olive, along with Nat, Captain Franks and what I hope is still a small army to protect her. If I go to her now, then I am forfeiting Cassie's safety, and almost certainly condemning her to death. On the other hand, if I fight my way to Cassie, then at least her fate is back in my control and I can fight to keep her safe, while having to trust that Nat will protect Olive.

Realising that I only have one choice, I jump over the orc as it falls and carry on up the stairs towards where Dan has crouched down to reload his gun, and I see Cooper firing over him at an orc that tried to rush forward, before turning and shooting another coming in from his right. I push up the stairs, two at a time, trying to close the distance between me and Cassie, when another orc steps in my path so I feint a thrust of my sword and as the orc attempts to parry thin air, I quickly spin the sword down, bringing it round and down into its shoulder, cleaving the orc almost in two.

As the orcs falls, I see two more charge towards Cooper. The first one drops but he doesn't get the second burst off in time and I watch as the orc plunges its sword straight through Cooper's chest. Dan turns and shouts at the orc, a sharp and pained sound, while emptying the freshly reloaded magazine into the orc's chest and kicking out at its falling corpse.

Despite killing the two orcs, his scream of anguish draws the attention of even more orcs that are starting to surround the group. I watch one of the soldiers push Cassie backwards, trying to get her up towards the room where they started, but their path is blocked by the orcs coming from the second portal. I'm out of time.

I cut down an orc on my left as I pass, and parry a clumsy swing from another on my right but then ignore him once I am out of his range. One of the soldiers notices me coming up towards them and fires a couple of shots into the orc I had left behind and I nod up to him in thanks.

The orcs are now in such great number, that the soldiers have all but escaped the room. Those still inside the studio, which is just Cassie's group, have stopped shooting blindly into the crowd, and are only firing on any that get too close. I can barely make Cassie out, crouched down behind Dan, just as a fresh wave of anxiety washes over me and my head starts to spin. I shake myself out of it, trying to focus on Cassie. On getting her back.

Charging forward with fresh determination, I thrust my sword between the shoulder blades of the first orc I come to, peeling it away from the pack, its weight pulling the corpse off my blade as it falls. Once free, I swing the blade down on top of the head of the next orc, but the force of the swing causes the blade to become wedged in the orcs gorget, forcing me to relinquish the stolen blade from yesterday. Feeling suddenly very exposed and unarmed, I quickly reach round and take the blade from the fallen orc, it's not like it'll need it anymore.

Standing back up straight, I find myself laughing when I realise I still have the handgun on my belt. Maybe I wasn't quite so unarmed, but I ignore it for now. The rest of the orcs are all looking at the group up by the room, so I get closer to the wall to try and reduce my chance of being seen. For a little while at least.

I can see that the soldiers are hopelessly outnumbered, all of them having fallen back to the exits and are just shooting any orcs that try to follow them through. I realise that they are keeping the orcs contained in here. There are now hundreds of orcs in the studio, all focused on one thing.

"Warchief!" I hear one of the orcs closest to Cassie call out. "You want to see this!"

The shout from the orc had completely drawn my focus, as I knew he could only be talking about Cassie. During my distraction, several orcs had noticed my presence and turned towards me. Three of them charge at me at once, a sadistic smirk on their faces. Three on one. They clearly like their chances.

"What is it?" The deep voice from before roars out behind me as I weigh up my limited options. The orcs are closing in.

"This girl has the Light too!" the orc shouts in reply, forcing me to glance up at the group of soldiers, and Cassie crouched behind them. I find myself willing her to look up at me. "And it is far brighter than the other one."

"Take her to Gro'alk," the Warchief demands. "Kill the rest."

I ignore the approaching orcs, as I watch the orcs closest to Cassie swarm the remaining soldiers, while a few of them fall to the hail of bullets from their guns, the orcs easily overwhelm the soldiers, not even glancing down at their fallen comrades. Do they even care? It's not long before I hear a gut-wrenching scream and I can see Cassie stood there alone, her hands covering her mouth as an orc pulls its sword out from Dan's neck and licks the blood straight from the blade. The sight of it makes me sick to my stomach. These orcs have no sense of honour, no humanity at all, and a shiver goes down my spine as I consider the darkness that must be inside them. The same orc sheathes its now clean sword and grabs Cassie by the arm, dragging her down towards the second portal as she starts to scream in protest.

"Cassie!" I shout up to her, trying to keep my voice level, as I watch her scanning the room in a desperate bid to see me. "I'll find you, I promise!"

"I know," Cassie mouths to me as she finally locks on to my position, tears rolling down her cheeks, and as the orcs pushes her towards the surface of the portal I hear her shout "Jake! I lo…" but she is gone before she can finish the sentence and I watch in horror as the portal collapses moments later.

Shaking off the initial shock, a wave of anger pulses through me and I lash out at the three orcs who are nearly on top of me. I block their swings one at a time, carefully picking my moment to strike. The right orc lunges with its sword and I parry the blade to my right and spin my body around, using the momentum to bring my sword in a full arc and into the back of its head as he passes me. I don't need to look back to know the orc and its head kept falling, albeit in different directions.

I start to swing my blade in a circular motion on my right, before crossing it in front of my body and into a downward strike against the orc to my left, forcing it to parry so I continue the momentum of the swing into another full lunge down into the next orc. Its parry is clumsy, knocking my sword sideways so I adjust my feet and start to twist my entire body round in a sort of pirouette motion, keeping the blade level at head height, the speed and force of the move taking both orcs by surprise. As I come to a stop, they both fall to their knees as their heads topple down from their bodies.

I take a moment to regain my balance before realising that the entire room has fallen silent and every pair of orcish eyes are now focused on me. With Cassie gone, I'm alone in the room. The soldiers are all either dead or behind the now closed the doors, sealing me inside. I make a point to bring that up with the Captain, if I ever see him again. Scanning the room from where I had last seen Cassie moments before, I eventually make eye contact with the Warchief stood with its arms crossed with a bemused look on its face, about ten feet away and just in front of the first portal.

"Tell me where they took her, orc," I warn the giant, dark skinned orc. My entire body is shaking. Not from fear, but anger. "Right now."

"I don't think so, little boy," the Warchief says with a snort, clearly amused by my threat.

"Tell me now, and you can walk away from this. All of you can," I tell the orcs gathering around the two of us to form some sort of make shift arena.

"Hah! Such idle threats. You do not scare me, boy, none of your kind do," the orc spits at me.

"The world of men is stronger than you give them credit for," I tell him flatly.

"I give them no credit at all, so that means little," the orc replies with a chuckle. "All you need to know is that the girl is being taken back to Warchief Gro'alk," the Warchief states. "But know this, boy, the fact she has the Light will be her death sentence. Gro'alk will take no chances with this one, not since it was Gro's fault we lost the first one."

"If this Gro'alk even thinks about touching her!" I shout, my anger and despair getting the better of me but the orcs laughter stops me from continuing my threat. It'll clearly fall on deaf ears.

I watch as the Warchief unsheathes his weapon and starts to walk towards me. I swallow down the intense feeling of anxiety that has been threatening to consume me since I watched Cassie disappear and wipe away the tears forming in my eyes, the thought of losing my family is too much. Taking a deep breath and trying to compose myself, a look around the room and try to absorb any little details that may help. The orc is carrying a great sword, held easily in its right hand, and we are surrounded by hundreds of orcs, all of whom look more than eager to kill me. But more importantly, the first portal is still pulsating behind the Warchief.

"You cannot hope to kill me, boy," the Warchief taunts, flicking the bones hanging from its armour. "I have been fighting for thousands of years, and killed all those that dared challenge me. Be it man, orc or elf. It is why I am a great Warchief of the orcs, and you are nothing but a petulant child of man."

"There is always a first time," I state, my voice portraying a level of calmness that was definitely not shared by the rest of my body. I was barely holding onto what little control I had left. This was not the time to lose that composure. I needed to find Cassie first. Then I could let go.

"Gwahaha, I like you, boy, you do have spirit!" the Warchief exclaims as it bangs his empty fist against its chest. "But that doesn't change the facts. You are weak, like all men, and you are alone."

"I won't stop, orc. I won't ever stop," I tell him, ignoring his taunts. All I can think about is getting to Cassie. The longer this goes on, the further away she is. "Not until I find her."

"No, boy, you'll stop when I drive my sword through your heart," the Warchief tells me, lifting his sword up to rest it on his shoulder.

I spin the sword in my hand, considering its weight, making sure I have a solid and comfortable grip on the hilt. The harsh reality is that my sword is only a third of the size of the one held by the Warchief, but it is also far lighter, so I need to use its speed to my advantage. I step towards the orc, and start to twirl the blade in front of me and down by my sides as I watch for its next move.

The Warchief casually takes several steps forward, and then without warning swings the great sword down from its shoulder in a surprisingly quick move, forcing me to jump backwards. But even as I do, the orc provides another staggering display of strength by stopping the blade at chest level and thrusting it towards me with deadly precision.

I just manage to parry the thrust with a leftward swing of my sword and step off to the right, bringing my blade back up in front of me. I clearly can't afford to underestimate my opponent as it turns towards me and uses the momentum to swing the sword horizontally at me. I duck underneath the blade, swiping my own along the back of it as I pass underneath in an attempt to ensure the blade carries on its trajectory, instead of coming down on top of me as I pass underneath.

I watch the orc perform a rather fancy looking twirl as the sword reaches the end of its arc before plunging the tip into the ground at the orc's feet. The Warchief is clearly enjoying this, but I can't afford to waste time indulging it. Every second I spend here, is another second further from Cassie. I jump forwards and swing my blade at its shoulder, which the orc easily blocks by lifting the blade up from its previous resting place. I jump to the orc's left side slightly before attempting to spin round behind it and thrust the tip of my blade at its now exposed back, but the sword just slams harmlessly against the plate armour, confirming what I already suspected; this sword is going to be utterly useless against the Warchief's thick armour.

The orc retaliates with a brutal swing from his left hand which I barely avoid by diving backwards to evade it, landing awkwardly on my back. I barely have time to recover, before having to quickly roll along my side to avoid the follow up strike from the Warchief as he slams his great sword into the ground where I had been laying just seconds before.

I roll onto my front and look back up at the orc, who is still leaning over with both hands on the hilt of the sword and realise the blade is stuck in the floor from the sheer force of the previous attack. Seizing the opportunity, I lunge forwards and plant my left foot halfway up the wedged blade, carefully keeping my balance as I swing my right leg up as hard as I can, aiming my foot at the orc's chin, the impact ripping the helmet from its head. As the dazed orc staggers backwards from the blow, I bring my right foot back down onto the hilt of the great sword and jump towards the orc while thrusting my own sword down and through the middle of its dark, and very surprised, face.

I manage to stay upright as I plant my feet on the orc's thighs and use my sword, still impaled in the orc's head, to balance myself as I ride down on top of his lifeless body as it drops to the floor.

As I stand up straight, I take a brief moment to compose myself while taking in the look of shock on the faces of the orcs all around me, before sheathing my newly acquired sword and turning to grab the hilt of the great sword in both hands, twisting it slightly before dislodging it out from the ground and bringing it to rest on my right shoulder.

With one last glance around the room, I turn to the remaining portal and without hesitating, I dive straight through.

Chapter Thirty One (Shadow War)

I charge up the large stone steps to the front gate of the keep, where two Royal Knights heave the large doors open for me to pass through without needing to break my stride. Inside, I see the large reception hall in front of me, large pillars of stone surround the outer edges with the Lor'ahan flags hanging from each balcony, the two wolves as bright as ever. Ahead of me is the grand central staircase, leading up to the first and second floors, where you would usually find the various city officials discussing matters of trade or governance, but today the entire castle has an air of silence, much like the rest of the city had done.

At the top of the stairs, I head off to a partially concealed alcove on the right corridor that hides a spiral staircase that leads to the top of the keep, where I knew my family would still be watching the battle. I take the stairs two at a time, I may be weary from the battle, but I have a renewed sense of purpose knowing that my family await me at the top. I must have made this climb a thousand times before, usually in various forms of childish competition with my brother Mal, so I know there are exactly 524 steps from the hall below to the top.

As I climb the stairs, I start to hear the sounds of nature coming through the arrowslits that are scattered throughout the stairwell and realise that this is the first time I have heard them since yesterday, before the orcs arrived at our gates. Approaching the doorway to the roof platform, I notice that there are birds flying around the parapets, squawking and singing to each other. I see the skyline crest over the top of the last few steps and I slow down my pace a fraction to savour this rare moment of tranquility, amongst the chaos. Even amongst all this death, there are still signs of life. Light, and Shadow. Always in opposition of each other.

As I step out onto the walkway, I can see my family still looking over the parapets at the battle still raging below. I start to walk over to them when I see my Serah turn back to talk to her mother, and I can't help but smile as she dances over to Cara. As she gets closer, her little arms raised, she finally catches sight of me from the corner of her eye.

"Papa!" she screams, with an innocence and excitement that only a child can possess, even under these circumstances. I hope she never loses it.

I see Cara turn to face me as well, her eyes may be filled with tears but her lips turn up into a smile that reaches right up to her eyes. Shortly after the little outburst, the rest of my family notice my arrival. I look over to my sons, clad in their armour and still carrying their shields and lances. Beyond them stands my mother, Queen Elaina, her eyes watering as well, but hers too, are filled with relief.

Using the Light, I dissipate my helmet and take a deep breath of the fresh crisp air as I approach my wife and daughter, pulling them both into my arms. I rest my forehead against Cara's and close my eyes, savouring the moment before turning to Serah and scooping her face into my hands as I plant a kiss on her forehead.

"Hello, little one," I say to her, looking into her green eyes. "I love you."

"Always, and forever?" she asks me, with a big smile.

"Of course," I tell her, kissing her forehead again and turning back to Cara.

" I love you, Cara," I tell her, resting my forehead against hers once more as I look deep into her bright blue eyes.

"And I you, my love," she tells me, angling her face forward to kiss me. We had been married for nearly 600 years, but every kiss felt like our first, all those years ago. The passion, the intensity, the love, it was all still evident each time our lips touched.

I reluctantly let go of Cara and Serah to walk over to my sons, who let their shields and lances drop to the floor in order to embrace me fully. I hold them both close to me, savouring their warmth and strength.

"My sons. Never can a father be more proud, than I am of you," I tell them. "You are my strength, as your mother is my love and your sister is my joy."

"We love you father," they both tell me in unison, releasing me to collect their weapons from the ground.

I turn to my mother, who is nervously holding her hands up to her heart, fiddling with the neckband of her dress. As I walk to her, she holds out both her hands and I take them in mine.

"My son. My handsome, brave, loving son," she says to me, the tears rolling down her cheeks now. "You may have been born second, but that never changed how we saw you, nor how we loved you. We are so proud of you, and of everything you have done."

"Mother, you raised me to be who I am. Everything I am is because of you, and father," I say to her, my voice faltering at the end as I remember watching him ride away from the keep moments before.

"You are everything a parent could have wished for, and so much more," my mother tells me, smiling now despite the tears that freely fall down her cheeks.

"I served my king and my city as best I could," I say, hesitating at the end as I turn to look out over the city walls, "but I fear it was not good enough. I have failed everyone. The city will fall."

"We watched as you rode out, and we saw you fall into the sea of darkness out there," my mother says to me, her voice breaking at the memory. "But we also watched you rise, bathed in light and we saw you fight once more."

"Many were lost…" I say, not attempting to hide the pain. "Including Petr."

"Petr will be waiting for you in the eternal forest," my mother says gently. "You honour his memory by fighting, and by living."

I nod solemnly, the crushing loss of Petr suddenly catching up with me, as fresh tears run down my cheeks. We had lost many today, and I grieved for each life lost, but here, now, alongside my family, the loss of my best friend was threatening to consume me.

"Tell me, what father is planning?" I ask her firmly, trying to turn my thoughts away from Petr. "He rode out to fight, but wouldn't tell me why, only that I needed to find you."

"He would have loved nothing more than to spend his final moments with you. But that cannot be, my darling boy. I'm sorry, truly I am. But there is not enough time for that," she tells me, looking over at Cara. "Not enough time for any of us."

"What do you mean, mother?" I ask her, panic rising inside me as I look from her to Cara and back again.

"I must leave, my love," Cara tells me, her eyes filling with tears. "I am to travel through the Dragon Gate and head south, away from the city as fast I can."

"Why, love?" I ask her softly, moving over to her, desperate to comfort her.

"I am to take Serah as far away from here as I can," Cara says softly. "We are to ride out and seek asylum within the realms of men. The king has already sent word to Chancellor Eldren, and requested that the council meets with me as soon as I arrive."

"It fills me with strength to know you will be safe, love," I tell my wife.

"Your father has tasked me with explaining what we know of this new threat, and what fate has befallen the elves at their hands," Cara explains, "They need to be warned, my love, so that they can defend themselves against this 'Shadow God' and all those that follow him."

I look at Cara and Serah, and do not try to hold back the tears that now flow freely down my cheeks. I am relieved to know that they will be safe from whatever fate awaits us here, but also distraught to know that I will likely never see them again.

"Who will protect you on your journey?" I ask them all, "The road is long, and without Mal's army, I fear that it is no longer as safe as it once was, even within our own borders."

"We will ride with them, father," Cen tells me, while Raf nods along beside him. "We will protect them. Our lives for theirs, should it come to it."

I am relieved to know that my family will be together once the city falls, and while Mal always opposed to our alliance with the previous Chancellor, I had forged a friendship with his son, who is now the Chancellor, and could trust him to ensure that my family were treated with the respect and courtesy that they were due.

"I hope with all my heart that it does not come to that, my son." I tell him, the pride I was feeling clearly audible.

"We cannot afford any further delay, my love," Cara tells me, tears once again rolling down her cheeks. "We waited as long as we could, in case you made it back in time. I'm so glad we had this moment together. All of us."

I look over at Cara, stood next to my mother who is now holding Serah, and I realise that in front of me stands the only three generations of the Royal Family of Lor'ahan that there will ever be. A Queen and her Princesses. Collectively we had lived for thousands of years, but in one day all that has changed. It would never be the same again.

With a heavy heart, I walk over to the elven beauty that I am honoured to have called my wife for all these years, looking into her bright blue eyes and trying to convey an eternities worth of love and happiness in the few moments we have left together.

"I love you Cara, Princess of Lor'ahan and Queen of my heart," I tell her, "You may be leaving but you do not go alone. My heart goes with you. Always, and forever."

Cara lets go of my hands, raising hers to my cheeks as she kisses me and I can feel the urgency behind it. Reluctantly, I feel her pull away and lean down to pick up Serah, before passing her over to me.

"My sweet Serah," I whisper to her, and putting my hand over her heart I say "Never forget that I love you, and then you will never feel alone. I always be with you in here."

I hold my daughter close to me, resting my chin on her head and stroking her hair, trying to take in every little detail of this moment, my last moment, with her.

"I love you, papa," Serah says to me, holding back the tears. "Always, and forever."

I watch as Serah takes back our daughter, holding her confidently in her strong arms, as she looks back at me.

"I love you, my prince, my husband, my best friend," Cara tells me through the tears, "I will see you again, in this life or the Eternal Forest that awaits us after."

I hold each of my sons in turn, before watching my family make their way to the doorway I had come through not long before. Even through the grief of losing Petr, watching them leave is a pain worse than anything I could imagine. My heart is aching, yearning, and my eyes are sore.

Yet I'm aware that my mother is still stood behind me. Turning to face her, I can see that she too feels the same pain as I do, but I know the look on her face. There is more to be said.

"The king will soon be riding out of the Wolf Gate, leading every last elven male of fighting age to engage the orcs directly in battle," she tells me.

"Father be damned," I curse out loud, closing my eyes. "He must know that he cannot possibly turn the tide of the battle. There are simply too many of them. The Shadow will consume them."

"Your Father does not ride out expecting to survive, my son," my mother says solemnly. "He means to buy time for Cara to lead the others from the city, without any risk of any orcs giving chase."

"Then the city will fall?" I ask her, the reality of the situation dawning on me. "All will be lost."

"Not all will be lost, my son," my mother tells me, motioning towards the gate that my family will be leaving through.

"Then what is father's plan for me?" I ask my mother.

"To witness the end of this battle, and then prepare for the next," she tells me, her voice full of love and pride.

"I should be at his side," I tell her. "He fights for my family, so should I."

"No, my son," she tells me. "Your place is here, you must see this through, for him. For all of us."

"What aren't you telling me, mother?" I ask her, my confusion mounting.

"Your father knows you better than anyone, he knows how you will react," my mother says, turning to face me, "You must promise me. That you will do as he wishes?"

"Mother, please," I plead. "Tell me?"

"Promise me, son," she states again.

"I promise. On the lives of my wife and daughter," I tell her dejectedly, knowing that I would never break that promise.

"Your Father plans to ride out the gates to attack the orcs directly. I was telling you the truth that they do not fight to win, but to buy more time for Cara and Serah to escape," she tells me. "Cara was telling the truth too, she rides for the Chancellor."

I stand there, waiting for my mother to continue with the plan. I can see that she is clearly upset, but there is more going on that I cannot understand yet. Something feels different, wrong somehow.

"Oh, my son. I am so sorry," she says to me, her eyes suddenly full of sorrow. "Please forgive us."

"Mother, please," I urge her.

"The elves within the city, those that could not ride out with your father," my mother begins to explain; "They made the choice to forsake their Light, before they fled the city with Cara."

The shock of what I had just heard staggers me. Moving closer to the parapets, I look over the edge at the city below, desperate to find any sign of life, but I remember the uneasy stillness of the city as I came through it earlier, and I know it is in vain.

"What? Why? How?" Is all I can bring myself to ask her, as I still struggle to process all that I have heard.

"They have chosen a mortal life," she tells me. "They made this sacrifice for your father, and for you."

I stand here, leaning against the closest wall, desperately trying to find rhyme or reason for what has been done. The elves. The wielders of the Light and protectors of this world, reduced to nothing.

"They have given their Light back, so that your father can wield it," my mother goes on to explain. "He alone has the strength, the power, to do this. The Light, it is bound to your father. He controls the flow of Light within all elves, and it is he that gives us our Light when we come of age."

"What do you mean? We are born with the Light?" I ask her.

"Not exactly. Our children do have the Light inside them, it is in very small amounts that were passed to them through our love. But, it is not until they come of age that they are given the blessing of the Light," mother continues. "And that is the true reason for the Festival of Light. He is sharing his Light with each new generation of elves."

"I never knew," is all I can think to say. The Festival of Light was a long-standing tradition. It was held on the first day of each passing season, and was a city wide celebration of all the young elves that had come of age since the last festival. There was singing, dancing, food, so much food. It was a joyous occasion, full of love for all elves, not just those directly involved. I could remember my son's festival like it was yesterday, I could even remember my own, although it was overshadowed by Mal as he was the Heir Apparent.

I still remember the look of love and affection on my mother's face, as our father had surrounded us in Light. I had always assumed it was just a formality, and that the Light was just for show. But it would seem my father has more power than even I realised. He wasn't just bathing us in his Light, but giving it to us.

"No one does, my son," my mother replies. "It was our secret, our burden, to bear. Your brother, as the Heir Apparent, was due to learn of it. But with his passing, that right passes to you now."

My mother continued to explain that the Light, the mysterious natural force that gives the elves our power, is anchored to my father. There were tales of where the Light came from, and where the elves came from, but that was all they were, tales. Until now.

"At the beginning, your father remembers being bathed in Light, and then awakening in the forest. He didn't know how or why he was here, but he travelled far and wide, learning as much as he could. Ever since that day, he has been able to wield the Light but over time, he has come to master it," my mother tells me. "Then one day he found me. I was wandering in the woods, having become restless, and we fell in love instantly."

I can see the same love in her eyes, as she recounts the story, and I am desperate to know more. Why had they never told me?

"Where did you come from?" I ask her.

"I think I came from the Light. Your father had been alone for centuries. He had watched as nature came and went, how the wolves had their families, and their children. He wanted nothing more than a family of his own. I didn't have the Light then, at least no more than Serah does now, from your love. So your father chose to bathe me in his Light and I too, became immortal."

"Soon, we settled here, in what would become Lor'ahan. Over the next few decades, more elves came from the forests, and your father gave them his Light, and the city grew. Then you were born, along with Mal, and we were overjoyed. Our family was complete, we could wish for no more. The elves decided then, that your father should be our king, and he should lead us. That is the true story of the elves."

"I wish I had known," I say, my mind reeling from all of the information.

"If only we had more time, then we could have told you all of this," my mother tells me, as tears form in her eyes. "I'm so sorry, my sweet boy."

"So father's plan is to gather all the Light?" I ask her, trying to focus. "So that he can be as powerful as he was at the beginning?"

"Ever since the battle started, he has been gathering the Light from all of us, and from all those that fell to the orcs." My mother continues, her voice straining. "Once he has gathered enough, he will have enough power. Enough power to… he intends to release the Light, all at once."

"The blast will kill him…" I sigh, as I realise what he is intending to do.

"It will. Our king will fall," my mother says, tears falling down her cheeks. "But on his terms, and more importantly, for his family."

"I want to argue, to come up with something, anything else. But I can't. It buys time for my family, while also weakening the orcs." I say out loud, trying to cling to some form of hope, "And the Light will live on through Cara and Serah."

"Yes, son, the Light will live on," my mother tells me, although I note an edge to her tone that causes a fresh wave of anxiety to rush through me.

"There is more…" I say to her, as I turn to look at her, realisation suddenly dawning on me.

"I am sorry," she says back to me, the usual brightness in her eyes all but gone.

"Mother, no," I say, trying to process this new revelation. "You gave up your Light too."

"I did it for you, my son," she explains, taking a deep breath before continuing, "Cara rides now, to meet with the chancellor and deliver the message that our city has fallen, of the sacrifice we made for this world and lastly, the plan your father has now put in motion."

Down below us, I hear the elven trumpets start up again and watch as they prepare to open the gates for my father to ride through, leading the remaining elves into the fray.

"Cara will deliver that message alone," my mother continues, "Your sons will take Serah into hiding. To keep her safe from any that may seek them."

"I don't understand," I tell her, trying to hide my fear.

"I know you trust them, my son, and we want to believe that trust was well placed," my mother states, "But they have shown time and again that their curiosity and greed is unquenchable."

"Then what of Serah, and my sons?" I ask bluntly. "And of the elves that left with them?"

"The elves will live a mortal life, alongside the world of men," my mother explains. "But for this to work, the Light must be focused within your father. And then within you."

"I still don't understand, mother," I say. "There must be another way!"

"Cara had already forsaken her Light before she left, as did your sons," she tells me, tears rolling down her cheeks. "As Serah has not yet come of age, she will continue to age, and then live a mortal life, but unlike the others, she will keep the Light she already has within her, to pass on to her own children."

This time, the shock is too much and everything around me starts to spin as I fall to my knees. How could

I have not noticed? I had looked in each of their eyes, but my love had blinded me to the truth.

"But you said the elves will live on?" I ask her, desperate to understand.

"The Elves will live on," my mother tells me with a small smile. "Through you."

"Father be damned!" I exclaim, although the realisation is starting to dawn on me. "Once our army falls, and father uses his Light to decimate the orcs. All of the Light will start to reform in any elves still standing."

"Yes, my son," my mother says, the strength returning to her voice. "That is the true purpose of your father's plan. The Light will begin to reform in the last of our people. In the last living elf. In you."

I stumble backwards, trying to concentrate on everything I have heard.

"Then you will have the full power of the elves inside you, save the small amount currently inside our little Serah," my mother finishes with a smile as she says my daughter's name.

I look up at my mother, my mind still trying to process all of the information, but when I meet her gaze, I realise my selfishness. I am not the only one hurting. She is about to watch the love of her life ride into battle, knowing that he will never return. At least I know that my wife and children will live on, albeit as mortals.

"I am so sorry, mother," I say, pulling her into my arms and I feel her hold me back, and we stand there for a few moments in silence.

Eventually my mother pulls away, and looking up at me, she explains, "You have a long road ahead of you, and many battles to fight before this war will be over. You are destined to lead our allies, old and new, against this army and you alone will have the power to confront their Shadow God."

Chapter Thirty Two

The strange sensation of weightlessness stops as suddenly as it started, followed quickly by that horrible feeling of falling, which doesn't last long as I find myself stumbling forward when my feet connect with the floor once again. I drop the great sword to help me keep my balance, and it falls loudly to the floor, the clanging sound echoing throughout this new place.

I look around and try to get my bearings. Where did the Portal take me? The entire area is bathed in darkness, save the small amount of light coming from the pulsating Portal behind me. The walls and ceiling look like rock but are also very smooth, my eyes follow the wall down to the floor, which is also some sort of smooth rock. Then a small laugh escapes me as I see two perfectly straight metal tracks. Train tracks. I'm not in the Underworld, I'm in the Underground. Again.

I hear a noise behind me, snapping my attention back to the Portal. Turning to face it, I can see two orcs stood either side with their hands held up towards it, along with two more orcs that have just followed me through, looking just as disorientated as I was. which was interesting. I made a mental note to bring that up with Harry, Adam, the Captain, or anyone actually, the realisation that I was completely alone suddenly dawning on me.

The two new orcs are staring at me, before being joined by a third. I need to get that Portal closed. Now. The other two orcs, which I now realise are wearing robes and not armour like every other orc I've seen so far, are probably responsible for keeping the Portal open, and presumably opening it to begin with. A fourth orc steps through the Portal, looking around apprehensively before drawing its sword and joining the other three stood there. Clearly my stunt with the Warchief had made them wary.

Still, I couldn't afford for more orcs to come through. Four was enough, or six with the two robed orcs. I quickly lunge forward, drawing my sword as I leap. I keep the blade swinging through its arc and slash at the first orc's face, and it falls away to the side, clutching its face as it falls. I quickly bring the blade back round to parry the left most orcs attack. I don't hesitate to flick my sword back towards the other orcs, heading off any attacks they may be contemplating, followed quickly by a thrust at the left most orc again, taking it by surprise, and my blade hits its mark as it pierces through the orc's thin armour and into its chest.

I let go of the hilt and thrust my elbow back into the face of the middle orc, knocking it back into the right orc as it stumbles backwards from the blow. I reach back for my blade, but as I turn back to the pair of disorientated orcs, another orc joins them from the Portal. Great.

I'm stood about ten feet from the three orcs, and maybe fifteen feet from the robed orcs. I look down at the dead orc at my feet, scanning for its sword, which is at my feet. Before the orcs can charge at me, I throw my sword as hard as I can at the robed orc to the left of the Portal, and as it swings through the air I bend down to grab the dead orc's sword, before looking up to see the sword looping round in wide circles as it approaches its target.

I don't linger to see the blade hit its mark, instead I turn to the three orcs who are all still watching the blade fly through the air. I leap towards the two orcs on the right, swinging the blade towards their heads and catch them both. The first orc's head is cleaved in two, but the second takes a glancing blow across its face. Now blinded, the orc screams in pain before starting to lash out with its sword, singly viciously but wildly. I dance backward, easily avoiding its attacks. I take a chance swing at the other orc to my left, trying to keep it away from me while I deal with the blinded orc as its thrashing blade could easily connect while my back was turned.

Now the orc is falling back, I chance a look at the Portal. With one of the robed orcs dead, it has now started to crack and shake, while the other robed orc is still rooted to the spot, arms outstretched, but it too is now shaking from the strain of trying to control the collapsing Portal. Smiling, I take a few steps back and quietly step round the blinded orc so that I can drive my blade between its shoulders. I pull my blade out of the now dead orc and twirl it at my side as I approach the last armoured orc, who launches at me with a snarl. I quickly parry its attack, and then spin to its left and slice my blade up its back, causing the orc to yelp as it falls to its knees. I walk up behind the orc and drive my blade down into the back of its neck. A far more dignified death that any orc deserves.

Pulling my blade free, I turn back in time to see the Portal finally collapse as the other robed orc stumbles to the side. The effort of trying to control the Portal clearing taking its toll. I make another mental note to join the one from earlier.

The orc pulls out two small daggers and lunges towards me, both blades darting out as it charges forward. I walk back a few steps, trying to keep some distance from the fast-moving blades. I need to pick the right moment. The orc is clearly fatigued, and as it approaches, the swings get slower and clumsier. Without any warning or build up, I swing my blade up and catch the orc on the shoulder, causing it to yelp in pain and drop one of its daggers. As it straightens up, I swing the blade back round and catch the other dagger, pushing it away from the orc, leaving it completely open so I plunge my sword through its chest. The orc makes a gurgling sound as it slumps to the ground, then once free of my sword, falling silent as its head finally hits the floor.

I lean down and cut off a strip of fabric from the orc's robe and use it to wipe the blade before sheathing it again. When I reach down to pick up the great sword, I look back at the orc and the realisation hits me… This was the first orc I had seen wearing a robe instead of armour. Why a robe? It only had daggers as well, not a sword like all the others. Was it a magic user? More questions, with no one to answer them.

I take a moment to look around, although there is little to see in the darkness now that the light from the Portal is gone. I had come through facing away from the

Portal, having gone through the same way the orcs had initially come out in the studio, it was a fair assumption that this was the direction they had come from. That this was the direction of their base.

I turn away from where the portal had been and start to run down the tunnel, although not particularly quickly. I don't want to make too much noise but more importantly, holding the great sword on my shoulder like this was making it more and more awkward to move. It was a bulky weapon, and my shoulder was already starting to ache from my old injury.

As I round another bend, I can see the tunnel open up ahead into a station. The signs on the platforms above indicate that I am back at Westminster station. This was where they were keeping Olive. This is where Gro'alk had set up camp. It made sense, but being back here again gave me a more than just a sense of deja-vu, the anxiety levels were building again. I had to get to Cassie.

But before I could think about that, I had to deal with the hundred or so orcs on both platforms, and on the tracks below, all of which draw their swords as they see me step out from the darkness of the tunnel. It would seem that they've increased their security since the last time I was here.

I take a few steps forward, but I don't want to get too far into the station, as the orcs up on the platform could jump down behind me and then I'd be in trouble. I stop and take the great sword off my shoulder, holding it in both hands now, which helps to alleviate the ache in my shoulder. Slightly. Almost immediately, the orcs all charge at me, while those up on the platform jump down to join them.

The first orc is maybe twenty feet from me when I hear a series of loud cracks from the tunnel behind me and the closest orc drops down dead, along with those around it, quickly followed by more cracks and more orcs dropping. I risk a quick glance back at the tunnel and see four figures walking towards me, their silhouettes look like they are almost dancing in the muzzle flashes from their weapons.

I turn back to face the orcs and lunge forwards, swinging the great sword round in wide horizontal arc as I land, cutting down several orcs. At the end of its swing, I bring the sword over my head and down into the orc closest to me, cleaving it in two. Lifting the blade up, I hold it up parallel to the floor, using its length to block several orcs' swords as they attempted to cut me down. I push the blade forwards, relinquishing the heavy blade, which knocks the orcs off balance, so I draw the small sword from its sheath on my hip and cut the three orcs down in a single deadly swing.

To my right, an orc is charging at me, but it doesn't make it any closer as it takes a bullet to the head. I quickly spin round and cut down another orc, while silently thanking the shooter, but there isn't time for any more than that. Several more orcs charge at me, causing me to take a step backwards while parrying their blades. Another orc joins them, followed by another. Gunfire behind me confirms that they are now preoccupied with orcs trying to overwhelm them using their superior numbers. Just like at the studio when the soldiers fell back to the doorways, the foursome behind me were keeping just inside the tunnel, creating a bottleneck, which would mean the orcs' numbers would count nothing against their automatic weapons.

But that didn't help me. These orcs are mine to deal with. I twirl the blade at my side, before quickly sheathing it and pulling the handgun from its holster and firing a bullet at each orc. Three of them hit their mark, the orcs dropping like stone, but the last one rushes forwards unharmed by my admittedly sketchy gun skills. Luckily, I still have nine bullets left, and two of them go into its chest, cutting its charge short.

I line up the next shot, dropping an orc mid jump from the platform, followed by another shot at an orc charging at me on the tracks. The last five bullets are fired into the dwindling crowd of orcs on the tracks ahead of me, before I push the gun back into its holster and unsheathe the sword once again.

I adjust my grip on the sword, and look up to see that all of the orcs have stopped advancing and are staring up at the platform. I follow their gaze to find a Warchief stood there, who is at least a foot taller than those on either side of this new challenger. How do they get so big? This question doesn't need answering, so I don't file it away with the other observations.

The Warchief lumbers forwards, jumping down to join me on the tracks below, and landing with a grunt. He is much larger than the one I fought at the TV Studio. What was the saying? Larger they are, harder they fall? Time to test that theory.

I twirl the blade at my side, cross it over in front of me and twirl it on my left before crossing it back again. No real reason. I was just buying time while waiting for the Warchief to play his hand. Plus I hoped the soldiers behind me were using the down time in the fighting to prepare themselves, get into position, reload, or just do whatever they need to do.

The Warchief draws the greataxe from its back, and spins it in a similar fashion to my fanciful sword twirls, which earns a small grin from me. I grip the sword tightly, knowing that an attack is coming. I need to be ready. Moments later, the Warchief leaps forward and drives the axe down, narrowingly missing me as I spin off to one side to avoid the attack.

I take a few steps backwards, away from the large orc, and as it straightens back up, I take a quick look back towards the entrance of the tunnel to see Adam, and 3 soldiers I don't know, step out into the light of the station. Adam and soldier one go up on the left, while the other two jump up on the right. I'm not sure, but I think I spot Adam pulling out a grenade from a punch on his belt, before he ducks out of view behind a barrier at the end of the platform.

I quickly adjust my gaze when I spot the Warchief looking at me curiously, not wanting to give away Adam's new location, nor his plan. Or what I think his plan is. So instead, I take a step forwards, towards my foe, and all I can think is; This orc is between me and Cassie. That right there, is why he will lose.

I lurch forwards, and five strides out, I jump to the left and watch as the orc draws its great axe to the right, in preparation of a swing towards where I was about to be. As soon as the Warchief is committed to the swing, I dart to my right and jump onto the tracks, my boots sliding along their smooth surface, and as I pass the now confused orc, I draw my sword across the side of its leg. The blood staining my blade confirming that I had aimed correctly, and I spin off the tracks in time to see the orc drop awkwardly onto its knee.

I quickly jump forwards and swing my blade up, cutting off the orc's hand and disabling it as its great axe falls to the floor, the orcs hand still gripping it tightly. I walk round in front of the orc, who is now clutching its severed wrist with the remaining hand. The orcs up on the platforms are becoming restless, no doubt driven by the sight of their Warchief being beaten like this. One jumps down to join us, but I realise that it's not even looking at me. It only has eyes for its Warchief's murderous eyes. Clearly the orc fancies itself as its successor.

"Adam, whatever you're planning, do it now!" I call out. Not wanting to turn away from the approaching orc.

"Get to cover!" he shouts in reply, and I hear the faint sounds of metal hitting concrete either side of me.

I step closer to the Warchief and plunge my sword straight into its shoulder, then using it as a lever, along with my own weight, I pull the large orc towards me and down, aiming my back for the gap between the rail and the wall leading up to the platform, and pull as hard as I can on the giant orc so that it would land on top of me.

Granted, not my best idea, as the orc is now laying on top of me, our faces inches apart, all while it snarls and snaps and spits at me. Over the Warchief's shoulder I see the opportunistic orc appear, blade held up, ready to drive it down through us both. I bury my face into the orc's shoulder, just as the entire station erupts in fire.

Chapter Thirty Three

The blinding light is followed immediately by an intense heat from the explosions going off all around me, the orc above me barely shielding me from the blast. I can feel the heat rolling down my neck and licking at my legs, as they are the most exposed. The Warchief is screaming in my ear and writhing in pain, but I keep my grip on the sword still impaled in its shoulder.

Moments later, the light fades as quickly as it started, and after another few seconds, I risk opening my eyes to look around. At first, I can't make anything out; everything is smokey, or is it blurry? I blink a few times, trying to clear my eyes, and slowly the station comes back into focus. I can see flames rolling along the roof, trying to find a way out along the newly formed cracks and crevices. Entire chunks of the station roof have collapsed from the blast. Or blasts. How many grenades had they thrown?

The Warchief is barely moving, its breath has become raspy, but the groans show that it's still conscious, and clearly in pain. I start to push the giant orc off me, but it is effectively dead weight at this point so it barely moves an inch. I try to heave it once more, when suddenly its weight disappears, at first I'm confused but then I realise that it's being lifted by someone, or something. My first thought is that the opportunistic orc survived the blast and had come to finish us off, but then Adam's worried face appears and I feel my whole body relax.

"That was one hell of a risky move, mate," Adam says to me, offering me his hand.

"It worked though," I tell him, a smile forming on my lips as I take his hand.

"I don't know whether you're brave or stupid, to be honest," he tells me, smiling now, as he helps me up to my feet.

I quickly look around and try to take in the destruction all around us. The platforms are covered in rubble and flames. The explosions have caused a fair amount of damage to the walls, and even the roof in places, but the general structure looks to be intact. For now, at least.

"I think Olive would agree that I am a decent mix of both, but definitely skewed more towards latter," I tell Adam, while patting myself down, and checking for any damage. I seem to be ok, these jeans have definitely seen better days, having been frazzled by the flames, and I think my hair is a bit singed at the back, but otherwise the Warchief did its job and protected me from the blast.

"Jake. That was the bravest thing I ever saw." Adam says, the awe showing in his voice. "I mean, seriously, you realise you just told us to throw grenades at you!"

"Well, I think you got them all!" I tell him, clapping him on the shoulder as I realise just how glad I am to see a friendly face.

"I'm not sure about the others, but I threw at least three grenades," Adam tells me with a chuckle. "So I would bloody hope so!"

"Four here," one of the other soldiers tell me, and I turn to look at him for the first time. He's familiar, but I cannot place his face. I know I should ask, but I have several far more important questions.

"Where is Olive? And Nat? What happened at the studio?" I ask him, rattling off my questions as quickly as I can think of them.

"Olive is fine, so is Nat. The Captain called us on his way back from the studio, told us they were with him," Adam explains.

"Thank you," I say, and I feel the relief wash over me.

"As for the other question; he also said some stupid kid had gone after a damsel in distress," Adam laughs, "And I only know one person stupid enough to do that."

"Stupid or brave?" I ask him.

"Probably both," Adam says with a wink.

"How is Harry?" I ask him, suddenly remembering our incapacitated friend, but from the haunted look that passes over Adam's face, I know it isn't good news.

"He's still in the coma, seems like the poison has taken a strong hold on him. Whatever it is, they still don't know. The doctors don't think it's from our world," Adam says, fixing his mask back to his usual half grin. "But I asked Olive to look after him while I'm gone."

"She will," I tell him, knowing Olive well enough to know she will. Without question. "She feels like she owes him, both of you, so she'll honour that request without hesitation."

"I figured as much," Adam says, "She takes after you, in a lot of ways."

"She's a good kid. I want to help him too, once we have Cassie back. Whatever it takes," I tell him, proudly. "And on that note. We have work to do."

"What's the plan, Jake?" Adam asks, but instead of answering, I look down at the Warchief at our feet, who is barely clinging to life.

"Tell me where they took the girl," I demand of the orc, kneeling down and resting my hand on its chest. "And I will show you mercy."

"You think it matters, boy?" the orc spits at me. "Anyway, Gro'alk will kill her just for having the Light inside her. She is too dangerous now."

"Just tell me orc," I demand. "Mercy, or pain. Your choice."

"Pain is pain," the orc says, through heavy pants. I replace my hand with my knee, pushing my full weight into it. The Warchief grits its teeth, but a whimper still escapes it.

"Gro'alk has her, at the top of the base," the orc whimpers, its resolve broken. "And he wants to meet you."

"Me? Why?" I ask the orc. "I'm no-one."

"You keep turning up and making a nuisance of yourself," the Warchief spits at me, "He wants you to watch as her Light is drained, and her life is taken."

"Then I guess I should go introduce myself," I tell him, and release the pressure on its chest.

I look up at Adam, who moves to draw his handgun but I shake my head. Instead, I pull a dagger that was on the Warchief's belt and push it up through the orc's chin, only pulling it out once it's taken its last raspy breath.

I use the knife to cut the daggers sheath from its belt, and then add it to my own as I stand up, along with the borrowed sword and handgun already hanging there.

"One last question, how did you know where to find me?" I ask Adam, having just thought of it.

"Given that we know Gro'alk was last seen here, and our surveillance hadn't shown any orcs leaving, even for the attack on the studio, it was a safe bet you would end up coming here," Adam replies. "Plus we were still at the hospital which is nearby, so didn't take long to get down here. These boys offered to come along too. They were the ones that you sent to get us from the safe house, so they know Cassie too."

"Thank you, all of you," I say to them, realising where I knew their faces from. I had seen them when Cassie took an age to get out the car and scared me half to death. "But I can't, and won't, ask any of you to come with me."

"You don't need to, we were always going to come along anyway," Adam replies, and they all nod along, before adding; "Plus I know that if Harry were awake, he'd either be here or have sent me anyway. I want to make sure Cassie is with us when he wakes up."

The mention of Cassie snaps my mind back to the aching chasm I feel in my chest. I need to get to her. Now.

"It won't be easy. There'll be more of those things the further we go," I say to the little group.

"Then we will deal with it, like we always do," Adam tells me, smiling as he claps me on the shoulder.

"No, Adam. That is my fight, and I mean to do it alone," I say to him, firmly. I have a plan, and I mean to stick to it. "But I do have a job for you, now that you're here."

"What is it?" Adam asks me, sounding intrigued.

"I am going to move through the station, searching for Cassie, however we know now that she'll be with Gro'alk," I tell them. "At that point, things are likely to get very, very messy. We will need an escape route, and the orcs are swarming all over this place now. As soon as I clear out an area, they'll just fill it again."

"Ignoring the fact that you want to kill hundreds of orcs on your own for a moment, what is it you want us to do?" Adam asks, his face a mixture of curiosity and concern.

"Well, given how good you all are with explosives," I say, which puts a very surprised look on their faces. "Do you have any grenades left on you?"

"I have some, yeah," he says, the smile growing on his face.

"I also have some C4," another soldier says, before quickly adding, "It was laying around, I thought it might be handy," to which Adam just laughs.

"Excellent. So I was thinking that we could use them to block all the tunnels that we don't plan on using," I say, pointing down the far end of the tunnel. "Like that one."

"You want us to destroy the London Underground?" one of the other soldiers asks, sounding bewildered.

"I want you to compromise the structural integrity of the London Underground. Slightly," I correct him. "And it's not like we are going to need it anytime soon, is it?"

"Haha, no, it isn't," Adam says, still smiling. "Leave it with us, Jake, we won't let you down."

"I know you won't Adam," I tell him sincerely. "You certainly haven't so far."

The soldiers all climb up to the platform one at a time, so that they can cover each other. Our earlier battle would have certainly been heard by the orcs in the deeper parts of the station. I retrieve my borrowed great sword from the ground, its blade was blackened from the blast but it was otherwise ok, and then slide it up onto the platform before jumping up myself.

"Stick together, all of you," I say to them. "I'll do my best to thin their numbers, but we have to assume that there are far more of them down here than we've seen before."

"How do you even propose to fight them all Jake?" Adam asks. "I mean, yeah, you can use a sword better than anyone I've ever met, but there's potentially thousands of them in there!"

"I need you to trust me, just for a little bit longer," I ask Adam, my voice suddenly sounding very strained.

"I do, Jake," Adam tells me. "I've followed you this far, haven't I?"

"For better or worse," I say, laughing. "Let's try and make it for the better, for a little longer."

"Sounds good to me, mate," Adam says, and I nod back.

"If they do come for you, fall back to the previous room and regain the advantage. You're own safety is more important than securing my exit. Got it?"

"Jake," Adam says firmly. "We got this, don't worry."

"I know mate, I trust you, its just… This is Cassie, you know?" I say to him.

"Then let's go get her back," Adam says, and smiling; "And blow up some stuff along the way."

Chapter Thirty Four

I lift the great sword up to rest it on my shoulder, the shooting pains down my arm acting as another reminder of my old injury. This is the most I've had to use my shoulder in a very long time, so I'm not all that surprised it's so sore. Olive would kill me if she knew I had missed the last few physio appointments, and the thought makes me smile as I walk away from Adam and the other soldiers who are discussing the best way to blow up the Underground.

As I pass through the archway at the end of the platform and into the large open area beyond, I see the two traitorous orcs from earlier still sprawled out on the floor, I guess they never got round to burning the bodies. Our rescue attempt obviously interrupted their plans. Luckily this ground floor is still clear, I assume any orcs that were out here either joined the initial battle down on the tracks or were caught up in the blast, so I move towards the escalators and begin the climb up to the next floor.

Up on the first floor, there are maybe ten orcs stood near the two entrances to the Eastbound platform beyond and they draw their swords as I step off the escalator. They must have stationed the majority of the orcs down below, fully expecting me to come in the same way as before. I'm glad I didn't disappoint, not that I had any choice on which way to go.

The orcs all charge at me, but I am ready for them. Despite the growing pain in my shoulder, I am focused solely on Cassie now, and nothing will stop me getting to her.

I swing the great sword down from my shoulder, cleaving the first orc in two and pull the blade quickly back up in front of me to simultaneously block swings from the two orcs now either side of me. I push the blade away from me, dislodging the tangle of swords and pull my blade back over my shoulder and take a step back while twirling the sword over my head to bring it down in a diagonal attack across the face and chest of the left most orc and then swiftly bring the blade back in a horizontal arc into the chest of the right hand one.

The next few orcs have slowed down, realising that maybe I am a genuine threat and should probably be dealt with using a little more care. I hold the sword out in front of me, ready to attack or defend, but I want them to make the first move.

"Run and tell the Warchief that the boy is here," one of the orcs says, and I see the furthest orc turn and flee up the stairs.

"Thanks for that," I tell them.

"For what?" The orc asks, puzzled.

"Showing me the way," I laugh.

I lunge forward and drive my blade into the confused orc's chest, pulling the blade out and spinning round to bring the blade back down in a powerful swing to cut the orc to my left all the way from its shoulder to its navel. I put my foot on its shoulder and push its corpse down and off my blade.

The remaining two orcs both look at each other and then back at me. With a roar, they both jump at me together so I lift my sword up horizontally to block both their strikes. I push their blades up and step underneath while turning my body around, all while drawing my other sword with my left hand, and holding it backwards, I slice the side of the right hand orc's chest and then as it tries to arch its back away from the blade, I continue to turn my body to give me the better angle and then twist back to force the tip of the blade through its back.

I stand up straight and pull the blade free, turning to face the last remaining orc. I now have the great sword in my right hand, resting on my shoulder, and the shorter sword held ahead of me in my left hand. The orc looks at me, and then flees down the escalators. About ten seconds later I hear a single gunshot ring out from the platform below. Jake 8, Adam 1.

I turn back to the stairs where the first orc had run off to, and start to follow it further into the station. I sheathe the sword again and adjust the great sword, as my shoulder is starting to seriously ache, I doubt I will be able to use the great sword for much longer. Not like this anyway.

At the top of the next set of escalators, there are another twenty or so orcs all stood in a line waiting for me. The element of surprise now completely lost, but in its place, it seems that I have handy orc shaped arrows pointing all the way to Cassie.

I lunge forward to engage the orcs, swinging my great sword in a wide arc at the full stretch of my arm, which is now on fire from the pain in my shoulder, forcing the orcs to jump backwards, except one who misjudged the distance at the cost of its head. At the end of its arc, I swing the sword back over my head and release it in a clumsy throw, right at an orc standing off to the right of the group and its final expression is one of total shock as the great sword pins it to the wall.

I draw the short sword and hold it up. While my shoulder is still sore, this sword is much lighter and doesn't cause anywhere near as much strain to wield it.

An orc dives forward, and I parry its attack to my right while bringing my left hand up to meet it and rip the sword from its hands leaving the orc unarmed. Using both blades, I bring them down in tandem in front of me, leaving a deep cross shaped slice across its face and the orc collapses to the floor.

With a blade in each hand now, I take on the remaining orcs without mercy. I start to twirl the blades in loose circles either side of me, while the orcs all try to take tentative swings at me that I can easily read and parry accordingly. I slowly and carefully move forwards, causing the orcs to form up around me in a loose circle, before positioning myself in the exact centre while trying to draw the twirling swords as close to my body as I can and wait for them to close in as tightly as possible.

As soon as they are all close enough, I change the momentum of the swords, bringing them back round to be above me, and in front of me, with my arms extended, the blades are held out so that when I spin my body round, they spin in full circles almost like a large, and deadly, blende, and I feel slight snags of resistance as each blade strikes a different orc, and watch through the blurred movement as they all fall one by one to the swift and unpredictable flurry of the blades swirling around me.

I slow down the blades when I see just the one orc left standing, who was just a fraction further back than the others and avoided my attack. It looks down at the dismembered orcs around him and back up at me, just as a loud explosion goes off below us and the entire station shakes. The orc watches as a large crack runs up the wall, before turning tail to run away from the concrete that has started to crack all around us. I step forward, using the momentum to help throw one of my swords at the retreating orc and it hits its mark.

I retrieve the blade from the dead orc's back on my way past, heading in the direction that it was about to run to. Unlike the other orc who was trying to escape into the lower part of the station, this one was attempting to run to safety. It was running towards its Warchief. Towards Gro'alk.

I walk up the last set of escalators and pause at the top to look at the sheer number of orcs ahead of me. It would seem that my earlier guess was wrong, the main bulk of the orc army wasn't below. It's here. There has to be a thousand orcs stood in front of me. I can see the archway across on the other platform which leads back up to an enclosed area behind it. Given all these orcs, that must be where Gro'alk is hiding, and therefore where Cassie will be too.

The entire station is made from reinforced concrete, and the earlier explosion from the lower levels had sent shockwaves reverberating around the station. If they didn't know we were here before, they definitely do now, every single orc is looking at me, weapons drawn.

I take a deep breath and hold both blades up in front of me, just as all around me the orcs start to cheer and roar, mocking me, goading me.

Chapter Thirty Five (Shadow War)

I stand looking over the parapet with my mother, the city is silent below us despite the bloody battle raging just outside the City gates. I turn my gaze south, towards the Dragon Gate but I see no signs of movement. Cara, Serah and my sons have already passed through, and the sense of that loss is threatening to overwhelm me.

Just inside the Wolf Gate, I can see my Father atop his horse. All around him, the remaining elves of fighting age are donning whatever armour and weapons were still available from the city armoury. Even from this distance, I can see that they are ill-equipped. But I guess it matters little, in the end.

"This will be brutal," I tell her with tears rolling down my cheeks. "Is there no other way?"

"If we simply let this orc army take the city, it will keep attacking each part of this world until they have total control," my mother says, her voice heavy with emotion. "We tried to stop them here, but it was always an outside chance."

"Could we not have fled, and made a stand at the city of men?"

"That was an option, one that we discussed at great length, but we would have had to concede too much to the orcs. Their numbers, and power would have grown," my mother attempts to explain. "What if our last stand was not enough? Then we would have no other options. The world would fall into Shadow."

My mind is whirring, trying to come up with a better plan. But I know it is futile. My parents had obviously discussed it all, at length. But even they didn't have the time to go through all of the possibilities. Was this really the only way? The best option?

"This plan, while it comes at such a great cost, also strikes a devastating blow to the orcs. It will decimate their army. Buying you time to find new allegiances, and re-forge old ones," my mother continues.

"But why me?" I ask her, my voice breaking.

"It has to be you, my son," she tells me. "You are not just the heir to the throne, but to the Light as well. It is bound to your father, but upon his death, it will become bound to you."

I stare down at my father, who looks up at the castle and I see him raise his hand to his heart and then to his mouth, and watch as my mother repeats the elven symbol of love back to my father.

He then looks at me, and even at this distance, I can see the love and pride in his eyes, the earlier concern all but fallen away. He has accepted his fate, and I realise that he is riding out on his own terms, knowing that his child will live on thanks to his actions, just as my children will.

"We have sacrificed so much for this world," I tell mother, and I hear the acceptance in my voice now.

"I love you, my son," she tells me, taking my hand. "Always, and forever."

Down in the courtyard below, the Wolf Gate is thrown wide open and I watch the last of the elves ride out to join the remains of the Royal Knights still fighting outside the City Walls. They are heavily outnumbered and I watch as they engage the orcs, I want to turn away, to spare myself the sight of the massacre below, but I will not dishonour the memory of those elves who are only fighting to buy time for those who can't, to flee.

I can see my father fighting several orcs, his presence has rallied the elves that were fighting outside the walls, but it is short lived as I notice that several Warchiefs are now approaching the area just in front of the gate, where he is defending with his personal guard. My father and one Warchief fight for several minutes, trading swings and parries with no clear victor in sight. With my father focused elsewhere, I see the city gates start to falter as the orcs start their assault against the city walls.

"It is time for you to leave, my son," my mother tells me, sadness etched back into her face.

"Where am I to go?" I ask her.

"Away from here, my son," she tells me. "You must re-forge the alliances of old."

"You mean the Warcouncil?" I ask mother. "But the Elementals haven't been seen for millennia, and I thought they only answer to father."

"When your father passes to the Eternal Forest, the Light will become bound to you. The Elementals Lords and Ladies answer to the Light," my mother explains. "The Light leads, and they follow. "

"How will I find them?" I ask her, desperate to know as much as I can, in the little time we have left. The Elementals were said to be born from the planet itself, each legendary species tied to an element of nature, as their protector.

"This will lead you to Lord Fenrir, and he will guide you, and he will help you to find the others," she tells me, handing me a small wooden carving of a Direwolf, its eyes made from some sort of sparkling green gem. The carving was meant to represent Fenrir, Lord of the Forest. He was father's oldest ally, and the first Elemental to join him. I had never met him, but I had listened to father's stories with glee as a child. My mother's voice brought me out of my memories. "But now, you must go. I will hold the castle, for as long as I can."

I embrace my mother one last time, then we both look down at my father, watching as he fights against two Warchiefs, and then make our way down the spiral staircase. As I reach the bottom, I see the large castle doors swing open, followed by a large number of orcs, quickly filling the hall. They'd breached the wall further down, without us noticing.

In the middle of the torrent of orcs entering the castle, stands the Warchief Gro'alk, who rips down one of the Lor'ahan banners and stamps on it. It is about to rip down a second banner, when it sees us at the top of the stairs.

"There you are, Princeling!" The large orc shouts to me. "Protecting the Queen. How touching."

"Will you run this time, orc?" I ask him, ignoring his taunt.

"Will you protect this one, boy?" the orc replies, his retort stunning me as I think back to Petr's death.

My mother confidently strides past me, before turning back, her eyes full of tears but also a strength I have never seen before. She lifts her hand up towards the Warchief, before saying to me;

"Some battles must be lost, for the war to be won."

Chapter Thirty Six

The first orcs charge at me and I parry their attacks, swinging my blades from left to right just to block the sheer number of attacks that the twenty or so orcs are throwing my way.. Each time one falls, another immediately takes its place. Already, this battle is futile.

Another explosion goes off below me, causing small chunks of concrete to fall from the ceiling and more cracks to appear on the walls. The next two explosions quickly follow as Adam and the others seal up the two archways on the first floor of the station; I think that is all the tunnels? I hope. Which means they should be positioning themselves in a defensive position to cover our escape route.

Behind all the orcs, I see a Warchief step through the archway on the other platform, before joining the crowd of orcs eager to join the battle. I continue to block the orcs' swings and thrusts, without opening myself up to any orcs that try to slip behind me. I need to keep them in front of me. After a minute or so, I see the Warchief climb up onto this side of the platform, unmistakable given its large frame in comparison to the grunts that surround it.

"This one is mine, on the orders of Gro'alk," the Warchief explains to the orc horde, who all take a step back from me and leaving me feel very exposed.

"I've killed every other Warchief that Gro'alk sent," I tell him. "Must not like you very much either."

"You have not fought a Warchief like me before, boy," It spits at me. "I am as old as Gro'alk."

"You talk just as much as Gro'alk as well," I say, trying to antagonise the orc.

It pulls a hand axe and hammer from its hips, one in each hand.

"I'm going to enjoy beating you, boy," the Warchief tells me, and I note that it didn't say kill, Gro'alk must actually want me alive. Interesting.

The large orc jumps forward, bringing the axe down in a heavy swing, forcing me to parry it to my right and spin away from the orc, but now I am too close to the orcs behind me and I feel them shove me back towards the Warchief. I lift my blades back up in front of me and try to circle round, but the Warchief remains rooted to the spot, not wanting to give up its position. Clever orc.

It lunges forward again, this time swinging the axe downwards and the hammer sidewards at the same time, I manage to parry the axe but the hammer slams into my sword at an awkward angle and carries on through it's arc, connecting with my shoulder awkwardly. I let out a yelp as the sword drops from my hand and I curl my arm up to my stomach, holding it there. With only one sword against an orc nearly twice my size and holding two weapons, it would appear that I am grossly outmatched.

"Drop your sword, boy," it says smugly, sensing my thoughts. "You lose."

I let the blade fall from my hand, and drop my head, watching the sword fall and rattle as it hits the floor. The orc hangs the axe and hammer back on his belt and takes a step towards me. It raises its hands to its helm and pulls it off, revealing a smile that makes its face twist grotesquely in the dimly lit station. With the helm in its left hand, I just register the orc curl its right hand into a fist, before it drives it into my cheek, knocking me to the ground and leaving me dazed.

I feel something grab my ankle and drag me towards the tracks. Several more hands start to grope my pack, and something sharp catches my shoulder before I feel my pack being ripped off me now that the straps have been cut. Moments later, my belt is also cut off. I can't help but feel beaten, broken and unarmed.

My thoughts are disturbed when I feel a sharp tug on my ankle, followed by the feeling of weightlessness before I drop painfully down the eight feet drop to land on the rails below. The awkward landing causes me to grunt as I roll away from the rail, and the Warchief who has jumped down to join me. As I roll onto my front and push myself up onto my hands and knees, it lashes out with a brutal kick to my abdomen that throws me into the wall of the platform, and I allow myself to crumple into a heap on the floor, before curling up into a ball to try and protect myself from any further kicks.

The Warchief kicks me twice, then stamps on me, laughing the entire time. It seems to be enjoying itself, at least. I feel its large, rough hands pick me up and effortlessly throw me onto the platform, where the orcs are still cheering, but are also now joining in with the kicking and stamping while the Warchief climbs up onto the platform. At least my shoulder doesn't seem to hurt as much anymore, its aches and pains completely masked by the aches and pains everywhere else.

"Get up," the Warchief spits to me, rolling me onto my back with its foot. "I said get up!"

I slowly roll over onto my front and climb up onto my knees before standing, hunched over, my right arm still curled up by my stomach. The Warchief grabs me by the back of my collar and pushes me towards the archway. Towards Gro'alk. Towards Cassie.

"Warchief Gro'alk!" the orc shouts as we enter the next room. "I have the boy."

I look up and see Cassie kneeling in the centre of the room, facing away from me. She is hunched over, but I can see her breathing heavily so I relax slightly. Just seeing her fills me with relief. I found her.

"Nice of you to join us," Gro'alk says to me. "I have heard so much about you, childling."

I stumble forwards, pushed on by the Warchief who still has me by my collar, and almost fall down as my foot catches a loose tile on the floor. Frustrated by my weakness, the Warchief pushes me hard and slams me into a concrete pillar and causing me to tumble to the floor, now level with Cassie.

Cassie turns her head slightly to make eye contact with me, and her entire expression changes. She had looked lost, frightened and had obviously been crying, but now she is looking at me, I don't see the hope I was expecting. Only sadness. I realise that she had accepted her fate, that she wouldn't make it, that she wouldn't see me again. But now seeing me, she is going to lose everything.

I look into her eyes, keeping my expression calm and composed, and try to let her see what I am thinking, she can read me like no-one else. I want her to know, need her to know, that she isn't alone. That I came for her. That I'll always come for her.

Chapter Thirty Seven

"You have been quite the nuisance, childling," Gro'alk says to me, as I sit hunched on the floor. "I am almost impressed with all that you have done. Luck may have got you this far, but it has now run out."

I sit there, hunched over, with the right side of my face resting on the pillar and my head turned down towards the ground. I just hope that Cassie saw the look in my eyes before.

"You came in here yesterday to save the other girl, the one with the Light, didn't you?" he asks me.

"Yeah, that was me," I tell him dejectedly.

"Tell me why?"

"Why? She is my little sister," I tell him.

"She told me her brother had died," he spits at me. "You humans, always lying."

"She didn't lie," I tell him, sighing. "Her brother did die, years ago. I adopted her."

"Hmph," the Warchief grunts. "Why help someone who isn't even your blood?"

"It's called love," I tell him, tears forming in my eyes. "And we will do anything for the people we love." I hope Cassie knows that answer was meant for her as much as it was for him.

"You humans are pathetic," he grunts. "You're almost as bad as the elves. They had that weakness too."

"Love isn't a weakness," I say firmly. "Love gives us strength."

"Love gets you killed," he laughs at me, turning to look at Cassie. "Gets others killed too."

I risk a glance up at Cassie, who is back to sitting hunched and looking down at the floor. I use this distraction to quickly look around the room, and can see about fifteen orcs in here, along with Gro'alk and the other Warchief. I notice Gro'alk turning back to me, so I quickly turn my gaze back to the floor.

"You survived the attack on the studio as well, did you not?" he asks, continuing his interrogation. "That must be quite the story."

"Not really," I tell him. "I wasn't alone, was I? There were a lot of soldiers there, all of them fighting to get us out safely. Which they did."

I notice Cassie flinch slightly as I say it, although it was imperceptible to the orcs around us. She knows that was a lie.

"You were lucky, again," he laughs. "This girl wasn't, though."

"What do you want with Cassie?" I ask him.

"She has the Light too, just like the other girl," he says to me. "Which I find very curious indeed."

"Why?" I ask, trying to keep him talking.

"The Light was lost millennia ago, childling," he says, laughing again. "When the Shadow God and his armies destroyed the elves."

"Clearly not," I say, trying to hide my smirk.

"Hence why it is curious," he spits, circling Cassie as he talks. "We had heard rumours, of course, that the Elves had hidden it. But until yesterday, we could find no trace of it anywhere."

"So that's not why you are here?" I ask him, confusion in my voice.

"For the Light?" Gro'alk laughs loudly now. "We do not care for the Light, childling. It's a hinderance, nothing more."

"Then what do you want?" I ask, forcing myself not to look up at him.

"Everything," he states, calm and collected. "The whole world, and everything in it."

"You won't get it," I say, sounding broken. "They'll fight you."

"Then they'll lose," he tells me. "We'll kill them all. Although those that surrender willingly, will be sent to the Underworld. To suffer as we have suffered in that hellish place. We were trapped for nearly eight thousand years, but it made us stronger, better. This time, we won't lose."

"You won't win," I tell him. "You lost before, right? You'll lose again."

"Gwahaha. Is that what your precious love is telling you boy?" he taunts.

"You fight for power, for control, nothing else," I say. "But you are up against an entire race that are fighting for the people they love, the world they love. They will not go down without a fight, but they also have something to fight for and that makes them far more dangerous."

"Our sources tell us that there are seven billion humans in this world," he says, which strikes me as a curious choice of words. Sources? What sources? I file that away with my other topics to discuss with the Adam, and Harry once he wakes up.. "Including your men, women and children, of all ages, from your infants to your elders. Only a fraction of that number can actually fight."

"They also have their technology." I say to him, purely to keep him talking.

"And we have our numbers. There are ten billion orcs in the Underworld," he says proudly. "And did you know that orcs are not born, but spawned and twisted from the Shadow. All of us ready to fight, ready to kill, on the day of our first breath, right through to our last."

"Oh my god," I say, shocked. I wasn't expecting that. So many. How?

"And that, childing, is why you will lose," Gro'alk says.

I sit there trying to process what I have just heard. There are ten billion orcs waiting to invade this world. The human race is heavily outnumbered and outmatched, even with their technology, they cannot possibly hope to win this war alone. Just like at the studio, their technology will count for nothing against an enemy that has impossibly large numbers, numbers that they are clearly willing to sacrifice to achieve their goal.

"Warchief, we found the others," I hear an orc say from behind me, and I feel my heart drop. "The ones who makes the explosions."

I turn my head away to look back over my left shoulder to see an orcs come through, holding someone in front of him. He has Adam.

Adam has blood running down his face, clearly he had tried to fight them off. I look at Adam, making eye contact with him and mouthing 'the others?' to which he just shakes his head slightly. My head drops as I realise that they didn't make it.

"So this is it?" Gro'alk says, laughing out loudly. "The elite warriors that the humans have been sending against me! A soldier, a weak childling and a girl with the Light."

I flinch at his words. More people have died, because of me. I had fought for Olive, and for Cassie. I'll fight for Nat, Harry and Adam too. They're my family. But those soldiers, they had families too. So does every single man, woman and child. I can't save them all. No one is that powerful.

"Luck may have been on your side," he continues. "But now, I will take everything from you."

I watch him walk towards the back of the room, where he picks up a great hammer that is as big as the orc itself. Gro'alk swings it round like it weighs nothing, despite the head being as big as Cassie, currently curled up on the floor.

"You all came here to save the girl. Whether it is because you love her, or you want the Light, it matters not," he says, grinning. "You came here for her, and now you will watch helplessly as I take her from you. You will watch as the Light leaves her body."

I see Cassie start to shake again, all I want to do is to run to her and hold her, and tell her that I love her. That I have always loved her.

But I stay seated, hunched against the pillar, looking at the floor.

"Do you have any last words, girl?" Gro'alk asks Cassie.

"Jake," she says, and I can't help but look up at her and can see that she has turned herself round to face me. "I've kept a secret from you, because I was too scared of losing you, and I'm sorry."

"It's OK sweetheart," I tell her, my heart yearning for me to go to her.

"No, it's not. It's not OK," she says to me, tears rolling down her face. "I've wasted years of my life keeping this secret… Years that I could have spent loving you."

"Cassie," I say to her, smiling. "I've kept a secret from you as well and it was the hardest secret I've ever had to keep from anyone, especially from you."

"I love you," Cassie tells me, tears rolling down her cheeks. "I love you, Jake.

"I love you too, Cassie," I tell her back, fighting back my own tears. "I always have."

"How touching," Gro'alk says, walking towards Cassie.

I watch as Cassie closes her eyes and turns back to face the Warchief walking towards her. He stands just in front of her smiling. I watch as he slowly lifts the hammer up above his head and starts to swing it down towards

Cassie. Everything seems to be moving in slow motion as I push myself up off the floor and leap forwards, closing the seven feet gap in a single bound. At the apex of my leap, my right hand goes up to my shoulder and grabs the hilt of the great sword now materialising on my back, I pull the blade from its brace and thrust it out in front of me as I land just shy of Cassie and hear the loud metallic clang ring out as the shaft of the hammer connects with my blade, stopping it dead a foot from Cassie's head.

"But that's not my secret."

Chapter Thirty Eight (Shadow War)

The Warchief Gro'alk walks over to us, grabbing a lance from one of his orcs as it passes. The giant orc starts to spin the weapon in its hands, before snapping the lance back behind its body and launching it straight at my mother. The throw is powerful and accurate, but I manage to leap forwards and push her out of the way just in time. I watch my mother hit the floor, right as the lance goes straight through my right shoulder and I feel the pain burst down my arm and into my chest from the impact.

"Jak!" I hear my mother scream, as I am thrown backwards from the blow, landing awkwardly and painfully against the back wall.

I roll over onto my side, and grip the shaft of the lance with both hands. I try to pull it free, but it is wedged into my armour, so instead I apply pressure to the shaft, the intensity of the pain forces me to scream as I snap the shaft in two, leaving just a few inches now protruding from my shoulder.

Up ahead my mother is stood between me and Gro'alk. Her arms out in front of her again, and I can hear her chanting an incantation under her breath. The Warchief storms towards her, its overly large hammer drawn up above him, but as it brings it down a fireball erupts from my mother's hands and blasts the orc back twenty feet, where it now lays sprawled on its back.

My father's greatest strength was the Light, but it was said that his greatest gift was his intelligence, it was often said that there was nothing that he did not already know. My mother's was her mastery over magic, as she had just proven. A rare gift among the elves, as only the Elementals could use their own magics, and the world of men had none. My brother's gift was his strength and cunning, it was what made him a good leader, and a good general. My mother always told me that my gift was life. Not my own, but my love of all life. My father said that my gift made me care about all living things, large and small. My mother said that I would protect those that could not protect themselves. My twin brother Mal just thought I had a hero complex. I guess in this moment, we had just proved them all true.

"You must flee, escape the city!" she calls back to me. "I will hold them off."

"Mother!" I shout to her, getting back up to my feet. "Come with me."

"Go, my darling son. Please, go," she tells me. "I love you, always, and forever."

Gro'alk has gotten to its feet and is marching back towards my mother, and I know I can't leave her to this fate. All life is precious. I charge forward, and past my mother, to meet the Warchief. I draw one of my sabres in my left hand and start to swing it at the orc, clumsily and painfully. My shoulder is on fire from the lance still wedged there.

The Warchief catches my arm and laughs at me as he rips the blade from my hand and kicks me down to the floor. I stand up and draw the other sabre, holding it out in front of me but Gro'alk continues to just laugh at me.

"I'm going to enjoy killing you, Princeling," the Warchief spits at me. "Just know that you will be joined shortly by your mother."

It swings the blade at me and I parry the attack, stepping round the orc and swinging my own blade which it easily blocks. I can hear my mother chanting again, but so does Gro'alk who twists round and slams my stolen sabre down at her, cutting off my mother's hand, and halting the spell.

I see her fall to the ground screaming, and I lunge forward to attack the distracted Warchief, but the orc sees it coming and punches me down to the ground with its offhand. I stagger slightly from the blow, but I see the orc swing my sabre at me and I twist away but it still catches me on the side of my face. I can feel the blood running down from the top of my right cheek, all the way down my jaw to my chin in a large J shape.

I scramble away from the Warchief, who is laughing again, and wipe the blood from my face. I try to compose myself but the pain is excruciating. I step back and turn to the pillar next to me, knowing that I will regret this, I slam my right shoulder into it as hard as I can, causing me to scream as the lance tip flies out onto the floor behind me. The pain is like a raging fire, but immediately there is also a sense of relief. I clench my right hand a few times, and while it is still sore to move, the damage is not irreversible.

I straighten up and move towards Gro'alk, who has now stopped its approach to where my mother lays on the floor.

As I pick up my sabre from the floor, I see mother begin to silently chant, her eyes closed in deep concentration for this particular spell. I am about to charge at the Warchief when a loud rushing sound erupts in around the room, startling the orcs all around us. The suits of armour start to rattle in the wind. As I look round the room, trying to find the source of the noise, I see an orb appear and I watch as it grows and grows into a large oval shape just to my right.

I look at mother, who smiles at me, and then a blinding light fills the entire hall. I turn and lift my hand to cover my eyes, looking out of the doorway, I realise that my father has fallen, releasing the Light into a powerful blast. Looking back at my mother, she is still smiling, and with a wave of her hand, I feel myself get thrown back as if I had been hit with Gro'alk's hammer.

"I love you, King Jak'ahan," my mother says, and it is the last thing I hear as I pass through the portal.

Chapter Thirty Nine

The look on Gro'alk's face is one of total shock.

I pull my great sword upwards, bringing the Warchief's hammer up with it, causing the large orc to lose its balance and stumble backwards. I twist my body round and slam my left palm into its chest, using some of the limited Light inside me to send out a pulse that knocks it back to the far wall, where the orc crumples to the ground with its hammer landing off to one side.

I immediately turn round and lift the great sword up in front of me with both hands, more Light surging from me and into the sword as I drive the tip down into the ground between me and Cassie, waves of Light emanating from the impact that knocks back each of the orcs stood in the room, before devouring them from within their armour.

While the other orcs all fall to the floor, the other Warchief managed to dive behind one of the pillars, narrowly avoiding the pulse of Light. I take my hands off the sword, leaving it impaled in the ground, and watch as the Warchief gets back up to his feet while drawing his axe. The orc regains its composure and throws it at me, but I easily catch it and spinning round full circle, I use the momentum to throw it straight back at the orc. It can't react quick enough and goes down with its own weapon sticking out of his shoulder.

"Err, Jake," I hear Adam say, and looking over to him, I see him pointing through the archway at the large numbers of orcs that were gathered in the room beyond. "They're coming for us."

I take a step forwards and grab the great sword without breaking my stride. I swing the large blade over my head, while filling the blade with more Light, before slamming it down into the ground which releases a large pulse of Light out through the arch and into the room beyond. The screams of pain from the orcs can be clearly heard, and no more try to enter the room.

Just in case, I hold out my hand and send out a pulse of light, but instead of letting it fly out to the room beyond, I hold it in the archway, where it stays, acting as a barrier against the Shadow beyond. One of the first things my father taught me was the basic nature of the Elements; everything has an equal and an opposite. Earth and Wind, Fire and Ice, Lightning and Water, Light and Shadow. My newly formed barrier of Light would stop any orc passing through it, because as Gro'alk had pointed out, all orcs were created from Shadow.

"I know that blade," I hear Gro'alk say from behind me, its voice groggy from the knockback.

I turn to see the orc reaching for its hammer and trying to pull it closer, as it still sits hunched on the floor, spitting out a mouthful of dark purple blood.

"I know that blade," It repeats. "I fought the elf that carried that blade. That elf is dead."

"My name is Jak, Son of Cen," I tell him. "Crown Prince of Lor'ahan, General of the Royal Knights, and Lord Protector of the Kingdom of Men."

"No!" Gro'alk stammers, the shock returning to its face. "The elves are gone. The Prince fell to the Shadow Gods might."

"Your Shadow God lied, orc," I tell the Warchief.

I turn back away from the cowering orc to look at Cassie, who has now stood up and is looking up at me, her eyes full of curiosity.

"Cassie. I need you to trust me, just for a little longer," I plead with her. "I love you, I always have, and I will forever more."

"Jake. I love you," she says to me, placing her hand over my heart. "I trust you."

"I need to show you the real me. The one that I have hidden from this world for so long." I explain to her, and I can her the pleading in my voice.

"I fell in love with the Jake that's in there," she tells me, patting my chest, "It wouldn't matter if you have two heads, I'll still love you. Probably," she adds with a wink.

I take a step back from her and close my eyes, taking a deep breath I let myself relax. I am weaker in this human form, only having a limited pool of Light inside me. It was part of the sacrifice I had to make in order to hide my true self. I allow the Light deep inside to flow out, covering my entire body as it builds up to a blinding radiance that fills the whole room.

As the Light dims again, I open my eyes to look down at Cassie and I can see the sheer wonder and amazement in her eyes as she looks up at me, I am no longer the thirty-year-old human that she had known for the last fourteen years, but a nearly nine-thousand-year elf.

I tower over her, standing at nearly seven feet tall and for the first time in millennia, I am wearing my full plate armour, enameled purest white as is the standard among the Royal Knights of Lor'ahan, although mine also has gilded gold feathers running along my helmet and pauldrons, as a sign of my rank as their General.

My shield is still secured to my back with the Royal Arms of Lor'ahan blazoned across its face - twin wolves chasing each other's tails in an eternal circle. Both my golden curved sabres are sitting comfortably in their sheaths on each hip, although my great sword is still in my hand, and not sitting in its brace between my shoulder blades as it was when I stood atop the city walls all those years ago. Before the war began.

I stand there for another moment, trying to read Cassie's expression as I look into her eyes, trying to sense what she is thinking. I hear Gro'alk stir behind me, so I reluctantly turn away from Cassie to face the Warchief that I have so much history with, one more time.

"So it really is you, princeling," Gro'alk says to me, smirking. "I always hoped we would meet again, I was even disappointed when I had found out you had died."

"I do hate to disappoint," I laugh at the Warchief, the sound of my true voice taking me by surprise, as it has been so long since I had last heard it. The elves typically have softer voices, but mine is slightly deeper and yet somehow more musical than Jake's. "You started a war that took my family from me, and now here you are trying to do it all over again."

"Why now?" the orc spits at me. "Why show yourself now."

"If my existence had been revealed, what would you have done?"

"The girl would be dead. Both the first one, and this one," the orc spits at me. "I would have killed them the instant I found them."

"That is why I waited," I told him. "Those two ladies, both Olive and Cassie, they are my world. I love them both equally, but differently. Everything I have done, is to protect them."

"You will fail them now, just as you did then," the orc says with a smirk. "I will take your head to the Shadow God," the Warchief says, smiling at me. "And I will be treated as a hero."

"You've threatened me with that before, orc," I remind the orc, and put the great sword back onto its brace on my back. "It ended with you fleeing for your life."

"Grah! I seem to remember that it was you that fled, princeling." It spits at me.

"Then you remember it wrong, orc," I tell the orc, wincing at the painful memory of that day, and all that I lost. "I didn't choose to go through that portal."

"Neither of us can run today," Gro'alk declares. "Unless you want to leave your friends to a fate worse than death, like you did your mother."

"My family sacrificed themselves to save this world," I tell the orc flatly. "I have tried to honour that sacrifice every day since."

Gro'alk lunges forward and swings the hammer down hard from its shoulder as I take a step back to avoid the crushing blow. I pull both my sabres from their sheaths, and hold them out either side of me. I am ready.

I thrust the right sabre at Gro'alk and twist away as it parries it with the buckler on its left forearm, using the momentum to bring my left sabre into a swing towards its shoulder but it brings the shaft of the hammer up to stop the attack so I immediately bring the right sabre in for a second hit right next to where the other sabre currently sits and the force of the blow knocks the hammer from its grip and it topples down to the floor.

The lumbering orc jumps away from me, looking around desperately for a replacement weapon, before picking up a broadsword from one of the orcs that fell to my earlier pulse of Light. Gro'alk straightens up and tries to walk around me in a wide arc in an attempt to get between me and Cassie, but I just stand there, not willing to move.

The orc charges forward again and swings the blade into an uppercut which I block with both sabres by crossing them in front of me. I move the crossed blades swiftly to my left, before bringing them over my head in unison and round into a horizontal swing that catches its left shoulder and spins the orc off balance, leaving two deep cuts where the pauldron had been moments before.

Gro'alk regains its balance, turning back to face me and thrusts its sword forward, which I parry to my right using my sabre, while thrusting my left sabre into the side of its torso, cutting straight through his armour and causing it to grunt as it stumbles past me, our positions now mirrored on the opposite sides of the room.

The Warchief drops the sword on the ground and picks up the great hammer again, before turning back to face me once more. I watch as the orc walks towards me, its eyes watching me, calculating and trying to decide on the next move. As it gets within range, I notice that the orc shifts the hammer on his shoulder slightly, getting ready to attack.

The head of the hammer swings down behind its body, making it appear that he will be bringing the hammer down into another uppercut, but I know that this is just a ruse. The memory of Petr's death is like a scar on my heart, much like those that I carry for my family, and just as much a reminder of my past as the physical scars I am forced to look at each day on my face and shoulder.

The hammer stops its swing as it comes up towards my waist and I watch as Gro'alk shifts the weight onto the balls of its feet as the orc tries to thrust the hammer forwards into my chest, but I twist away from the attack, rolling along the side of the weapon. As I come out of the final spin, I drive my left sabre into the right shoulder from behind and twist until the orc screams and drops the hammer. I let go of the sabre, leaving it impaled there as I walk back round in front of him.

"That was for me," I tell the orc, who has now slumped down onto its knees.

I watch as the mighty Warchief clumsily grabs at the blade of my sabre now sticking out of the front of its shoulder and tries to push it back out the way it went in. The orc winces and groans as it slowly works it's way back out, dropping to the floor. Gro'alk bends down slowly to pick it up with its left hand, before quickly swinging it up at me, but I easily parry it to my left and twist away before bringing my sabre in an upwards strike right that connects with his wrist, severing its hand in one clean motion.

"That was for my mother," I tell the orc.

I watch the orc stumble backwards, clutching the stump of its arm. I bend down to retrieve my other sabre from the floor, and walk towards Gro'alk, who is still backing away from me. I leap forward and slice its left thigh with my right sabre before bringing both sabres back in the other direction to slice the right thigh, and with both legs now cut deeply, it drops to the floor to kneel in front of me.

I sheathe both sabres and turn to walk back to where Cassie is stood, who is just watching me with deep interest and curiosity, although I can't quite tell if I also see fear. I am no longer the same person she knew. Am I still the one she loves? The thought fills me with anxiety and I force myself to focus on the Warchief.

I grab the hilt of my great sword and pull it from its brace, twirling it behind me before stopping it to rest on my shoulder. As I do, I notice that it no longer aches; now that I have reverted to my elven form, the Light is able to work on healing my millennia old injuries once more and reverse the degeneration that occurs each time I take human form.

This time had been far worse than ever before, as I had been Jake for over fourteen years. Usually I would only stay in one place for a year or two, before moving on with a new identity and a new look. But that was before I met Cassie, everything had changed when I had met her.

I turn away from Cassie and walk back towards Gro'alk, who remains knelt at the back of the room. As I approach the now disabled and unarmed orc, I bring the great sword down from my shoulder and use both hands to thrust it straight through his chest and into the ground behind him.

"That was for Petr," I tell the orc.

I can hear his breathing turn raspy and shallow, the life slowly leaving its body. I look into the eyes of the orc that has been the source of so much of my pain and misery for so long, and all I feel is pity. It has only ever known war and death, It has never known love.

I step over to the discarded hammer and pick it up with both hands. It's heavy, even for me, and horribly balanced, but it hardly matters, I don't intend to keep it. I rest the hammer onto my shoulder as I walk back to face the kneeling Warchief, much as he did with my father all those years ago.

"And this…" I say to orc. "This is for the elves."

I lift the hammer up over my head and bring it down with all my strength, crushing his head and shoulders before it stops with a clang as it connects with the great sword still impaled in its chest. I lift the hammer again and toss it to one side, before pulling my great sword from the Warchief's corpse and sliding it back into it's brace on my back.

I look down at the mangled corpse in front of me and close my eyes once again, taking a deep breath and thinking of my old family, my old life. I have finally found the source of my scars, and my pain. I have avenged the ones that I loved, and I finally feel at peace with that life now.

I open my eyes as I turn to look back at Cassie, at my new life. I start to walk towards her, while using the Light to make my weapons and shield dematerialise again. I also use the Light to strip me of the bulkier parts of my armour, the gauntlets and vambraces fade from my arms leaving them bare, along with the pauldrons on my shoulders and the chausses on my thighs which reveal the deep green elven cloth I wear underneath. Lastly my helm fades away, revealing my true face.

I still look like I did in my most recent human form, as I had chosen to retain my dominant facial features as Jake. The key differences are that I am taller now, and slightly broader but I would still be classed as lean. My hair is longer too and hangs down in front of my eyes, so I brush it away with my fingers.

However, the most obvious change is my eyes, which are now bright green; for it is the eyes that show the Light that the elves have inside them. They can take many forms, Cara's eyes pulsed like they were brimming with energy, whereas Serah's seemed to almost glow like the stars in the night sky. Not mine though, mine burn like an intense green flame.

I look over at Cassie, and then just behind her stands Adam, who I have known for barely a few days, and yet he has done more for me than I could have ever have asked of anyone. He had no reason to follow me, no reason to trust me. But still he fought at my side, time and time again, following me straight into hell. Not since Petr had I known such loyalty.

I give Adam a nod, but my attention is immediately drawn back to Cassie. It feels like I am seeing her again for the first time. My elven eyesight allowing me to rediscover every little detail. Her beautiful blue eyes full of wonder and love, her lips curled into a smile that reaches all the way up to her eyes, her nostrils flaring slightly as she takes a deep breath each time she looks at me, every single aspect of her made even more beautiful now that I can see her through my own eyes.

I start to walk over to her, and as I do so, she takes a step towards me and I feel my heart flutter. I lift my right hand up to her cheek, and move my left hand round her waist to the small of her back, all while looking intensely into her eyes. Cassie raises her hands up to my chest, tracing the shape of the two wolves depicted on the armour.

"I love you, Cassie," I tell her, again.

"I love you more," she whispers to me, as I lean down to kiss her.

The moment our lips touch, everything else fades away, all I can think about is her. I feel the Light surging inside of me again, although I can't understand why. I kiss her again, more passionately than the last, and before long the Light has spread through my whole body. I am vaguely aware that the Light is enveloping us both now, as it passes through me and into Cassie.

As the Light becomes blinding, I can hear it humming, or is it singing? I'm not sure, but at that exact moment I hear Cassie take in a sudden breath and a small whimper leaves her lips. I reluctantly pull away from her and carefully watch her face, willing her to look at me. Everything around us is pure white, everything except for her.

As the Light fades around us, Cassie slowly opens her eyes and I feel a smile growing on my face, for her eyes are now pulsing the brightest blue that I have ever seen.

Epilogue

Looking down at Cassie, into those bright blue eyes, I have to force myself to remember where we are. Where are we? I reluctantly draw myself away from Cassie to look around the room, which has now returned to its former darkened state, with Adam looking both confused and surprised. Right, that's where we are, in the Underground.

"I have a lot to tell you," I say to her, looking back into her impossibly blue eyes. "But we should probably get out of here first."

I walk over to the archway and dissipate the barrier of Light. Just like all elven magic, it only falls when we do. A memory hits me, painfully, as I remember falling through the portal my mother had created the last time I had seen Gro'alk in the castle hall, and watching in horror as it had closed before she had joined me. That was the last time I had seen her.

As I look through to the next room, I can see that all of the orcs have now fled from the station, but I know this peace will not last forever. Word of my appearance would surely reach the Underworld, and soon. Gro'alk may have been a powerful Warchief, but in reality, it was only working in the service of their so called 'Shadow God', who I know now commands an army far greater than I could possibly have imagined. This war is far from over, it has only just begun.

Adam walks over to me and claps me on the shoulder as he walks past and picks up his gun and pack from the corner. Followed by Cassie, her eyes still glowing brightly as she looks all around her, taking in the little details that would have been lost to her before. I have never seen her so full of life, full of energy.

As her eyes meet mine, she smiles at me again, a big smile that reaches up to eyes.

"Jake, is this what you see?" she asks me, her voice full of amazement.

"It would be, if I could ever bring myself to take my eyes off you," I tell her with a wink, and she blushes slightly as a small smile forms on her lips. Then she bounds forwards, wrapping her arms round me and stretching up on her toes to kiss me. As she leans away, I can see that she is smiling properly now, her lips reaching up to her eyes again, as she takes my hand and pulls me forwards; "Tell me *EVERYTHING*."

"I don't even know where to start," I tell her, honestly. "The first Shadow War started thousands of years ago, and I had thought it was over."

As we walk back through the now devastated Westminster station, I begin to tell her about the elves, about Lor'ahan, and about my family. Cara, Raf, Cen and little Serah, my parents, and Petr. Then I went on to explain about the first days of the Shadow War. How the elves made their stand at Lor'ahan. My initial encounter with Gro'alk and the other Warchiefs on the battlefield, and the death of Petr. I told them of my father's plan, and of my family's sacrifice to ensure the first victory against the orcs and their 'Shadow God'. Cassie listened intently, taking in every detail, but not saying a word until I had finished.

"I'm so sorry Jake, I cannot even imagine what you went through," Cassie whispers to me, tears forming in her eyes.

"It's why I fought so hard to keep you safe, and to get you back," I tell her, smiling. "You, Olive, even Nat. You're my family now."

Cassie takes my hand and we walk in silence, until Adam breaks it.

"It's all starting to make sense now," Adam says, "Why you were always so willing to run into hell."

"I'd do anything for my family, mate," I tell him, "Speaking of which, we need to get to Harry."

"Harry?" Adam asks, confusion spreading across his face.

"I owe him a cure," I tell him, with a wink. "When I came to see you in the hospital, I gave him the tiniest bit of Light, to keep the Shadow at bay."

"The Shadow? So it's not a poison?" Adam asks.

"Yes, and no. The orc weapons are forged in Shadow, as are their arrows. The elves are immune to their weapons, as our Light can repel it. Men are not as lucky," I tell him.

"Will he be ok?" Adam asks, and I can hear the concern in his voice.

"He will carry the scar for the rest of his life, but he'll live," I tell him, and I know from experience. Gro'alk had thrown an orc spear through my shoulder, and while my Light could keep the wound healed as an elf, it would degenerate while in human form. The scar on my face was caused by an elvish weapon, my own sabre in fact, so that was a reminder that I carried always.

"Thank you, Jake. I mean it, thank you," Adam says, his relief clearly showing.

"You two are practically family too," I tell him, with a smile. "And I think it's time to get our little family back together."

"Agreed," Cassie says, and I see Adam nod too, lost in his thoughts. "I do have questions though, lots of them.

"Fire away," I tell her.

"Why did I have the Light? And Olive too?" she asks me, and I see Adam perk up at the question.

"That is a great question. Olive is easier to explain, I think," I tell them. "You see, my mother told me that my sons would hide Serah and let her live out her mortal life, untouched by war and safe from those that may seek her out for having the Light."

"Her Light would be passed from first born child to first born child, on and on, over hundreds of generations," I explain, or try to at least. "I spent millennia trying to find one of Serah's descendants, once the Shadow War was over. But I never could, my sons had hidden her well." I can hear the pride in my voice at that comment.

"So you think Olive might be your great, great granddaughter?" Adam asks me, while I can feel Cassie's blue eyes burning into me, waiting for the answer. So full of life.

"Pretty much," I tell him. "I looked everywhere, twice, but couldn't find any Light. Then one day, I'm walking down the road, minding my own business, and there she was. Huddled in a shop window, cold, hungry, probably fed up, but also burning brightly. There was no doubt that she had the Light, and that could only mean one thing."

"So you took her in," Cassie smiles at me. "Adopted her as your sister."

"I did take her in, but I didn't want to force it," I tell them. "She was free to make her own choices, to leave or stay, to love me or not."

"That explains why you two are so close, and so similar," Adam says.

"You weren't just adopted family, you are actual family," Cassie says. "After she lost hers, she not only found a home, but she did find family after all."

"I hope so," I tell them. I loved Olive, just as I had loved Serah. Thousands of years may lay between them, but they were so similar. I'm torn from my thoughts of Serah by Cassie looking sheepish and anxious.

"What about me?" Cassie asks, the shyness offset by the curiosity in her bright blue eyes.

"That's slightly more complicated," I say to her. "My mother told me that elven children do not have the Light from birth, but that it was given to them by my father when they came of age."

"But your father is dead?" Cassie says, "And I'm not an elven child, like Olive. Am I?"

"Yes, he is and no, love, you are not,

" I say to her, with a chuckle as I see her relax, clearly relieved that she isn't also possibly related to me. "But elven children do have Light inside them, like Serah did. We think that their parents share their own Light with their children, gifted to them through their love."

"We?" Cassie asks, and it takes me a moment to realise what I had said.

"Ah, yes, '*we*'" I say to her. "After Lor'ahan fell, and the elves were lost to the war. I had to find new allies. One of them was an old friend of my father, Lord Fenrir. He shared what he knew of the Light, what my father had told him, and then we had to fill in the gaps ourselves."

"So I didn't have the Light when we met?" Cassie asks.

"No, you were just a perfectly ordinary human girl," I tell her with a wink. "Well, until I fell in love with you. Then everything changed…"

"You said that the stronger the love, the stronger the Light," Cassie says, leaving the question unsaid.

"Remember that day, in the form room?" I ask her. "It was raining outside."

"And I had been dumped, so we were sat at the back," Cassie continued. "You were just holding me, keeping me safe."

"I was," I tell her. "I always will."

"All that time?" Cassie asks.

"Pretty much," I tell her. "And now, well, now you are like me."

"So I'm immortal now?" she asks me breathlessly, clearly trying to process this information. "Like you?"

"Yes, Cassie, we both are," I tell her, smiling down at her. "Welcome to the club."

"So I won't ever lose you?" she asks me, looking up at me with longing in her eyes.

"I'll love you," I tell her, lifting my hand up to her cheek. "Always, and forever."

"That is one hell of a story, Jake," Adam says to me, as we reach the last set of escalators.

"And that was just the beginning," I tell him. "But let's go find Olive and Nat before we get into that. I definitely owe them the full story as well."

"That's a fair point," Adam says, and Cassie nods absently as she looks around, unable to stay focused on anything with her improved eyesight. It would take a while for that amazement to fade.

"I cannot wait to see the look on their faces when they see you now!" Adam says laughing, and I can't help but join in. I'm glad that he has accepted me, and I didn't doubt that Harry would too. But I knew from experience that the world of men wasn't as accepting of those that were different. It was why I was Jake to begin with.

"So what's next?" Cassie asks me, dragging herself away from a film poster thirty feet away, that I am sure she read in full, even the small print.

"Gro'alk is dead, and that will have been a bitter blow to the orcs," I explain, all while staring into Cassie's bright blue eyes. I didn't want to look anywhere else. I couldn't look anywhere else. "Their Shadow God won't take that news lightly."

"What do you think is going to happen?" Adam asks.

"A second Shadow War is coming," I tell him. "We have won the first battle; they won't want to lose the next."

"It's going to get worse, isn't it?" Cassie asks me, her smile fading.

"I'm afraid so, love," I tell her. "But we aren't alone in this war."

"We aren't?" Cassie asks, looking up at me with a curious look in her eye.

"The elves stood alone last time, and sacrificed themselves in the early days of the war, to buy time for the remaining races to fight back and ultimately drive the orcs into the Underworld," I explain. "It is time to re-forge those old alliances."

"Like Lord Fenrir?" Cassie asks me curiously. "Does he have descendants too, like Olive?"

"Exactly like Fen," I tell her, before adding with a smile. "He does have descendants, although I think he prefers to call them children."

"He's still alive?" Cassie exclaims, "He's immortal too?"

"He certainly is," I tell her. "All Elementals are"

"Where will we find him?" Adam asks me. "And what exactly is 'he'?"

"I know exactly where he is, and what he is. A Direwolf, by the way, and he is definitely going to want to meet Cassie," I say, before adding with a smile. "Again."

Before Cassie can ask me what I mean, we are stopped in our tracks as dark clouds start to roll unnaturally across the London skyline. Powerful magics are at work here. While I had sealed the gates to the Underworld myself, those magics mean nothing now that the Shadow God is able to open portals to this world directly. But how are they doing it? A portal is starting to open just ahead of us, so I step forwards drawing my twin sabres with a flourish, and put myself between the orcs and Cassie.

I have been Jake Shepherd for fourteen years. And in that fleeting time, I have felt more alive than I had in the eight thousand years that came before it.

For in those fourteen years, I had found something worth living for, worth fighting for. I was no longer alone.

TO BE CONTINUED…

◆ ◆ ◆

Thank you for joining me on this new journey, I hope you enjoyed reading it as much as I have writing it.

The next instalment, Torrent, is currently being written and will be available towards the end of 2018.

You can find out more information at:

www.TheShadowWarSaga.com

Thank you!
Lee

◆ ◆ ◆

Printed in Poland
by Amazon Fulfillment
Poland Sp. z o.o., Wrocław

41662242R00197